GHOST
OF A
Chance

CYNTHIA
EDEN

CHAPTER ONE

"You're staring again," Marilyn Montgomery whispered. Only her voice was one of those overly loud, fake whispers. The kind that far too many people could actually hear.

At her friend's words, Tess Barrett jerked her gaze off the sexy-as-hell guy that she had — *yes, so guilty* — been staring at for probably way too long. The club was crowded. No, more like packed. A band blasted from the stage. Drinks flowed. Laughter filled the air. Couples danced and kissed, and she was even about ninety percent sure she'd seen one man and woman having sex in the back of the club. There were all sorts of things happening around her.

But *he* kept pulling her attention.

"He's hot." Marilyn took a long swig from her beer. Her red nails gleamed against the long neck of the bottle. "Got that whole *I'm-a-badass-and-I-want-to-do-bad-things-to-you* vibe going on."

Tess felt her face flush. "He does not." *Yes, yes, he does.*

"I wouldn't mind doing some bad things with him," Latonya Wilson added with a soft sigh as her dark gaze drifted over to the man in question. "It's been way too long since I've done bad things. I *need* some bad things in my life." She raised one perfect eyebrow at Tess. "What about you? How long has it been?"

Since she'd done something bad? *Um, a very long time.* Tess reached for the water in front of her. Water because she was on call. Water because even if she wasn't on call, she wouldn't be drinking. She didn't drink. Didn't hook up with strangers. Didn't break any of the careful rules that she had for her life.

She bit her lower lip and tried not to glance toward the bar once more. What was the deal with her? The guy was good-looking. Yes, absolutely. Hard jaw covered by a delectable growth of stubble. Messy hair that was a little long. Killer body. The white t-shirt he wore was seriously stretched by his shoulders and powerful arms. When she'd been, ah, staring, Tess had noticed that his long legs had been encased in faded denim, and his fingers drummed idly on the bar top.

"Uh, oh." Marilyn straightened in her chair. She was stage whispering again as she noted, "Now, he's staring…"

Tess stiffened her shoulders—

"At you!" Marilyn finished almost gleefully.

What? Tess's head whipped around. The jerky, startled movement was totally not a cool and casual thing to do. She was probably supposed to play some teasing game with him and not gape in his direction. Wasn't that expected club behavior? If so, she failed miserably because her head whipped toward the guy, and she gaped at him. Yet as she gaped, Tess saw that her mystery man was, in fact, staring at their table.

"He's not staring at me." She forced herself to look away. *Again.* "He's probably looking at one of you." Latonya was absolutely gorgeous. Tall, curvy, and with a flawless face, the African American doctor had been known to always leave a trail of men in her wake. And as for Marilyn, the woman looked a whole lot like her namesake, Marilyn Monroe. Like the famous star, Marilyn didn't suffer for male attention. Never had, never would.

Marilyn laughed. "His eyes are on you. And don't look now—seriously, do *not* look again because you'll give off a desperate vibe if you do that—but he's heading this way."

"Bad things," Latonya muttered under her breath. "If he offers, please go do some very bad—"

Latonya didn't get to finish her words because he was there. Tess just *felt* him. She eased out a low breath and kept her eyes on the table in front of her. Marilyn knew the dating scene.

Heck, Marilyn *ruled* the dating scene with an iron fist. If she said don't look, then Tess shouldn't look. She should dig deep and find some way to be chill about this whole situation—

"Oh, so *now* you won't look my way?" His voice was low and deep. It sank through her body and made Tess feel warm in all kinds of fun places. It was because his voice was pure warm yumminess that it took so long for his actual words to register and when they did finally sink in…

Tess winced and glanced at him.

Golden eyes. Huh. That was interesting. *Okay, gorgeous.* Across the club, she hadn't been able to tell that his eyes were such incredible gold. Unusual. And he was even better looking up close. How was that possible?

He smiled. A half-smile that didn't light his eyes.

She wanted to smile back. Instead, Tess just kept staring. When it came to dating, she was pretty much a total novice. Her fault. She poured herself into her work, and it wasn't like there was a whole lot of time or energy left over for the dating scene. She didn't have hours to spend getting to know someone. She didn't want to be swiping left or right or whatever on her phone. She didn't have time for movie nights. Or candle-lit dinners. Tess usually came home from work, collapsed, and then repeated that pattern a whole lot. Unsexy. Unexciting.

"Would you like to dance?" he asked.

She shook her head no.

He blinked.

Tess felt Marilyn kick her under the table. Hard. What the hell?

"Did I...misread the situation?" His voice was so damn sexy.

Marilyn kicked her again.

"I don't dance well," Tess blurted. "And the place is so packed — I mean, there's not really any room on the dance floor for us." She was still staring at him. His bone structure was fabulous. A thing of beauty, not that he probably wanted to hear that. But she knew a lot about bones and bodies and —

"I can take you to a place where there is plenty of room." He extended his hand toward her. "And I don't care how you dance. You can break every toe I have. I just want to get to know you better."

Oh. That was rather — nice? Gallant? Sexy? Maybe all of the above? She didn't take his hand, though, because caution held her back. "Where exactly do you want to take me?"

He turned his head, just a bit, and glanced toward the second level of the club. "VIP space."

She hadn't even known there *was* a VIP space. It was her first visit to the club. The club had opened two weeks ago — some sort of grand re-opening under new management situation — and Marilyn had raved about it, so Tess and Latonya had finally broken down and headed into the place with her earlier that night.

"No one will bother us up there. Like I said, there's plenty of room." His hand was still extended toward her. "And no one else will see you dance, just me."

Well, okay, that sounded good so…Tess stood up. She was average height, currently wearing her flats, and when she stood, she had to tilt her head back to see his incredible eyes. Tall, muscled, sexy — he was checking off everything on her fantasy lover list. Check, check, check. And his voice…

Wow.

Tentatively, her fingers reached for his. When she touched his skin, a surge of awareness poured through her. An instant, primal response that she'd never felt before. The surge should have been some sort of warning to her.

It wasn't.

"I'm James. James Smith."

"Tess Barrett."

He nodded. His gaze slowly drifted over her face. He kept her hand held carefully in his. "Ready to dance?"

Um, no. "I can't leave my friends while I head up to VIP land." That was a loser move.

Another nod from him. "Of course. I'll make sure they're given the best champagne we have in the club and that they are escorted upstairs as well."

She heard a little squeal from Marilyn. Marilyn loved her champagne.

"Though you and I will be in a private room," he added. "I think it's better if we're alone. Like I said, only I'll be watching you."

Her head cocked. "So how do you have all of this magic VIP pull? Are you someone famous?"

"In certain circles." For a moment, humor seemed to gleam in his eyes.

Her eyes narrowed.

He squeezed her hand. "My club. My rules. I can get anyone into VIP that I want."

Oh, wait…his place? Did that make things better…or worse?

He gave a little wave, and a muscled guy in a black shirt and pants hurried toward their table. "Mason will take care of your friends." His gaze held hers. "And I'll take care of you."

There sure seemed to be a whole lot of double meaning in his words.

He turned away, but kept hold of her hand.

"Bad things," Latonya threw out.

James stopped. Stiffened. Glanced back. His gaze slid to Latonya. "I assure you, I have no intention of doing anything bad to your friend." His stare rose to catch Tess's once more. "You're safe with me."

Her life was all about safety. One of her rules. But in this instance… "She wasn't worried. Latonya was telling me to *do* some bad things."

Latonya made a choking sound.

His lips quirked. "You want to do something bad? I am sure that can be arranged."

She swallowed and followed him…followed him through the crowd and up the stairs and down a little corridor before they were secluded in some seriously lush space. Not an office. More like…a private entertainment room? Huge couch. Giant windows that looked out over the club. She could swear the room even smelled expensive.

"No one can see in. We can look out, but the glass is specially tinted so no one below can look in." He hit a button on a nearby control panel. The band's music drifted into the room. "And I can control what we hear, too."

She shifted from foot to foot. Now that they were, in fact, alone, he seemed even bigger.

"How about that dance?"

She put her hands on his shoulders. The band had slowed down. Had he given some sort of cue to them? Was this all part of some typical seduction plan that James had? Pick a woman, take her upstairs, while the band plays something slow and sensual and James works his magic?

"How many women have you brought up here?" Tess asked, voice sharp.

His eyes crinkled a little. She had the feeling he wanted to laugh. "You say what you think, don't you?"

"Why would I say anything else? I mean, do you want me to say what other people think?"

He did laugh then.

Crap. She'd been literal. She did that sometimes. Marilyn and Latonya helped her work on mistakes like that. It had been a while since she'd screwed up. Not like back in her early med school days.

"How many?" James seemed to consider her question before he announced, "Zero."

Her hands tightened around his shoulders. "Are you being honest with me?"

His hands slid to curl around her waist. "I've brought zero women here. Well, actually, scratch that. I brought you up here. So that's one."

"Why did you bring me up here?"

He began to sway ever so slowly with her. She moved, too, trying to match her body with his.

"You wanted privacy. So I gave it to you." A pause. "I can give you whatever you need."

He had no idea what she needed. Unfortunately, neither did she. "You're a stranger."

"No, you know my name. I know yours. We're on a first name basis. Hardly strangers."

He made her want to smile. That didn't happen often. "Why did you approach me downstairs?"

He moved a little closer. So close that his body brushed against hers, and she liked it. His crisp, masculine scent surrounded her.

"Why were you staring at me, Tess?"

"Because you're gorgeous." Something the man obviously knew. "You probably have people staring at you all the time." She lifted her eyebrows. "You didn't answer my question."

"That's because I thought the answer was apparent."

Not to her.

"I saw you. I wanted you. So I came to you."

Okay. That was... "Is that your usual routine?" They were swaying sensually together. Dancing. And everywhere that she touched him, heat licked at her.

"I have no usual routine."

She leaned a little closer to him. His words were probably a lie, but she liked touching him. She liked the way she felt against him. Warm on the inside, when she hadn't even realized just how cold she'd been.

"I want to kiss you."

Her breath caught at his low, rough words. "I want that, too."

His eyes gleamed down at her. "You don't play games, do you?"

"I don't know how to play them."

He blinked, as if she'd caught him off guard.

"I'm not about lying or seducing or being coy or whatever. I don't have time for stuff like that." And if she did have time, she'd probably fail miserably at those endeavors. "So I'm probably saying the wrong things, but that's who I am."

She pulled in a bracing breath. "I'd like to kiss you, too."

His head lowered. Not fast. Slowly. As if he expected her to change her mind. Uh, not happening. Hadn't he heard her? She wanted his mouth on hers. Truth be told, she was a little foggy on when she'd had her last kiss. Maybe at the hospital Christmas party? Under the mistletoe? But that kiss had been sloppy and quick, and hardly awe-inspiring.

Was an awe-inspiring kiss too much to ask for?

His lips brushed over hers. Tenderly. Carefully. A light sampling that made her body hum and want more.

But it was *not* awe-inspiring. At least, not yet. Nice, though. He had warm, firm lips, and she liked the way they felt against her and she liked —

He kissed her again. Only this time, the kiss wasn't so careful. Her lips parted for him, and his tongue thrust inside. The kiss was deep and slow, and her heart slammed into her ribs because something that had been sleeping inside of her seemed to wake up in a flash. Her short nails dug into his shoulders as he hauled her ever closer. And she'd *thought* that she was close before. But this was different, like, a thousand times different.

He lifted her up. She'd figured he would be strong enough to hold her easily. She'd been right. He was. *Serious turn on.* Tess admired a strong man. Her legs curled around his hips in an instinctual move that Tess would have *never* thought she'd make with a stranger. She could feel the ridge of his arousal pushing against the front of his jeans and pressing against her, and she lifted her hips, riding his cock in a fast glide.

He growled, and it was a guttural sound that sent a shiver through her.

She kept kissing him. Kept loving the way he felt. She didn't normally react this way. She didn't get lost in a kiss. Certainly not with a stranger, and he *was* a stranger, even if she knew his name.

James.

His mouth tore from hers, and he kissed a path down her neck. She choked out a moan that was his name even as her hips rocked against him again.

Then she realized what she was doing. *Oh, crap, am I dry humping him?* Her hands curled tightly around his shoulders. "Wait."

He stilled. His head lifted. His eyes blazed down at her, and there was no missing the lust that had turned his features savage.

Oh, God. She was in way, way over her head.

Slowly, she unhooked her legs...*from around his waist!* Her feet touched the floor, but he was still holding her waist. His touch scorched her.

"I-I don't...this isn't how I usually act." She'd stammered. Wonderful. Tess sucked in a breath. "You're a really, really good kisser." In fact, she'd describe him as...*awe-inspiring.*

He gave her a half-grin, though the lust didn't fade from his eyes. "So are you, Tess."

She liked the way he said her name. All rumbling and growling and hot. She liked a lot of things about him but... "I don't hook up with strangers for sex." Lifting her chin, Tess took a few steps back from him.

His hands fell away as she retreated. She missed his touch. How weird was that? But she did.

"That's good to know. I don't, either."

Oh, wait, had she just insulted him? "I didn't mean—"

His half-grin became a full grin. "It's okay."

Her gaze darted toward the door. "I should leave." Like, right then before she did or said anything else horribly embarrassing. She turned on her heel.

"If you change your mind about sex with a stranger—though I did tell you, we aren't strangers—I'll be here."

She froze. Had he really said that? Or had she just had one major auditory hallucination? Her head turned, and she peeked suspiciously back at him.

His smile was gone, and he was watching her with an intense, focused gaze. "I have the feeling that you and I would be incredible together."

Oh, my. She had that feeling, too. The feeling that they could burn up the sheets, wreck the bed, and go crazy together. She'd never gone crazy with a lover. But then, she'd never met someone like James before. Someone who made her instantly think...

Sex. Pleasure.

He stalked toward her.

She backed up until her shoulders hit the door.

He leaned toward her. Flattened one palm on the wood behind her head. "I like you."

She more than liked him.

"Connections like this don't happen all the time."

Was that a line? It could just be a line, but...

She'd *never* felt a connection like this. Connection. Attraction. Whatever he wanted to call it.

In her head, she could hear Latonya whispering... *"Do bad things with him."* Tess bet bad things would feel incredible with James.

"I'd like to get to know you better, Tess. We can date. Go out for dinner or—"

"I don't—I don't have time for that."

His jaw hardened. "I get it." He dropped his hand.

She caught his hand. Held tight. "No, you don't. I truly don't have time for dates and things like that. My life is crazy." *Hospital shift after shift and—* "I don't have time for a relationship."

He nodded.

She was holding too tightly to his hand. Mostly because she wanted to hold tight to him.

She was also fibbing, a little. Work was hell, absolutely true, but it was her choice to be in that particular hell. She'd wanted to be an ER doctor. She'd worked hard to become one, busted ass over the years, and now she was living her dream. Yes, the job took up a huge amount of her time, but...

But even without the job, she wouldn't let a guy get close. Because if she had a relationship, then she'd have to share details of her past with her partner.

She didn't want to share her past with anyone. Her secrets were hers and hers alone. "I can't let anyone in." She let his hand go. She really did suck at lying, so why not just put all the cards on the table? Not like they were going to see each other again. It was kind of freeing to think that she could tell this man anything and not worry about being judged. She was only with him for this moment, so... "I don't talk about my past with lovers. I don't share my life. I don't have much to give. I'm pretty much the worst girlfriend ever because I don't trust easily." Understatement. She didn't trust at all.

He crossed his arms over his chest, cocked his head, and stared at her.

So she kept going. "I won't introduce boyfriends to my family. I don't talk to my family. Well, the family that's left." A shrug. That family was distant and scattered. They'd never looked for her. She wouldn't look for them. "I don't want some long-term commitment because I don't think about the future. I'm not looking for love or happily ever after. Honestly, I'm just tired of being alone and I'd like to escape for a little while with someone who can make me feel good."

Oh, crap. Her eyes widened. She'd been on a sharing roll there, and she'd gone overboard and *overshared.* Tess knew it with certainty. That whole *I'm just tired of being alone* had sounded desperate to her own ears.

Time to leave. Now. "Good night." She spun around again.

"I won't be introducing you to my family, either. There is no family. And if there was, trust me, you wouldn't want to be around them."

Her shoulders stiffened.

"I don't believe in love or happily ever after. It's just a nice way of explaining really dirty, hot sex."

Uh, okay.

"I can take you out to fancy dinners, if that's what you want. But if you want to skip the wining and dining because that's not your thing, then I want to know what *is* your thing."

She risked a glance back at him.

"Because I liked the part about making you feel good."

Her throat was super dry.

"But I think I can do better than just good. I think I can make you feel pretty damn fantastic, if you give me the chance."

What was he saying? She licked dry lips. Didn't turn fully to face him, but her gaze never left his face as Tess asked, "Just what is it that you're proposing?"

"Sex without strings. I've got a clean bill of health, and I'm happy to prove it, and I'll be sure to take care of the protection."

"I'm clean, too." Her words sounded as if they came from far away. "I can prove it, too, but protection — yes, we still need that." She didn't take chances. Didn't take risks. Not ever.

So what am I doing still talking to him?

"I'm not seeing anyone else," he continued as his stare held hers. "And I won't be, not while we're together."

This was all surreal. They'd just met. She shook her head.

"You won't, either." His voice roughened. "If we reach an agreement, it's just us, until we're done."

"This isn't happening."

His lips thinned. "Why not? You think two people normally kiss and ignite like that? Because I have to tell you, that was damn unusual for me."

It was the first time ever for her. But she gave another slow shake of her head. "I don't...*this isn't me.*"

He nodded. Took a step back. His nostrils flared, as if he'd just pulled in her scent. "You change your mind, you know where to find me."

She yanked open the door. Hurried toward the stairs. Before she'd even reached them, though, Latonya appeared. She was smiling and holding a flute of champagne.

"That was fast for a—" Latonya stopped. Frowned. "You okay?"

"I need to go home."

Latonya glanced over her shoulder. Tess followed her gaze. James stood in the open doorway, his arms still crossed over his chest, and that hot, golden stare of his on Tess.

"Did he hurt you?' Latonya took an aggressive step toward him. "Because I will make him—"

Tess grabbed Latonya's arm. "He didn't hurt me. I'm just tired. I have a big shift tomorrow, and I have to go home." *Go home because my knees are jelly, and I'm thinking way too much about taking him up on his offer.*

Sex without strings.

"I'm coming with you." Latonya glared at James. "This place is dull anyway." She made her voice extra loud—deliberately, Tess was sure.

As if on cue, Marilyn appeared. Her champagne flute was empty. "What's up?"

"We're doing a pissed walk out," Latonya muttered as she slammed her flute—and Marilyn's—down on a nearby table. "Let's do it like we're the queens of the universe."

Wait, no, they didn't have to act pissed. There was no reason—

Too late. Marilyn was regally leading the way down the stairs, sniffing as if she'd smelled something bad. Latonya nudged Tess forward, and, after one final look at James, Tess moved. But with every step, she swore she could feel his gaze on her.

All too soon, they were outside of the club and on the busy Savannah street. The wind was a bit brisk, and Tess sucked in a bracing breath.

"Bad boys are the *worst*," Latonya said as her worried gaze slid over Tess. "I was just kidding earlier. That wasn't like, advice you were supposed to follow. Those kinds of guys really aren't for you. They'd chew you up and spit you out."

Marilyn narrowed her eyes on Tess. "Do I need to go back inside and kick someone's ass?"

She loved her friends. "No. And I promise, he didn't do anything bad."

"Hmmm." Latonya didn't look convinced.

He offered. Such a tempting offer.

Latonya and Marilyn hooked their arms with Tess and they all headed down the street. "Bad is over-rated," Latonya told her. "Speaking from real experience here. You stick with one of those safe, solid doctors at the hospital."

She wasn't interested in them. They pushed for more than she wanted to give. She didn't *have* more to give.

Safety…what was really safe these days?

"You don't need trouble. You don't need that guy back there." Now it was Marilyn talking. "I shouldn't have pushed you to come here. This isn't your scene."

What was her scene?

With every step that she took away from the club, an ache seemed to settle in Tess's chest. She had the weird, sinking feeling that she'd just lost something. But that was crazy. She hadn't found anything in that club.

So there had been nothing to lose...

Right?

***

Well, that had sure as fuck been unexpected.

James Smith released a slow breath as he headed into his office on the second floor of the club. The club—hell, the place was just a hobby. A way to pass all of the free time that he suddenly had at his disposal. When he'd acquired the space, he'd decided the place needed an upgrade. He'd exposed some brick, ripped out some walls, and brought in a popular, local band. He'd made sure the staff completed updated training, and bam, suddenly, the club was *the* place to be.

He normally hated crowds. So for the last two weeks, he'd been watching folks in his club from a distance.

But this hadn't been a normal night.

She hadn't been normal.

She'd been wearing jeans. A flowing, black blouse. Her thick, dark hair had been pulled up in a bun, and loose tendrils had escaped to fall artfully around her delicate face.

Delicate. That word seemed to fit her, or at least, it had…as he'd viewed her across the club. He'd felt her gaze on him, had turned to see who was checking him out, and been surprised by the absolute punch he'd felt in his gut.

When he'd seen her, he'd just wanted.

Not normal. Not at all. He normally had much better control. With his, uh, *former,* line of work, he needed control. A lack of control would screw up a mission. Worse, it would get you killed.

He'd seen her, and he'd wanted to lunge off the barstool. Wanted to head straight toward her, and, before he'd even realized that he'd been moving — James had been on the way to her table.

Then he'd gotten a look into her dark chocolate eyes.

Not fragile. He'd seen a core of steel staring back at him. She'd been direct and blunt and he fucking *loved* —

"Ahem." His assistant cleared his throat.

The guy had trailed James into the office. He'd *known* Barnes was there. Just as he'd known Barnes would give that gruff, *ahem,* once his patience wore out. Refusing to smile, James glanced his way. "Something I can do for you?"

"I'm assuming you want the standard report?" Barnes asked.

Barnes had actually been with him—on and off—for a year. James had initially tried to ditch the fellow, but Barnes just kept turning up, kinda like a bad penny.

You don't kill the guy – one time – and he decides to stick to you like glue.

But at the question from his assistant, James hesitated. The standard report. When James became involved with anyone—even on the lightest of levels—he had an investigation conducted. He always had to look for enemies. Betrayals. It was the nature of the beast for him.

When you were a fucking ex-assassin, there were plenty of people out there who wanted to get some serious payback.

While Tess had certainly seemed genuine enough, he couldn't take chances. But... "Not standard."

Barnes blinked.

"I want in-depth." He could still taste her. Still smell her. Vanilla cream. He wanted to lick her all over. James rolled back his shoulders. "I want to know every single thing there is to know about Tess Barrett."

Barnes took a few quick steps forward. "Is there a problem?"

Yes, I want her too damn badly. But she'd run away. She might not ever come back to him, and that would be a freaking shame.

If she did come back, though…

I made her a promise, and I intend to deliver on my word.

He'd make her feel far, far better than just good. He'd have her screaming.

"Ahem."

Right. Barnes. He focused on his assistant. Barnes had on his new glasses. Completely, unnecessary glasses that he thought made him look older and more distinguished. His black hair was slicked back from his forehead. His suit was perfectly pressed.

"Is there a problem?" Barnes repeated. For a moment, his ice blue eyes hardened.

It was easy to forget that the guy — barely twenty-one now — had once turned on one of the biggest crime families on the West Coast. Barnes looked different now and that was all part of the fellow's plan. And the reason for the slicked back, dyed hair. And Clark Kent-like glasses.

Barnes was always afraid that someone else would come after him.

He didn't have to worry. James had his back.

"No problem," James responded slowly. "Just…I want to know everything."

"Why?"

"Because I like her." And letting her walk away, hell, he couldn't shake the feeling that when he'd done that, he'd made one of the worst mistakes of his life.

CHAPTER TWO

She shouldn't be in the club. Tess brushed past the bouncer who barely glanced at her and headed into the thick crowd on the dance floor. She shouldn't be in *his* club again. She should be at home but—

She'd lost a patient that day. A sixteen-year-old boy who'd flipped on his ATV. God, she'd tried so hard to save him. He'd died on her table, and his family had been gutted. *She'd* been gutted. The pain was still knifing through her, and she knew she was supposed to hold it together. Doctors didn't break down and cry in front of everyone. They kept working. They got the job done.

She'd stayed at the hospital until her shift ended. She'd treated other patients. She'd talked with nurses and hospital administration. She'd done her job even though her insides were ripped and hurting.

But as soon as the shift had ended, she'd run. *To him?*

The band blasted. Her hand flew over her cheek, swiping at the wetness there.

Why was she in the club? Why wasn't she at home, in her rented condo, hiding where no one could see how torn apart she was?

Why—

"Who the hell made you cry?" James stood in front of her. He'd shoved his way through the crowd. "Tell me the name, and he's dead."

He is dead. I tried to save him, and I couldn't. Another tear trickled down her cheek. "I-I changed my mind."

She needed oblivion. She needed release. She needed—

Him.

Tess stared up at James and his blazing eyes. Now she knew exactly why she was in the club. She'd gone there for him. Because simply being closer to him seemed to ease the ache in her chest. She could breathe again without it hurting.

His hands lifted and curled around her shoulders. "Tell me the name."

He thought someone had hurt her. She got that, and his protectiveness warmed her even more. Though he'd obviously been kidding when he said if she told him the name, the guy was dead. "It was...a bad day at work." Understatement. Major, major understatement.

His eyes narrowed as he searched her face. Then James gave a jerky nod. "You want a drink?"

Someone bumped into her from behind. James growled and pulled her closer, sheltering her in his arms. It was nice to be there, surrounded by him. More of the cold faded. "No drink." Tess tilted her head back. "I came for you."

His gaze drank her in. "Not yet, you haven't. But you will."

He — oh. *Got it.*

"Let's get out of here," he told her.

Away from the crowd and music? Sounded wonderful.

"Be sure," he rumbled.

She was sure. She'd run to him. But Tess licked her lips and asked, "The deal we agreed on before?" Her voice was soft.

He heard her, though. She knew it.

Sex without strings.

James nodded.

"I'm sure."

Then they were heading for the exit. People got out of his way as he kept her tucked against his side. She was warm and safe because she was with him. Her feelings didn't make any sense, she knew that, but in that moment, Tess didn't care.

When she'd been hurting, she'd thought of James.

She was going to do this. Going to let go and see what happened. One night. What could it possibly hurt?

The bouncer held the door as they hurried outside. A long, black limo waited at the curb. She'd vaguely been aware of it when she'd rushed into the club, but now it came into sharp focus as James steered her toward it.

"Wait — it's yours?"

The driver had gotten out. He hurried to open the back door.

"Something new I collected." James murmured. "That's what I do. I collect things."

That was interesting. "What sort of things?"

"Everything."

She ducked inside the limo. The seats were made of leather, soft illumination filled the interior of the vehicle — coming from faint lights that had been strategically placed in the back — and champagne was chilling nearby. A lump rose in her throat. "You were expecting someone." *Someone who isn't me.*

He slid in behind her. The driver shut the door. James eased closer to her, and his hand brushed over hers. "Yes."

This was awkward. And some of her delicious warmth faded. "You were going to hook up with some random chick tonight?" Anger — jealousy — twisted in her stomach.

James gave a low laugh. A sexy rumble of sound. "There is nothing random about you."

Wait — he...*crap. I'm the random chick?*

Her gaze faltered. She couldn't meet his stare as her eyes darted to the champagne. The driver was cranking the limo, and she had the fast and frantic urge to lunge out of the vehicle before it started to move down the road.

James caught her hand in his. Threaded his fingers with hers. "I hoped you'd come back. I wanted to be ready if you did. If you didn't show tonight, then I just would've had the limo waiting tomorrow. I would have kept it waiting, for you."

Her head turned toward him. "Is this a line? I have a really hard time telling if what you say is the truth or a lie."

"Most people have a hard time deciding if I'm lying or not." He shrugged.

"That wasn't an answer." The car was moving. Her chance to jump out had passed.

"How about this...I haven't lied to you yet. And I won't."

"*That* sounds like a lie."

He turned over her hand. Began to trace a light path over her palm.

She shivered.

"Ask me anything. I won't lie. It will be a new experience for me. Being completely honest with someone from the very get-go."

She had no idea where the driver was taking them. Tess didn't remember hearing James give any instructions to the fellow. "Where are we going?"

"My place. We'll have complete privacy, and you can tell me all about your bad day."

Her head shook in a quick, negative motion. She didn't want to talk about the kid she'd lost.

"Or…" Another slow trace on her palm. Since when were palms so sensitive? "Or we can have crazy, wild sex and you can scream my name while you come over and over again."

Her breath choked out. "Option two sounds like a winner." *Ding, ding.*

He laughed. "See? Us being totally honest with each other is working out great so far."

He was so different from anyone she'd met before. "You're not, like, secretly a killer or anything, are you?"

He stopped his pattern on her palm.

"Who are you really, James Smith?"

His gaze held hers. "I'm a former assassin turned club owner. I also dabble in the personal protection business with a new semi-friend I have. You should know, I don't make friends easily, but I do seem to create enemies every other minute. In fact, I have enemies all over the world. I can kill a man in a thousand different ways without batting an eye, but I swear to you, I won't hurt you. I will keep you safe, give you pleasure, and you will never need to fear me a day in your life."

He was…

Laughter broke from her. Light and free, and it felt so good to laugh after the sorrow that had surrounded her. *Former assassin turned club owner.* Sure. Like she believed that one. He was getting her back for her oversharing the night before when she'd spilled out everything to him. "So much for total honesty." The smile lingered on her lips.

He didn't smile back at her. "I meant what I said." James lifted her hand and brought it to his lips. He pressed a kiss to her palm. Then nipped, lightly, and she jolted. Heat flooded through her body. "I will give you more pleasure than you can stand," James promised, "and I will *not* hurt you."

"I won't hurt you, either," she whispered. Emotions weren't going to be involved. Just sex. They'd play it safe, and no one would get hurt. As for pleasure… "I don't have lot of experience." A stilted, painful confession. "So I'm not sure how, um, good I can—"

He gave her palm another nip. "You're not just good. You're going to combust with me."

That was a bit of pressure. And combusting sounded painful. She didn't exactly remember her other lovers going wild with her and them burning any sheets. School had been her life for so long. She'd graduated high school early, gone straight to college, and been far younger than the others in her class. The guys hadn't glanced at her. When she'd gone to med school, that was when she'd dated some. But there had been so much work and studying, the relationships had fizzled fast. The sex had been okay. Nothing to make her scream, though.

She'd like to scream.

She'd like to make him go wild. "I'm a fast learner."

Oh, God, had she just felt his tongue lick her palm?

She stared into his eyes and got lost. *Focus, woman.* "I'm a fast learner," Tess said again. It was true. "You show me what you like, and I'll make sure you enjoy me."

He slowly lowered her hand. "Baby, I have no doubt that I will enjoy you." He leaned forward. Kissed her. And it was exactly like before. His mouth touched hers, her lips parted for him, and her whole body went molten. She burned and ached and wanted.

She didn't think about death or failure or being alone.

She thought about him and about all of the things that they were going to do together.

"I am going to enjoy every single fucking inch of you," he promised against her mouth.

***

She'd come back to him. He'd hoped she would, and yeah, he'd even had the limo ready, just in case. Why not be optimistic? He'd known she felt the same red-hot attraction that he did.

But James hadn't been sure of Tess. And the more he'd discovered about her, the more uncertainty had chipped away at him.

She was so fucking out of his league. He shouldn't have his blood-stained hands on her, much less plan to do all the dirty things he imagined.

Barnes had been fast with his intel. He was a great hacker, after all.

Tess Barrett. Age twenty-four. A freaking certified genius. She'd blown through school early. Graduated college and med school with a ton of honors. And now she was working as an ER doc in town.

She saved lives.

He fucking took them. How twisted was that? He'd tried to warn her. In the limo, he'd been one hundred percent honest with her. That shit had felt good. He'd never been one hundred percent honest with anyone before. Not that his doc had believed him. Why would she?

Assassin turned club owner. Hell, that sounded like bullshit. Being a club owner wasn't exactly his long-term goal. He wanted to get fully into the protection business, and he'd been working that angle hard lately, trying to convince the right people that he could be trusted.

But it was hard, considering his reputation.

When the world thought you were the bad guy, no one wanted to let you get close.

Right then, Tess turned toward him. A faint smile curved her full lips. "I love your place."

He loved looking at her. She was freaking beautiful. Did she get that? Her hair was up in a bun again, and a few tendrils had escaped. Her nose was small and straight, her jaw curving, and her cheekbones high. She had the sweetest little dip in her chin. A dimple that he wanted to lick.

Hell, who was he kidding? He wanted to lick every single inch of her.

"Did you 'collect' this place, too?" Tess asked as she tilted her head.

Actually, he had. People paid for his special skills with all sorts of things. He didn't just kill. The assassin job was in the past, and he'd friggin' done that work for Uncle Sam. A dirty and twisted career path that he didn't like to remember. "I did." He rolled one shoulder. Glanced around at his new home. Exposed brick lined the walls. He loved the brick. It was sturdy and lasting, and it stood strong against the world. They were on the second floor of a building he owned. The bottom floor was empty, for now. The second floor was pure freaking open concept. Yeah, okay, so maybe he watched home improvement shows to relax. Who didn't? He'd torn down some walls here just like he had at his club. Pounded the shit out of stuff and put in a ton of windows to look out at the city.

Turned out, his hands were good for more than killing. He could make things, too.

Tess carried a small bag with her, and she slid it onto the nearby chair. She gazed at him a moment longer, as if thinking things through, before she moved toward the nearby floor-to-ceiling windows. "The view is incredible."

He had one killer view, all right. He could see her completely. Tess was clad in her jeans and a loose sweater. Though she looked good in her outfit, he wanted her clothes gone. Wanted her naked. And in the bed that waited.

But she seemed nervous. He could tell by the way she rocked forward onto the balls of her feet every few moments. And by the way she still had on her clothes. The clothing was a dead giveaway. If he'd had his way, they both would have been naked five seconds after walking through the doorway of his home.

"You want a drink?"

She rocked forward onto the balls of her feet again as she kept gazing out the windows. "No, thank you."

Right. She'd told him the night before that she didn't drink. He scrambled for something to say.

"Uh, James, you're not going to like...pull out any bondage stuff, are you?" Now, as if she'd gathered her courage and come to some decision, she spun to face him. Bit her lip. "No handcuffs?"

He had some in the bedroom. Tools of his trade. "You want them?"

"No! I was just, you know, making sure. Making sure we were *not* going to use them."

It took considerable effort not to smile at her. Sometimes, she was so freaking adorable. And sexy. "Don't knock the cuffs until you try them."

Her eyes widened. Her tongue swiped across her lower lip. Well, well, was that a bit of interest?

Mental note. Come back to that one day. He locked down his muscles. Breathed slowly. And tried to ignore the fact her vanilla cream scent hung in the air and tempted him. "I'm not pressuring you for anything, baby. If you want to walk away, I can get my driver to take you home."

Once again, she rocked forward onto the balls of her feet. Forward, then back.

He waited for her. He wanted to reach out and lock his arms around her. Pick her up and carry her to his bed.

Never let her go.

Whoa. Where the hell did that thought come from? This wasn't about keeping her. They'd just met. This was…

She gave a determined nod. Her hands went to the bottom of her sweater. She yanked it up and over her head, and dropped it on the floor near her feet.

Fuck, yes. She was *gorgeous.* Her breasts pushed against the black bra that she wore — looked like it was made out of satin, but he'd bet her skin was softer than that material.

Then she kicked off her shoes. Tossed away her socks. Her hands went to the front of her jeans —

He hurried toward her. Caught her hands. "Wh-what's wrong?"

The little stutter made his heart surge in his chest.

"You're in front of the window. It's dark out there but every light in this area is on bright."

"Oh, no." Horror filled her gaze.

"And I don't really want to share you with any lucky sonofabitch who might be strolling by outside, so…" He scooped her into his arms. Just like he'd wanted to do. "Let's go to the bedroom."

Her arm looped around his neck. "You're strong."

"And you're sexy as fucking hell." He put his mouth on hers. Tasted her nice and deep and wanted so much more. "I need you," he growled. *"Now."*

He hurried toward the bedroom. Pretty much ran. Since when had he been that desperate for a woman?

Since her.

"Yes, let's do it fast," she whispered. "Before I lose my nerve."

Dammit. She said the most honest things, and if he'd had a heart, James would have sworn that it softened a little bit. For her. He carried her into his bedroom and carefully lowered her onto the massive bed. He wanted to reach for the waist of her jeans and yank those things off her. But, instead…

"You can tell me to stop at any time, and I will." She needed to understand their situation completely. The rest of the world could say he was a fucking nightmare, but he was more. She needed to understand that she would always be safe with him.

Her breath came faster. "I don't want to stop."

"What do you want?"

She reached for the waistband of her jeans once more. Undid the snap. Lowered the zipper. "I want you."

"And I want to hear you scream for me." He caught the jeans. Dragged them off her legs. She was wearing black, satin panties to match her bra. He put a knee on the bed and leaned over her. His fingers slid over the satin. Nice and soft. His fingers eased on down, moving between her legs. She spread her legs more for him as his fingers stroked her sex through the panties. "You ready?"

Tess nodded.

He curled his fingers around the top of the panties, then tugged them down her legs.

"I'm not, um, super into foreplay, so we can just get straight to—"

He put his mouth on her.

She sucked in a sharp breath as her hips bucked up against him. "James!"

He licked. Kissed. Stroked her with his fingers and tongue, and he'd been so right. She was way softer than the satin, and she tasted divine. He could lap her up all night long.

But the more he licked, the more her hips rocked against him. Her hands grabbed for his shoulders.

To push him away?

He lifted his head.

She was staring at him, all wide eyed, flushed, and freaking gorgeous as she said, "Please, don't stop!"

Hell, yes. His mouth went back to her. Back to devouring her because she was delicious, and he could feel her body tensing up with her pending orgasm. His dick shoved against the front of his jeans, long and hard and fully erect. He was so damn turned on, and he kept licking her. Kept driving her higher and higher until she came.

"*James!*" Her voice was high and pierced with pleasure.

The climax rocked her body and he wanted it to last and last so he kept right on going with his mouth and fingers. The first orgasm had been only the start. Sort of a…break-the-ice situation.

Now he was ready for the real show.

His fingers stroked over her as he lifted his body.

Her breath was panting out. The lamps were on in his bedroom—the curtains were pulled closed, so no chance that anyone was looking in the windows—and he could see her perfectly. She still wore her bra. He got rid of it in an instant. Her pink-tipped breasts thrust toward him. Her nipples were tight and he just had to take a taste. A quick lick.

She tipped back her head and moaned.

He licked again. Sucked harder.

He was positioned between her spread legs, and his eager cock wanted to be in her. Buried balls deep. He wanted to feel the contractions of her release around him when she came again.

"You still have on your clothes," she panted. "How do you still have on your clothes?"

He almost smiled. Even though he wanted her more than breath, he almost smiled.

Until her hands reached between their bodies. Until her fingers stroked his cock through his jeans.

Then he forgot about smiling.

He'd been holding tight to his control but—

She unsnapped his jeans. Pulled down the zipper. He was a commando kind of guy, and his cock sprang toward her. She wrapped her hot little fist around him. Pumped once, twice, and then she said, "I can lick you, too. I'm a fast learner, just tell me—"

The image of her mouth on his cock sent him over the edge.

Yeah, he was fucking her. Right then and there.

He pulled away from her long enough to kill the lights and ditch his clothes. He grabbed the condom. Ripped that bitch open and had it on in record time. He lunged for the bed—for her. She reached for him with greedy hands and he took her mouth, driving his tongue past her lips because he needed to kiss her again before he took her body.

He fucking loved her mouth.

He positioned his cock at the entrance to her body. Lodged the tip right there. He needed to plunge hard and deep, but he held back, locking down his muscles because he didn't want to hurt her.

She tore her mouth from his. "You are driving me crazy! I want you inside, *now!*"

He plunged inside. Sank into the tightest, hottest heaven of his life. She moaned, he let out a guttural groan, and he kissed his control good-bye. "Hold on," James gritted out.

Her legs locked around him. Her hands curled over his shoulders, and her nails bit into his skin. He withdrew, thrust — and was lost.

His thrusts were frantic. Deep. Her moans and gasps drove him on. He was insane, totally swept away by her. He could feel his orgasm building, growing stronger and stronger, but he needed her to come again before he exploded. His hand snaked over her body, moved to her clit where he stroked her ruthlessly, driving her need higher and higher until —

"*James!*"

He loved her scream. Loved the way her sex clamped around him and sweet shudders shook her whole body. He let go and the pleasure took him, gutting him in a release that went on and on. When it finally ended, fuck, he was barely holding his weight off her. He wanted to crash down and hold her tight.

Never let go.

No, no, that shit didn't happen. He didn't cling to anyone. Didn't want to *keep* anyone. That wasn't how his life worked. He collected things. Not people. People came and went.

He unclenched his jaw. Slowly withdrew. She gave a little gasp, and he stilled instantly. "I'm sorry, baby. Did I hurt you?"

"No. That was awesome."

He smiled. In the dark, she wouldn't be able to see his smile. Or the marks on his body. There was a reason he'd turned off the lights before he'd stripped. He didn't want his scars to scare her.

He'd grabbed her hands whenever she'd tried to run those soft fingers of hers over his chest and back, so she hadn't realized how damaged he was.

Damaged. Such a good word. Because he was damaged — on the inside and out.

He eased away from her and padded to the bathroom. He didn't need a light. Hell, he could see damn well in the dark. A trait that had come in handy more times than he could count. So it was easy to get in the bathroom. To ditch the condom. To grab some jogging pants and a t-shirt and return to the bedroom to find —

Tess, rooting around in the dark. Swearing when she stubbed her toe on the bed post. He stood near the wall, crossed his arms over his chest, and then flipped on the light.

"Gah!"

She jerked upright, blinking owlishly. God, she was sexy. Her hair had come out of the bun, and the thick, dark locks tumbled over her shoulders. Her breasts bounced toward him, well, they bounced until she yanked her sweater over her head and tugged it down to her thighs.

Then she dove for her jeans. Put them on in a flash. Grabbed for her shoes—

"I'm getting the impression that you're in a hurry," he murmured as he kept his pose against the wall.

"I, um…" Her hands fisted at her sides, *after* she put on her shoes. "You went to the bathroom without saying anything so I thought that meant we were done."

Not even close. They were only getting started.

"I figured I'd get dressed and hurry out so I wouldn't be in your way."

"We should be very clear on something." His arms dropped. He pushed away from the wall. Stalked toward her.

Her shoulders stiffened, and her chin notched up. He hadn't got to lick that cute-as-fuck dimple on the bottom of her chin yet. He would. Soon.

She didn't back up at his approach. Tess waited and watched him.

He stopped right in front of her. Wanted to put his hands all over her. "You're not in the way. You will never be in my way."

Her teeth bit into her lower lip.

He growled.

Her breath came a little faster. "That was...a lot more than I expected."

Her honesty was about to drive him to his knees. There was no pretense with her, and it was so different to be with someone who just said what she thought. Everyone was always trying to lie in his world. Hell, *he* was a world-class, grade A liar. But she wasn't.

She wasn't anything like him.

I should keep my hands off her.

Instead, his hand rose. His knuckles slid over her cheek. "It was exactly what I expected."

A little line appeared between her eyebrows. "Is that bad?"

"No. Not even close." His lips skimmed over hers. "The sex was just as fantastic as I knew it would be." And he'd be wanting more. A whole lot more with her.

She leaned toward him. Her scent swept around him. When she left, he knew the vanilla cream would linger on his sheets. On him. And he liked that. He wanted her scent on him. Wanted his scent on her. That way, other bastards would stay the hell back.

Whoa. Hold up. He wasn't getting jealous, was he?

"I swear I can still feel you," Tess whispered. "On the inside."

Okay, obviously she was trying to drive him insane.

She stepped back. "I have to go."

He wanted her to go right back to bed.

"This is more than I—" She waved a hand vaguely in the air, then that hand dropped and pressed to her chest. "Everything is all tense and swirling, and I think I need to step back."

He wasn't going to stop her. But… "Do I get to see you again?"

Her gaze held his. "No strings?"

"I don't see any. Do you?"

She shook her head. "I'd like to see you again." Her gaze darted to the bed. "I'd like…I'd like that a lot."

He waited for her stare to return to him. When it did, James offered her a slow smile. "Give me your phone."

She glanced around. "I swear, um, I had a bag somewhere."

Now he laughed. He vaguely remembered her putting down the bag in the other room. He turned, going after it, and Tess hurried to follow him. She spied the bag on a chair near the big windows, and she hauled her phone out of it. She unlocked the screen and handed it to him.

He put in his contact info. And for his name…

He handed the phone back to her.

She frowned down at the screen. Hell, even her frowns were sexy. *"My guy?"* She looked up at him. "You're —"

"I'm the guy you call when you need something. Anything. I'm the guy you need."

She pushed the phone back into her bag. "Give me your phone."

He glanced around. Spied it on the table. Did *not* remember putting that damn thing there. He'd been distracted by her. James unlocked the phone and handed it to her. She seemed very serious as she added in her contact information.

Then she gave the phone back to him.

Truly curious now, he glanced down at the —

Laughter tore from him.

"My best sex ever."

"Are you laughing because it's not true?"

His gaze shot to her face.

Her cheeks had flushed. "Because I was just kidding. I mean…"

James shoved the phone into his pocket. He caught her arms and hauled her closer. "Actually, it is fucking true." He kissed her. "I like you."

"That's good. I think I like you, too."

Another kiss. He didn't want her to go. He wanted her back in that bed, with him, tearing up the sheets all night long but…

But there were shadows under her eyes. He still didn't know what in the hell had sent her running to him, but he would be finding out. She needed to rest, he could see that. "I'll call for the limo."

"That's not necessary. I can catch a cab."

"I want to make sure you get home safely. It's part of my deal."

She lifted one eyebrow. "Wild sex and safety?"

A nod.

"It's a good deal. I'll take it."

And I'll take you.

The thought was possessive. Mostly because he was starting to feel very possessive about his doc. But he kept playing the gentleman. When the limo arrived, he headed downstairs with Tess. Didn't pounce on her during the trip to her place. James thought he deserved serious props for that one.

He escorted her to her second-floor condo. He liked her building, a converted warehouse that offered one large condo on the bottom floor and another on the second. Aesthetically, the building was nice, but the security was shit. When he asked about her downstairs neighbors, Tess told him they were a retired couple on an extended trip to Europe.

"Thanks for the ride home," Tess murmured as she stood before her door.

He had the distinct feeling she was *not* inviting him in.

"And thanks for the, you know, awe-inspiring sex."

He couldn't help his smile. "You stay stuff like that, and it will totally go to my head."

"I enjoyed being with you."

Now those words made his heart feel funny. James bent forward and kissed her long and lingeringly, before reluctantly letting her go. "You know where to find me, Tess."

A nod.

He waited until she'd shut and locked her door before he headed back downstairs.

And when he was in the limo, riding in the back alone…

His mask vanished. He ripped out his phone. Dialed Barnes. "I want to know what the fuck happened to Tess today," he snapped, not bothering with a greeting. "Find out what hurt her — *who* hurt her."

"Uh…boss?"

"Because no one hurts her. Understand me? *No one.*"

He ended the call. Stared down at his hands. Thought about the way they'd been all over her body.

The hands of a killer…Tess should have believed him when he'd told her about his past. In his way, he'd been trying to warn her off. Trying to tell her that she should stay away from a guy like him.

Too late now. He'd had a taste of her.

He wanted more.

CHAPTER THREE

My shift is over. Tess hunched her shoulders as she shot off the text to James. *Still want to meet up?* A nurse bustled past her. Tess smiled a quick greeting at Sean. He was one of the best nurses on the floor and always friendly to everyone.

Her phone dinged. Her gaze darted away from Sean and back to her phone.

Absolutely.

Her heart raced a little faster.

Another ding.

I'll be waiting outside for you.

She shoved the phone into the front pocket of her scrubs. She hurried to the locker room and changed as quickly as she could, donning jeans and a sexy, flirty red top that she'd picked up on impulse. The top was totally not like anything she usually wore, but she liked it and it made her feel a little extra bold as she put on the heels that she'd brought to wear for her meet-up with James.

Heels. She could not even remember the last time she'd worn heels. She was mostly a flats kind of woman.

Tess put her phone in her small bag, then slammed her locker shut. The clang seeming extra loud to her ears.

A low whistle followed the clang.

Her gaze jerked to the right.

Latonya smiled at her. "Someone's being sexy."

Someone was *trying* to be sexy. "Does it look okay?" Tess pulled on the shirt. It dipped super low, revealing the swell of her breasts, and maybe it was too much.

Latonya swatted away her hands. "Stop doing that. Okay doesn't even begin to describe the situation." She surveyed Tess with a critical eye. "You look killer. *Killer*."

Relief surged through her.

"Now, spill. Tell your dearest friend in the world who the guy is and why I haven't heard about him before." Latonya still wore her scrubs. A stethoscope circled her neck. Tess knew Latonya's ER shift was just about to start. They'd met during their first year of med school and had become quick friends. Latonya's easy warmth had pulled Tess in before she'd ever even realized what was happening. And, unlike so many others, Latonya had never pushed Tess to reveal her past. She'd just accepted her.

"Give me details about this man who has you pulling out the heels. *Heels*. I think I may just be having a hallucination."

"No hallucination, and you *have* heard about him." No one else was in there, so Tess decided to say, "Bad things."

"What?" Her eyebrows wiggled down.

"I'm meeting up with the owner of the club. Remember him?" She smoothed her hair. It was still in the bun. But…

Tess pulled it down.

"Oh, damn. The hair is coming down. This is like every makeover show in America. The hair comes down because you're about to get freaky."

A laugh sputtered from Tess. "Stop." *And I am so about to get freaky, I think.* She shoved up the sleeve of her blouse and glanced at her watch. "I need to go. He's waiting."

"Oh, Tess, let him wait. Men need to wait. It makes them appreciate us more." But she headed toward the door with Tess. Slowly. "And are you serious? You're dating Tall, Sexy, and Bad?"

Tess shoved open the door. "His name is James."

"Um, I like my name for him better. It has more personality."

Tess's heels tapped over the tiled floor. "And I wouldn't call it dating, exactly —"

Latonya grabbed her arm and hauled her closer. "What would you call it?"

Tess allowed a slow smile to curl her lips.

In response, Latonya shook her head. "That smile both makes me happy, and it worries me."

"He's outside," Tess whispered as she glanced around the busy hospital corridor. "I have to go."

"Yes, well, you'd better give me a whole lot of details at the first opportunity."

Not going to happen. Tess wasn't a detailing-sharing type, and Latonya knew that.

But Latonya gave her a firm glare. "Drinks with me and Marilyn. Pencil that shit in."

Someone called out for Latonya, and she hurried away.

Tess turned on her heel and tap-tap-tapped her way to the exit as—

"Dr. Barrett?" A tall, blond-haired man in green scrubs came to a hard stop.

Wonderful. *Not.* But she straightened her shoulders and halted so she could stare at Dr. Devin Goddard. It was a running joke in the ER that the guy's nickname was God Complex. He truly thought he was the greatest thing going in the hospital. He let the staff know that fact on a regular basis, and he absolutely made sure all the *female* staff members were regularly apprised of his many, many merits—or, what he perceived to be his merits.

"You look…different." His gaze dipped over her.

God Complex was a competent doctor, she'd give him that. But he'd tried to make passes at her from day one, and she'd more than proven she wasn't interested. The last thing she wanted to do was have a chat with him about her attire.

While James was waiting.

"It's my non-work outfit, Devin. I have those, you know." She stepped forward.

He blocked her path. Smirked. "Are you going out on a date?"

"No, I'm going to church. Excuse me." She pushed past him.

"What? Seriously? Hey, wait—Tess!"

She was at the sliding glass exit doors. The security guard on duty gave Tess a quick wave, then he shot an eye roll toward Devin.

Tess double timed her steps—or tried to, the heels were wobbly—as she hurried along the sidewalk and toward the—

Limo?

Yes, the limo waited. The familiar driver stood by the door. Ryley. She'd been introduced to him on her ride home. Ryley Hutch inclined his head toward her.

She lifted her hand and waved to him. A little nervously. Her steps slowed.

"That doesn't look like church."

She jumped.

Spun.

Devin had followed her out of the hospital. He glared at the limo. "It's waiting for you, isn't it? And that isn't church." He put his hand on her shoulder. Turned his gaze to her. "I didn't think you were seeing anyone. I mean, *I* asked you out—"

He had. Very arrogantly. Very *I'm-doing-you-a-favor*-like. And she'd declined. At least five times.

"You said you weren't dating. You said you didn't have *time* to date."

"You'll want to remove the hand." The masculine voice was low and lethal, and it sent a shiver over Tess's skin.

She hadn't heard James approach. But, suddenly, she could feel him. His warmth was right behind her.

"Unless she asked you to touch her, you move the fucking hand, right now. Or I move it for you."

Those words were even lower. Even rougher.

Devin snatched his hand back. "Tess said she was going to church. You don't look like fucking church!"

"You sure about that? Push me, and I can take you to God."

Tess pressed her lips together so she wouldn't laugh. Devin was glaring. Gaping. Glaring some more.

James took her hand in his. Twined his fingers with hers. "You look absolutely beautiful."

Her head swiveled toward him.

"Love the red." He grinned down at her. "Makes your skin look like cream, and your hair seem even darker. You've got this whole super sexy Snow White thing happening right now."

She had to laugh. That was crazy and oddly sweet at the same time.

James turned his head to stare at Devin. His smile vanished. "Why are you still here?"

"I was on my way to my car. My Jag." Devin drew himself up to his full height. Shoved his nose high into the air. Using his most arrogant voice — the voice he used to make interns jump and quake — he demanded, "Who are you?"

"Who the fuck are you?" James tossed right back, not missing a beat. Then he shrugged. "Wait, never mind. I don't care." His gaze slid back to Tess. "You ready?"

More than ready. She nodded.

He led her toward the limo. Ryley held the back door open for them. She slid inside, and James followed behind her.

The door slammed shut a moment later. Through the tinted window, she could see Devin still standing there, staring after them.

"Tell me he isn't one of your exes." James sprawled on the seat.

"He isn't one of my exes," she said immediately.

He blinked. "Did you just tell me what I asked to hear? Or is it the truth?"

She put her hand on his chest. He was dressed up tonight, and she was glad she'd worn her heels and the sexy top. He wore crisp, black dress pants. A white dress shirt, unbuttoned at the collar, and a black coat that fit his wide shoulders perfectly. "I told you the truth. I've never been interested in Devin Goddard."

"He's interested in you."

The limo was moving.

"He is interested in anyone with a pulse."

James's mouth kicked up into a half-smile, but his eyes remained serious. "If you just wanted to have sex with someone, he was right there, the whole time."

"I didn't want just someone." She stared into his eyes. "I wanted awe-inspiring."

Now his eyes did gleam. "Baby, you keep saying stuff like that and —" But he stopped.

She didn't want him to stop. She wanted to know exactly what he'd intended to tell her. "And what?"

He swallowed. His lashes — the man truly had incredibly thick, dark lashes — shielded his gaze for a moment before he said, "You keep saying stuff like that, and I'll want to fuck you right here."

Her gaze darted to the privacy screen. It was up. "Can the driver hear us?" Because if Ryley could hear her, she'd be mortified.

"No."

"See us?" She couldn't even believe she was *thinking* this.

"No. Ryley can't see back here right now."

She bit her lower lip.

"You got another question for me?" James asked, voice all smooth and rich and deep.

Do it. Tess let go of her lower lip. "Will you fuck me here?"

That grin of his came again, slow and body-melting. "Baby, it would be my pleasure to fuck you *anywhere.*"

Her chest felt warm. Everything from her day was forgotten. The stress. The worry. She kicked off her heels.

"Those were hot as hell, by the way. Love them," James praised.

She was smiling again. She seemed to do that a lot with him.

She shimmied out of her pants. And her red panties.

He released a low whistle. "Baby, you are pure perfection."

She didn't feel like perfection. Nerves rushed through her body, but she wanted this. She wanted him. Tess straddled him, her knees sinking into the leather seats. Low music was playing—the music finally penetrated in her mind. Some jazzy music that was oddly sensual.

Her tongue swiped over her lower lip as she gathered up her courage. She'd never had sex in a moving vehicle before. Wait, correction, she'd never had sex in *any* vehicle before. Totally new experience. Her fingers went to the top of his pants. A few moments later, she had his pants open, and his long, fully erect length thrust toward her.

She glanced up, surprised that he was already so—

James chuckled. "Seriously? You asked me to fuck you in the car. If I hadn't already been turned on, my dick would have gone to instant full erection." He leaned forward and pressed a kiss to her neck. "But I *was* already turned on. The instant I saw you in your heels and your hot red top, my dick applauded."

She curled her hands around said dick. "An applauding dick, huh?" She didn't ever remember teasing a lover the way she did with him. It just was easy. Comfortable. "That is something new."

"You have no idea."

Oh, she had lots of ideas. Lots of things that she wanted to try. The limo was moving smoothly so...

She slid off the seat. Her knees hit the floorboard.

"Tess?"

Her mouth went to his dick. Her lips parted. She took him inside.

"Fuck. Baby, you are going to wreck me."

Well, she sure hoped no one wrecked right then. Because explaining things to the responding officers would be awkward as all hell.

In the next instant, Tess forgot about any hypothetical officers and concentrated on the matter at hand.

He was long and thick. Hard and warm. She feathered her mouth over the head of his cock. She licked that broad head, then sucked him inside. Not too deep, because she was learning, but—

"You are such a fast fucking learner," he growled.

She did try.

She smiled around his dick, then took him a little deeper. Sucked harder. Faster and—

She was on the seat.

Tess blinked. He'd lifted her up and positioned her so that she straddled his thighs, and her hands grabbed onto his shoulders as she tried to balance herself.

"I need to fuck you," James told her. His voice wasn't teasing. It had gone guttural.

A shiver worked over her.

"Now."

Now sounded great to her.

He yanked out a condom from his wallet. Shoved it on. She expected him to immediately thrust his cock into her, but he didn't. His fingers slid between their bodies. He worked her clit, strumming her with a touch that had her moaning. Only then, when she was moaning and arching toward him, when her own body was desperate for release, only then did he thrust inside of her.

He filled her completely. Every single inch.

Her eyes squeezed closed. She barely breathed. His hands had moved and locked around her hips.

"You control it," he rasped. "Fast, slow, or any fucking thing you want. Show me."

Her eyes opened.

She could see the lust burning in his golden stare. But he was waiting for her.

She pushed up on her knees. Then sank down. Again and again. His cock glided into her, almost out, in again. Every time she sank down, she was moaning. She'd started slow, but as the heated moments rolled past, she went faster and faster because her body was spinning out of control. Release was so close. She could feel it, could almost grab tight to it and —

She came. Exploded. Shattered. Splintered. She felt her body burst with pleasure, and her head tipped back as she chanted his name.

His hold tightened on her. He thrust deep once more, twice, and then he was growling her name and kissing her throat. Pressing his lips to her and coming inside of her.

Her arms locked around him. She held him. Didn't want to let go.

Didn't want to move at all.

And then she realized…

Oh, God, we aren't moving.

She shoved against him. Her head whipped up.

A satisfied smile curved his lips. "I should pick you up from work every night."

He should — Tess shook her head. "We're not moving."

"Um, no."

"Why aren't we moving?"

He caught her hand. Lifted it to his lips. Kissed her knuckles. "Probably because we're at our destination."

"How long have we been *not* moving?" Her breath panted out. And, purely by accident, her sex tightened around his cock.

He groaned. "I need a new condom before we go again—"

"James!" She darted off him. Grabbed for her pants and underwear. Did a snake-like shimmy to get them on. "How long has the limo been stopped?"

He ditched the condom. Cleaned up with a wipe he had in some mini-compartment. She probably should have used a wipe, too, but she'd already dressed and was looking for her shoes.

He hadn't answered her.

When she tossed him a frown, he winked. She could see his wink because the car was lit by soft lights inside. The same mood illumination that had been turned on the first night she'd been in the limo.

"I think it's been stopped for…a little while."

Oh, no. She shook her head. "The driver knows what we were doing!"

James just shrugged. "Does it matter?"

She frowned. "I've never had sex in a car before. It matters to me."

He reached for her hand once more. Curled his fingers over hers. "I was the first?"

"You probably have sex in the car all the time. You probably —"

"I was the first?"

"Yes, dammit! Did you even hear what I —"

He opened her hand. Pressed a kiss to her palm. "The driver won't say a word. You don't have to worry about Ryley. The man is a vault. Now, come on, I have a surprise waiting for you."

A surprise? "I don't like surprises."

He pushed open the car door. Pushed the thing open! As if she wasn't in the middle of a freak out.

"You don't like them? Really?" James glanced back at her with a teasing grin. "Because you just seduced me in a car. I'd say that definitely counted as a surprise."

Her jaw dropped.

He was out of the limo.

She grabbed her shoes. He'd been all *loud* as he exited so she was sure the driver had gotten an earful. Clutching the shoes to her chest, she rushed out after him.

The driver wasn't there.

The limo was parked. In a garage? In...*his* garage. She recognized it. They were in his building, the first floor.

"You told me you weren't in the mood to date." His tone seemed oddly careful. "So I thought you'd like to stay in."

She still held her shoes. "Where's the driver?"

"I gave Ryley orders to leave once he got us home."

Her cheeks stung. "So you knew what we'd be doing in the car."

"No, but I knew that I didn't want to share you with anyone, so I figured he could bring us here and cut out."

She put on her shoes. Stood there, her knees feeling all wobbly.

He held out his hand to her. "Come on. You'll like this." One shoulder rolled. "Maybe."

Now she was curious. She took his hand and let him lead her up the stairs. They were silent as they made their way to his door, then inside his home.

When they got inside...

The table was set. Not just set...

She sucked in a sharp breath. There was a freaking guy in a chef's uniform standing there. Candles glowed from the table, and it looked like she was walking into a full, four-course meal.

"You didn't want to go out."

Her head turned. James was watching her, with a hooded gaze, as if he wasn't quite sure how to proceed and was treading carefully.

"So I brought dinner in," he finished.

"You...you didn't have to do this." He'd brought a *chef* to his place?

A silent chef who was standing there, waiting.

"I can't cook for shit," James told her. "Trust me, if you were going to eat tonight, I had to do this."

Another laugh slipped from her. How did he do that? How did he catch her off-guard that way?

He glanced over at the chef. "It smells like heaven, Charles. Thank you."

Charles inclined his head. "Always a pleasure." He headed toward James.

James shook his hand, and she caught the very casual pass of money between them.

"Have a good night." Charles beamed at her. "I hope you enjoy the cuisine."

"Ah, I am sure I will. Thank you."

A few moments later, he was gone.

The feast waited.

She still didn't move. "This feels very...fancy."

"You look very fancy."

She shifted her high heels a bit. *It's just a look. It's not the real me.* The real her, the girl she'd been so long ago, had been as far from fancy as it was possible to be.

"You're a doctor, Tess. I'm sure you've gone out for plenty of fancy meals in your life."

She hadn't told him she was a doctor. She'd told him that she worked at the hospital. That he could pick her up there. But there were hundreds of jobs in a hospital. "How do you know I'm a doctor?"

He turned away. Headed for the table.

The delicious smells were making her salivate.

"Just a guess. I suppose you could be an administrator. A nurse. A social worker. An IT tech or—"

"I'm a doctor." She didn't move.

"Then I am a fantastic guesser." He pulled out a chair. Waited.

She needed to relax. "You have obviously not spent a lot of time having meals in a hospital cafeteria. Fancy isn't the word that comes to mind." Slowly, she crossed to him.

Sat at the table.

There were so many knives and forks and spoons around her plate. Definitely fancy. She knew how to use them all. She'd learned.

I'm a fast learner.

But once...

Once she'd been homeless. She'd literally scavenged for food. She'd thought the old boxes of cereal her mom received from the local food pantry were gold.

"Tess?"

She blinked.

Her vision had gone a little blurry there for a moment.

"You don't have to eat a bite." His voice was oddly gentle. "I can order a pizza. It will be here in twenty minutes." He cursed. "Look, I didn't mean to upset you. I just — forget it. I don't know what the hell I thought. I overstepped. It won't happen again and I — "

"You didn't do anything wrong." She wanted to tell him about her life. To put those dirty parts of her past right out there. She'd *never* told a lover about her time being homeless.

Why was she even considering it now?

No strings. Just sex.

He didn't want to know about her past. They had a deal. And she *didn't* share that part of herself with anyone. How could she even be thinking about revealing that pain to him?

"Sit down," she urged him with a smile that didn't feel real. It didn't feel real because it wasn't. "You don't want the food to get cold."

He took the chair next to hers. Didn't reach for the food. "Tell me how I screwed up so I don't make the same mistake again."

Her throat wanted to close up. "You didn't do anything wrong." She was the one being hit by bad memories.

He didn't look convinced. But he also didn't push her.

She reached for the glass full of water near her plate. Her fingers trembled a little, but he didn't notice. Or, if he did, James didn't comment on it.

"Tess, you don't have to share a damn thing with me. That's what we're about, remember?"

He began to eat. Slowly. Savoring the meal. Filet mignon.

She started to lower the water.

"But, if you do want to tell me anything, another perk of our no strings deal is that I won't ever judge a word you say. You could tell me you killed a man, and I wouldn't give a shit."

She knocked over the water. To her horror, it poured across the table, soaking what appeared to be a very, very expensive table cloth. "I'm so sorry!" Tess jumped to her feet and started patting up the water with her napkin. "I'll fix it! I'll clean it! I'll—"

He caught her hand in his. "It's water. It will dry." He stared at her. "It's okay."

Her past was everywhere tonight. Strangling her. It hadn't been this bad in ages. *And this is why I don't do dates.* Because she screwed things up. It was better if she stuck to her work. Her routine.

He gave a hard, decisive nod. "I'm ordering pizza."

"No. This meal must have cost a fortune and—"

"It didn't cost a thing. The chef owed me."

"I *saw* you give him money."

"A tip." He didn't blink. "His culinary services were something that I collected."

"The way you collect everything." Her head tilted. "Why do I suddenly feel like I'm something you're collecting, too?"

"You would be the best piece of my collection."

Her stomach dropped. "You can't collect people. That's not how it works."

His fingers uncurled from her wrist. "I know." His expression was guarded. "Why don't you go sit near the TV? I'll order pizza, and we can watch anything you want."

There was no need for him to do that. "I can eat this. It's a beautiful meal." She sat down. Squared her shoulders. "And you didn't mean it, of course." She picked up her knife. Her fork.

"I usually mean the things I say." A pause. "But you'll have to be a little more specific. What is it that you think I didn't mean?"

She forced a light laugh. "If I killed someone, you'd care."

Silence.

From beneath her lashes, she risked a glance at him. He was slowly chewing and seeming to mull her words in his head.

Of course. Just as she'd thought. He would —

"No. I don't think I'm really in the position to judge."

What?

"But I am in the position to order pizza. What do you feel like? Pepperoni? Sausage?"

"Cheese," she whispered.

He pushed away from the table. "On it."

She stared down at the knife in her hand.

And wondered…what would he do if he ever learned that…once upon a time, she *had* killed someone?

CHAPTER FOUR

"So…this is awkward." James flashed a smile at the gorgeous doctor who stepped into the exam room.

Dr. Tess Barrett blinked her insanely seductive, dark eyes. She looked at the chart. She looked up at him. "James?"

"Um. That's me."

"But the name on the chart says —"

"Jamieson? Yes, well, sometimes, I go by that." Not because it was his real name. Just another alias.

A nurse bustled in behind her. He recognized the nurse as the blonde who'd been with Tess the first night they'd met. Marilyn Montgomery. Barnes had assembled some basic data on her when he'd dug into Tess's background. No criminal background. Wealthy family. She'd been working at the hospital for as long as Tess had. Actually, the background info had said that Tess met Marilyn *before* they had both become employed at the hospital.

Marilyn came to a quick stop and blinked her big, blue eyes. "Wait. *He's* the stabbing victim?"

Now James winced. "I mean, really, it's more of a slice than anything. A little nick." That needed stitches. He could have actually taken care of that on his own but...

He'd wanted to see Tess.

Tess hadn't returned his calls that week. He wasn't being a stalker. He wasn't into that shit. He had a wound, and he needed it fixed, so he'd gone to the hospital.

Seeing her was a...bonus?

A carefully planned bonus?

Tess rushed toward him. Her fingers reached out and trailed over his arm. The wound pulsed from his wrist to his elbow. "You need stitches," she said.

He nodded.

"Marilyn—"

"On my way," the blonde fired back as she bustled out.

As soon as the door closed behind her, Tess released a fast breath. "What happened?" Her eyes were filled with worry.

"Someone sliced me." He shrugged.

"You can't say that so casually! You can't just—"

"It's not a big deal. You'll stitch me up. I'll be as good as new."

She had gloves on her hands. And worry deepened in her eyes. "Who did this?"

Oh, he liked the touch of fire roughening her voice. She was upset on his behalf. That was promising. "A guy at my club." Partial lie, partial truth. "Don't worry, he's been handled."

"Someone at your club *stabbed* you?"

"It's more of a slice really." Though he'd been stabbed before. A time or two. Or seven. "And it was a lucky cut. I was distracted." Because he'd been thinking about Tess and how he'd somehow screwed up with her.

He needed to fix the screw up. Immediately. Because, sure, it was no strings between them but...

He'd missed her this week. So he just damn well said, "I missed you."

Marilyn walked in at that exact same instant. "Oh." She cleared her throat. "Should I leave you two alone?"

Tess held his gaze. "We need to stitch him up."

And then they did just that. Cleaned his wound. Examined him.

Marilyn actually stitched him up, and Tess watched him with a little line between her brows.

"It's not deep," Tess told him. "When was your last tetanus shot?"

He rattled off a date.

"If you were attacked," Marilyn said as she pulled the thread through his skin, like that shit was a normal occurrence—oh, wait, for her, it was, "then we should notify the police so that they can—"

"No police." His voice came out hard and flat.

Tess and Marilyn shared a look.

"If the cops ask, I'll just tell them that my knife slipped while I was cleaning."

Tess rocked forward. "You'd lie to the police?"

She sounded so utterly appalled. How adorable. He'd missed that adorableness of hers this week. "Of course not," he assured her.

Her shoulders sagged.

"I was *cleaning* up my club. Can't have trash in there."

Marilyn hummed.

She also finished stitching him up—and immediately darted back several steps. What? Was she afraid of him?

"Uh, Dr. Barrett?" Marilyn wiggled her eyebrows. "How about we talk outside?"

Tess nodded. "I'll be right there."

Marilyn fled. A very fast fleeing. He'd had no idea she could move that quickly.

He glanced down at his stitches. Nice job. Tight and even. "Any orders for me, doc?"

"I shouldn't have stayed in here. I shouldn't have treated a man that I was—"

He looked up.

She'd clamped her lips together.

"Marilyn did the stitching. Don't see how you did anything wrong." He flexed his wrist. He'd have to be careful not to pop those stitches. And if he did—oh, well, so what? He'd already accomplished his primary mission by coming to the hospital.

"Why did you come here?" Tess stood, as if rooted to the spot, just a few feet away.

"Because I was bleeding. I thought the ER was a good place to go."

"No."

"No?" He lifted a brow. "You shouldn't come to the ER when you're bleeding?"

She surged toward him. "You came here, to *this* hospital, because you wanted to see me. You even asked one of the nurses outside to assign you to me. You charmed her, and you got me put in this room with you."

"Did I charm her?" James considered that. "I can have my charming moments."

"You can also have your asshole moments." She put her hands on her hips. "What are you doing?"

"Listening to a grumpy, but beautiful doctor?"

She stared.

He sighed. "Fine. I wanted to see you. In your natural environment, so to speak." He waved vaguely. "And I asked for you because I didn't want to get that asshat from the other night. What was his name...Goddamn?"

"Goddard." Her hands were still on her hips. "You wanted to see me?"

Yes. "I called twice. You didn't answer. I was worried that I'd pissed you off the other night, so I wanted to tell you, face to face, that I'm sorry. For whatever the hell I did wrong, I'm sorry."

She glanced down at the floor.

Even in those atrocious green scrubs, she was gorgeous.

"You left right after the pizza. Caught a cab and vanished." Even though he'd wanted to take her home. "You were barely talking to me before you cut out. I didn't mean to upset you."

Her lashes slowly lifted. "You didn't do anything wrong."

"No?" *Then tell me why you shut down. Tell me why you shut me out.*

She bit her lower lip.

He pushed off the exam table. Moved so that he was right in front of her.

"I'm not who you think," she whispered.

Oh, sweetheart. I know exactly who you are.

And he'd come there, with blood on him, because he wanted her to know who he really was, too.

"I'm not fancy. I'm not fine dining. I'm not the rich lifestyle." Her breath came faster. "I grew up with nothing. Less than that. And I still lock down every time I'm at a table and there's too much food or too much silverware because I feel like a fraud and I don't fit in and all I want to do is—"

His chest *ached.*

But she stopped. "Forget I said that."

Hell, no, he wouldn't.

The door burst open. Marilyn was there, but her cheeks were flushed and her eyes were frantic. "I need you! *Now!*"

"I have to go." Tess whirled. "I'm sorry!"

No. He didn't want to lose her. "Tess!"

But she raced away with Marilyn.

***

"He's as high as a freaking kite," Marilyn warned as they raced down the corridor. Tess could already hear the shouts and commotion from up ahead. "God Complex was supposed to be attending but he left Julia in there, and Sean rushed in to back her up."

Julia and Sean were both outstanding nurses.

"The patient is freaking out, and he needs a doctor right—"

They rounded the corner. Burst into the exam area.

The patient was massive. Big in bulk and height, and he'd just thrown Sean across the room.

"*Security!*" Tess shouted.

At her shout, the patient—wearing torn jeans and a ripped, black shirt—spun toward her. His eyes were bloodshot. His pupils the size of pinpricks. His nostrils flared.

And he charged.

He lunged right for her. There was no time to do anything. He grabbed her and locked his hands around her throat.

He yanked her up against him. "Bitch, you won't have me strapped down! You won't—"

"Let her go. Right the hell now." The snarling, lethal voice cut right through the patient's roar.

Tess's eyes darted to the left. That was James's voice. He was steps away, in the doorway. Devin was there, too, and another nurse and—

The man's hands tightened on her throat. She couldn't breathe! Her fingers clawed at him.

"I fucking warned you." James lunged forward.

The patient tossed Tess down, the same way he'd tossed Sean. She hit the floor and scrambled back up, just in time to see James drive his fist into the wild patient's stomach. A left to the stomach. A right hook to the jaw. And the patient went down *hard*. He crashed onto the floor, and James shoved his hand in the guy's hair. James yanked back the fellow's head. "Weren't you ever taught how to treat a lady? You *never* put your hands on a woman like that. *Never*." He drew back his free hand and curled his fingers into a powerful fist, obviously intending to—

"Freeze!"

Security had finally arrived.

Tess's hands still clutched her burning throat. "He's...not the bad guy." She shook her head. "James...let him go."

But he didn't.

She strained her throat to say, "It's the...the man in the black shirt. He's the one who attacked me, he's—"

The patient's eyes rolled back in his head. His whole body started seizing. Jesus.

She shot forward. Began calling out orders as she pushed James back so that she could get to work on the man who was ODing in front of her.

She forgot everything else. Everyone else. Her hands were rock steady as she attended him. As she fought to save him.

A low keening tore from his throat.

"It's going to be okay," she assured him as her neck throbbed and burned. "I've got you."

***

She was trying to save the man who'd just choked her. James stood behind Tess and watched her with a clenched jaw as blood dripped down his wrist. Tess was intent and focused, and he didn't think that she even realized he was there.

"Medical personnel only!" Now the prick was in there—Goddard—shouting orders and pointing his stubby finger at James. "Everyone else, *out!*"

James didn't move, not yet. He had a warning to give. "You should probably keep a fucking security guard in here. Because if she gets hurt again, I'm kicking *your* ass, too."

The prick blinked at him. Gaped.

Marilyn moved in front of James. "You tore open your stitches."

He shrugged.

"Let me fix them. Come on. We'll go back to your exam room."

He didn't want to leave Tess. What if she needed him again?

Marilyn touched his shoulder. "The security personnel will stay, no matter what Devin says. She's good. Tess will be safe."

Tess didn't look back at him. She was too focused on the man who appeared to be foaming at the mouth right then. "What'd he take?" James asked.

"We have no clue at this point. Hopefully, Tess can help him." Marilyn nudged him forward. "You have to go now. Your blood is dripping onto the floor."

I want to stay with her.

But he backed off. Headed into the hallway as hard tension filled his body. "Screw the stitches. I'm fine."

"Of course, tough guy, I'm sure you are." Marilyn shook her head. "But I'm going to do my job and I'm going to patch you up. Because if I don't and Tess finds out that you left here, bleeding, she's going to worry about you. She'll probably turn up on your doorstep, determined to treat you herself."

He lifted a brow.

"That's what you want, isn't it?" She sighed. "But I'm still stitching you up." She clutched his shirtfront and hauled him after her. He could have resisted. For the moment, he didn't. This was Tess's friend, and she could give him more insight to Tess. And Tess *was* safe. The security guards had remained in the room.

They should have been in there from the word go.

"Tess can show up at your door for plenty of other reasons," Marilyn continued in a casual tone. "Doesn't have to be because you're bleeding."

They were back at the exam room. She headed in first, and he followed. As soon as the door shut behind him...

Marilyn dropped her semi-caring nurse act. "What the hell is your deal?"

He waited. He knew he was in a proceed-with-caution scene.

"Why are you with my friend?"

That was an easy one. "Because I happen to think she's sexy as hell."

"Okay. Good answer." She tapped her foot. "You attacked the guy who outweighed you by at *least* seventy pounds, and you didn't hesitate."

"Why would I have hesitated? What does his weight have to do with anything?"

"Didn't look like that was your first fight."

"It wasn't."

"You own a club."

"Technically, I own a few clubs."

Her blue eyes were challenging. "You might as well have 'bad boy' stamped on your forehead."

"Nah, that would be too obvious."

Her lips twitched. But then her face smoothed. "I like the way you rushed to save her."

He'd just reacted, hadn't thought. Tess had been in danger, and *no one* would hurt Tess. "If the bastard lives, I might break his fingers so he understands that you don't *ever* put your hands on a woman."

She laughed. Then… "Oh, God, are you serious?" Her eyes became saucers.

He smiled at her. Not a particularly warm smile.

She grabbed fresh gloves from the dispenser. "I can't tell if you're serious or not, and that is freaking me out."

He tended to often freak out people. Part of his charm.

"Tell me…tell me that you will *never* hurt my friend."

That was easy. "I will never hurt Tess."

She grabbed his arm. Swabbed with some disinfectant or alcohol pad or something. "Tell me that you're not dangerous."

Now he chose his words carefully. "I'm not dangerous to Tess." Was that good enough?

Marilyn gave a firm nod, so he supposed his promise had, indeed, been good enough.

"Is the area still numb? You need another shot?"

"Stitch away. I don't care about the pain."

"Tough guy. I suppose you think that's hot?"

He didn't really think about it one way or the other.

"It *was* rather hot the way you saved her. I'm sure Tess will appreciate it, you know, when she's not trying to keep that guy alive." She went to work on his wound once more. "And you got to play the hero right in front of Dr. Goddard's face. That man is such an ass. He's been nosing around Tess from day one. It's time he figured out that he has no shot with her."

See…this was why he'd gone back to the exam room. Tess's friend was giving him good intel. Intel that hadn't been in the report provided by Barnes. "I'll be sure he gets the message."

"Hmm." Her head tilted to better study his wound.

The needle slid into his skin. "Tess has had a hard day." *He freaking strangled her.*

"Tell me about it. But you know, it was even worse a few days back. Wait." She looked up.

"Was that last week? Time moves so fast in the ER." Marilyn shook her head and went back to work.

"What happened?"

"She had a sixteen-year-old boy die on her, and, Tess *always* takes the deaths hard, but for it to be a kid…"

Fuck me. That must have been the night she showed up at my club with shadows under her beautiful eyes.

A low sigh. "Anyway, let's just call it the job from hell and be done with it, huh?"

"What can I do to make her feel better?"

Her stare slowly lifted. Held his. "If it's only some random hook up, why do you care?"

"Who told you it was random?"

"Tess doesn't look for relationships. She doesn't *do* long term."

"Why?"

Her lips parted.

Come on. Tell me –

"You'd have to ask her." The needle slid in again.

James gave her points for being a good friend to Tess.

She worked in silence the rest of the time. Then as she finished up, Marilyn revealed, "Tess really likes chocolate fudge. It's her one weakness."

"Thank you."

A jerky nod. She put up the supplies. Ditched the waste. Pointed at him. "If she comes to you tonight, handle her with kid gloves."

"She won't have to come to me tonight. I'll be waiting for her."

***

Her shoulders sagged as Tess headed down the hallway. Tension gathered in her neck — or, hell, maybe that wasn't tension. Maybe it was the pain from the bruising that had started. She felt like absolute hell.

"Where is my brother?"

Her head lifted. She'd just made it to the ER waiting room. A man in an expensive suit, with close-cropped, light brown hair, loomed in front of the check-in desk.

"He was brought in over two hours ago! I just freaking found out, and I want to see him, now!"

"Who's your brother?" The administrative assistant was as cool as you please. Unfortunately, in the ER, dealing with frantic — and pissed — families was an all too common occurrence. When people were scared, they often acted angry. "I need a name."

"Frederick Waller. He's about six-foot-four, three hundred pounds. He..." His voice lowered but Tess had crept closer. "He was brought in because I think...he took something that he shouldn't have."

Tess released a low breath. "Excuse me?"

He whirled to stare at her. He didn't look a thing like his brother. His eyes were a pale, clear green. No sign of the bloodshot red that had filled Tess's patient's gaze. This man's face was clean shaven, his suit neat and obviously tailored. "I treated your brother. I'm Dr. Tess Barrett."

His gaze slid over her. Went to her neck. Lingered. "What happened to you?"

"Your brother."

His stare flew back up to hers.

Should she have been more tactful with her response? Too late. She was out of tact and energy. "He's stable, for now. But we almost lost him tonight. He's in recovery, and I'm sure that you will be able to see him shortly. I have to say, your brother needs help. Serious counseling and intervention, and I hope you get that help for him."

His attention shifted back to her neck. "Those are finger marks."

"Yes. He attacked me and a male nurse before he began to seize."

"Seize? Oh, hell."

"He almost died tonight. In fact, his heart did stop. We got him back. He has a second chance. I hope he can use that chance wisely."

His lips thinned. He shook his head. "He's had a million second chances. Never does a damn thing with them." He offered his hand to her. "I'm Morgan Waller. And thank you."

His hold was warm and strong. She shook his hand once, then pulled back.

"He's my half-brother," Morgan admitted, the words gruff. "Always told my dad I'd look after him. But some people don't seem to ever learn, do they? There's only so much you can do for them." He straightened his shoulders. "Fred is one of those people. I'm sorry he hurt you."

"You done, Dr. Barrett?" The question came from the admin who'd been watching them.

She was *so* done. Tess nodded briskly before she told Morgan, "Someone will take you back to see your brother soon. Please just take a seat in our waiting area until then."

The admin shot her a relieved glance.

Tess shuffled forward as she headed for the exit. As soon as those doors parted, and the cool air hit her…

Paradise. The air soothed her overheated skin and even made her neck feel better.

Her gaze darted around the lot. Was it wrong that part of her hoped that a limo was waiting? Or, hell, didn't even have to be the limo. She just…

Wished that James was there.

But it was late—far after her shift should have ended—and he wasn't there. She didn't know when he had left. She needed to get home and collapse. Tess headed for her reliable Jeep.

"No prince charming tonight?"

Devin's voice stopped her.

"Though the way he acted, I'd hardly call the guy a prince."

Her spine snapped straight as she whirled toward him. "I didn't see you jumping in to help when the guy's fingers were squeezing my neck."

He notched up his chin. "I was about to help you. Your thug beat me to the punch."

"Thug?" Was he serious?

"Heard he came in with a knife wound. Don't you think you should have reported that to—"

"Why the hell am I always finding you around my Tess?"

James? Her head swung to the left. The quick swing made her neck ache, but she ignored the ache because James *was* there. He strode briskly from the parking area. And he—did he have a bag in his hand? He did. A white bag that he lifted toward her as he closed the distance between them and brushed a kiss over her cheek.

"Sorry I was a few minutes late. Wanted to make sure the fudge was nice and fresh for you."

He'd gotten her fudge? She took the bag—all greedy fingers—and tore it open. The rich, blissfully chocolate scent filled her nostrils. "I love you."

"I'll remember you said that."

Her stare snapped up. "Um, I didn't mean—"

He simply nodded.

Her hold tightened on the bag. "I love fudge. How did you know?"

"A friend told me." He wrapped an arm around her shoulders and pulled her to his side. Then he glanced over at Devin. "You didn't answer my question."

"I was *leaving* the hospital. I wasn't following Tess. I don't need to follow women."

"And you don't know how to step in when they're being hurt, either, do you?"

"I was going to —"

"What the fuck ever. Listen up, buddy. You *ever* just stand there while someone attacks Tess, and I will make you wish you'd never been born."

Devin rushed forward. "You're threatening me. *Me?*" He puffed out his chest.

James held his easy pose. "I don't threaten. I act."

"Thug! You're nothing but some —"

James laughed.

Devin glared at him, then focused on Tess. "You saw him in action."

Yes, she had. She'd seen him rush to help her.

"He's dangerous. Uncontrolled." Devin peered over James's shoulder. "Where's the fancy limo?"

"Didn't feel like being fancy tonight."

A shiver slid over her.

James rubbed his fingers over her knuckles as she clutched her precious fudge close.

He wouldn't know, he *couldn't* know that when she'd been a child, a bakery owner had once seen Tess pressing her face to the shop's colorful window. The baker had given her a free piece of fudge that day. Told her to come back any time she'd needed a treat.

She hadn't gone back often.

Just when she'd been sad.

She liked seeing the warm bakery. Liked the smells and the sights. And the kind man who'd worked inside. The man who had never looked at her with pity or scorn.

"I brought my motorcycle instead," James said, still as cool as could be. He stared at Tess. "Are you ready, baby?"

"Of *course,*" Devin muttered. "You would have a motorcycle."

James turned his head. "Are you still here? I thought you were leaving the hospital."

"I *wanted* to check on Tess. Things got rough and she was injured, and I wanted to make sure she was going to be all right tonight."

James returned his focus to Tess. "Don't you worry." His words were for Devin, but his gaze never left her. "I'll stay with Tess tonight. I'll make sure she's a lot more than merely all right."

She wanted to leave with him, right then. But… "I can drive myself home. You don't have to take me on your motorcycle."

"I don't have to do anything. Neither do you. After the day you had, I thought you might want to drive fast. Roar down the road. Feel the wind in your hair as you scream your heart out into the night."

Her heart surged in her chest.

Devin sniffed. "You obviously do *not* know her well. That's not the sort of thing that Tess enjoys. She's far too refined to ever —"

"Yes," Tess said to James. Staff members often left their cars in the lot overnight. She'd make arrangements and just take a taxi to work the next day or something. "I'd like that very much."

"Then get ready to scream."

She didn't miss the sensual promise in his words. She was sure Devin hadn't, either. The guy wasn't that thick.

Or, maybe he was. But she forgot about him. A few moments later, she was straddling the big, beast of a bike that James owned. "Another piece of your collection?"

"Umm." He didn't climb on the bike. "Why don't you have some fudge first?"

She was already digging into the bag. "Excellent idea. Where did you even get this stuff, anyway? I mean, I would think most of the local shops would be closed at this time of the night."

"With the right incentive, I got a shop to open."

Did she want to know what incentive he'd used? Probably not. She put a piece of the fudge to her lips. Took a bite and… "Oh, God." She couldn't help her moan. Tess's eyes squeezed shut. "This is heaven." Another bite. It was melting on her tongue, and it was that rich, decadent chocolate. The best kind of chocolate fudge. Though, honestly, she'd never met chocolate that she didn't love.

She had another piece. What the hell? It had been a day.

Another moan slipped from her.

James was dead silent.

Should she offer to share with him? Nah. That fudge was hers.

"I will buy you fudge every night for the rest of your life, if you want."

Her eyes flew open.

"Because you are the sexiest thing I've ever seen when you eat that fudge." He shook his head.

Perhaps she should share. Especially since she thought *he* was pretty sexy. "I didn't thank you for saving me earlier."

"Because you don't need to thank me."

"When someone saves you, it's polite to say thank you."

"And are you always polite?"

"No."

One of the parking lot lights illuminated his wicked grin. "Good."

She closed her precious bag of fudge. "I don't want to drop this while we're driving." She'd never been on a motorcycle before, so Tess already knew she'd be holding on for dear life.

"Got you covered." He tucked the bag into a little compartment she hadn't even noticed. Then he stared down at her. "You've got a little fudge on your lower lip."

Oh, that was embarrassing.

Her tongue snaked out to lick it away.

"*Fuck.*"

His mouth took hers. He leaned over her, devoured her mouth, and he had her moaning. Yep, this time, that moan wasn't from the fudge. It was purely from him and from the way he made her feel.

Her hands curled around his shoulders. She opened her mouth wider. Her tongue slid against his.

"Don't be polite when I get you home, doc," James growled against her lips. "You tell me every single thing you want."

"You." She didn't have to wait until she was home. She knew what she wanted. "It's you."

He kissed her again, and then he climbed onto the motorcycle. He made sure she was settled with a helmet before he revved the engine, and the bike shot forward. She held on tight. They raced through the streets and the wind battered against her as the motorcycle growled. Her thighs trembled from the powerful vibration and as they drove fast—

"Scream," James told her.

She thought of the man who'd attacked her.

Of the way he'd almost died beneath her hands from his drug overdose.

Thought of the sixteen-year-old boy she'd lost in her ER…

"You know you want to…*Scream.*"

Tess opened her mouth. Her neck was sore. Maybe she shouldn't but…

She screamed.

It felt so good. Almost as good as when she screamed as she came with James. *Almost.*

***

He'd watched them from the shadows. They had been so focused on one another that they hadn't even glanced his way. He'd taken one look at the woman, and he'd known.

It's your turn.

She thought she was safe. Thought she had a lover who could protect her. She had no clue.

All of this time, he'd been waiting.

Fate had just given him the perfect opportunity.

He just had to learn more. A smart man always knew all the players involved in the game. And he'd seen someone at the hospital that he already suspected might prove to be useful.

The motorcycle was long gone. He lingered. Considered his options. The best punishment was the one that ripped apart your whole world.

Once upon a time, *his* world had been ripped apart.

Time for payback.

He turned on his heel and headed back into the hospital.

CHAPTER FIVE

"Are you going to come inside?" Tess tucked a lock of hair behind her ear as she stood beside the motorcycle. She was also clutching her fudge bag again. So freaking cute. The woman obviously loved her chocolate fudge very, very much.

He stepped away from the bike. His body brushed against hers. "Is that an invitation? Or were you simply asking about my plans for the night?"

"An invitation."

He glanced at the big, brick building behind her. He'd dropped her off at her door before, but never gone inside her condo. Tess inviting him in her home seemed like a big step. Or hell, maybe it wasn't.

But… "I want to come inside."

"Then let's go." She turned quickly and hurried toward the building. Once inside, she marched for the stairwell, but he caught her arm and pointed her toward the elevator instead.

"James?"

They entered the elevator. "I have this fantasy we'll have to live out soon. It involves me, you, and sex in an elevator." The elevator doors slid closed.

Her breath caught. "Didn't realize that was a fantasy for you."

"Didn't realize it either, until you stepped inside. Full disclosure, I pretty much want to have sex with you everywhere so…"

She put her hand on his chest. "It's not normal, is it?"

The elevator already had them on the second floor. He should have pushed the stop button when he had the chance. "What isn't normal?"

"This." She motioned between them. "Us. The way we react to each other. Like…how is it possible that I want you more now than I did the first night?"

"Because you know exactly how good we are together." As for anything else… "Fuck normal." He brushed his lips over hers. "I've never been normal a day in my life, and I don't think you have been, either."

They made it to her condo. She unlocked the door and reset the alarm while he took stock of things. First thing he noticed? He'd already been unimpressed by the security of the building in general, but in her home? "Your security is shit."

She spun. "What?"

"I know some people who can install a state-of-the-art system for you. I can have them here tomorrow. First thing." He motioned toward the piece of crap that an eight-year-old could disable. "Anyone with five seconds and pliers can get past this thing."

"It's a safe part of town. That's why I moved in. There's a security camera downstairs, too."

He'd seen it. It would be easy enough for an intruder to dodge that *one* camera.

"I don't need a new system." She put the fudge down on her white, marble kitchen countertop. "But thank you."

Tension tightened his shoulders. He wanted her safe. Especially after the attack earlier. "Things like that happen a lot to you?" He sauntered toward her. A slow saunter when he really wanted to pounce.

"Things like the attack?" Tess shook her head. Turned so that her back was to the counter and her eyes on him. "Luckily, no. We have good security at the hospital, and we're trained to handle unruly patients. Things just got a little out of control."

"That's an understatement." He tipped back her chin. His fingers lingered against her. "I can see his fingerprints on your skin." *That* fucking pissed him off. "I should have killed him."

She caught his hand. "Don't say things like that."

Because life mattered to her — even the life of the bastard who'd hurt her. "He tried to strangle you, and then you saved him." James shook his head. "You remind me of someone I knew a long time ago. She had that same *I'll-risk-myself-for-everyone-else* mentality that you do." Anger stirred. "She got hurt because of it. *You* got hurt tonight. Some people don't need saving." His hand slid down her throat as his fingers feathered over the bruises. The rage he felt was jarring. He hated seeing those marks on her flesh. He wanted to *destroy.*

James could feel his control unraveling. It was disconcerting. No, fucking terrifying. He didn't lose control. Not ever. His life had been built on careful control. On watching and waiting, on holding back. On knowing the exact moment to strike.

To kill.

He stared at his hand. On her throat.

Tess spoke softly, calmly, as she told him, "I don't get to decide who to save. I have to save *everyone* who comes before me. Good, bad, something in between—it's not my place to decide. I became a doctor because I wanted to help people, the same way that I'd been helped."

He barely breathed. They weren't supposed to share about their pasts. Or at least, he knew Tess didn't like to share. But—

"I was thirteen when I was brought to the hospital. No money. No family. I had *nothing.* But the doctors didn't care. They didn't turn me away. They saved me that day when I was so desperate. And I vowed that I would pay it forward. I'd save someone else. I'd pay my debt. Some way. Eventually."

Tears gleamed in her eyes. He hated that. Tess shouldn't cry.

"But I lose patients. Some days, I help. Some days, I can't do anything. And some days, I feel like I'm completely lost and back to being that same thirteen-year-old girl who was in the hospital, collapsing, because some asshole pumped her veins full of drugs and tried to kill her." A swift inhale. "*Tried to kill me.*"

His heart stopped. The whole world went black for a moment.

He'd known about her being in the hospital, about how close to death she'd come as a teen— that had been in the report that Barnes got for him but…

"So, no, I couldn't let that man OD in front of me. I don't care who he is or what he did, saving him is my job." Her pulse raced frantically beneath his index finger.

"What happened to the sonofabitch?" The question was deep and grating.

Her eyebrows pulled together.

"The man who tried to kill you when you were a kid. What happened to him?" Because *that* hadn't been in the report. Her admission to the hospital had been in the report. The fact that she'd been ODing had been in the report. *At thirteen.* But that someone had done that *to* her? That some bastard had tried to kill Tess?

You're a dead man, you sonofabitch.

She glanced away. "Why are we talking about this? My past doesn't matter. Neither does yours. I shouldn't have brought it up."

"You shouldn't be afraid of your past."

"Who says I am?"

His hands moved to curl around her waist, and he lifted her up.

Her eyes widened. "James?"

He put her on the counter. Slid closer, moving between her legs. "I don't want you afraid of anyone or anything."

She swallowed.

"Are you afraid of me?" He held his breath as he waited for her answer.

For a moment, he didn't think she would answer. The tension stretched between them.

She smiled. "Because you're an ex-assassin turned club owner?"

Tess still thought he'd been teasing. "Yes."

"No." She shook her head. "I'm not afraid of you. In fact, I feel oddly safe with you." Her left hand slid down his arm, moving to rest near the bandage that Marilyn had applied. "But as your doctor, I'm telling you that you shouldn't be exerting yourself. Don't pull out these stitches again."

"Screw the stitches." He went in for a kiss.

"No."

He stilled.

"I want you to try something first."

Oh, he was all about trying things with Tess.

She pulled a piece of fudge out of the bag.

"I'm not really much for sweet things," he told her gruffly.

A soft laugh escaped Tess. "Appearances are deceiving. You think something might be sweet and good, but then you take a bite and you discover something rich enough to rock your whole world."

"Rock my world, huh? All right. I'll try a bite." *Then I'm trying you.*

She put the fudge to his lips. His tongue snaked out. Licked her fingertips.

A shiver slid over her.

He took a careful bite of the fudge. Damn. She was right. It was rich. Damn good.

She lowered the fudge. Waited with her head slightly cocked. "Well?" She put down the fudge.

"Delicious." Truth. "But not nearly as delicious as you are." Another truth.

He kissed her. Yeah, she was about a thousand times better than the fudge. She moaned into his mouth, and he pulled her to the edge of the counter, rocking her against the hard edge of his dick.

He'd been holding tightly to his control. Playing the calm, easy going guy on the ride over and up to her place, but the reality was…

His self-control was in shreds. He kept seeing that bastard with his hands on Tess's throat. Kept seeing her with fear in her eyes. Kept thinking about how easy it would be for her to die.

No.

He tore his mouth from hers. Moved to her neck. With the last bit of his control, he used care and feathered kisses over the bruises on her. "I want to kill him."

"James…"

"Want to destroy anyone who hurts you." He knew his words were wrong. Too savage and dark, but she didn't get it — that was who he was. He was savage and dark, and he wasn't a *safe* lover, not by any means.

Yet she *was* safe, with him. He would always keep her safe.

He moved back. Tugged off her shoes and hauled off her jeans and underwear. He yanked open his own jeans and shoved on the condom he'd brought —

"Be careful," Tess scolded, voice all husky and sensual — a sensual scold, hell, he hadn't even known that was a thing, "don't tear open the stitches —"

"Sweetheart, I don't care about the stitches." He kissed her again as he positioned his cock at the entrance to her body. "All I care about is fucking you."

His fingers slid into her. She was wet and hot and ready for him. Hell, yes.

He sank deep.

Her legs locked around him.

There was no more talking. He was acting on pure, animal instinct. His thrusts were hard and deep, and she met him. Over and over again. A beast was inside of him, driving him to take and take. The sex was supposed to be casual, no strings.

Yet he'd felt anything but casual when she'd been threatened.

Possessive. Protective. Primitive.

Everything was spinning out of his control. And for once, he didn't care.

Her delicate inner muscles clamped tightly around him. Her body stiffened as her nails sank into his sides. "*James!*"

He loved the way she cried out his name when pleasure hit her.

Her sex contracted around him as the climax pulsed through her. He waited, waited until he'd rung every single drop of pleasure from her that he could, and only then did James let go.

He surged into her one more time. Sank as deeply as he could, and he came so long and hard that when the climax finally ended, he was hollowed out, blissed out…

And in deep, deep trouble.

***

"Good-bye, sweetheart."

Tess heard the words distantly. She turned in her bed, burrowing deeper into the covers.

"I'll see you tonight. Stay out of trouble for me, will you?" A kiss pressed to her temple.

James. He was leaving. He was—

Her eyes flew open. Holy crap. He'd *stayed?*

She could see sunlight trickling through her blinds. The night had ended, and James stood—completely dressed but with his hair sexily rumpled—near her bed.

He'd stayed all night with her.

She remembered him carrying her to her bedroom. Tucking her under the covers. She'd pretty much been boneless and limp at that point. From pleasure. From exhaustion. From the adrenaline rush that had finally left her. She'd assumed he'd left, too.

He'd…stayed?

She sat up, pulling the sheet with her. She should say something to him, and she finally managed to stammer, "Y-you stay out of trouble, too."

He laughed. A rich, deep rumble of a laugh. "But I like trouble." He winked at her. "And it usually has a way of finding me."

There were so many things she didn't know about him. Things she hadn't asked. Things she'd thought wouldn't matter. Truth be told, she hadn't expected them to still be together at this point. Sex once, yes, maybe twice, but…

Her need for him wasn't lessening. The more she was with him, the more she wanted him. That was dangerous. She knew it. It was dangerous to depend on anyone too much. "I...can't see you tonight."

"Okay." He nodded.

That was it. No pressure. Just acceptance. Things with him always seemed so easy. Nothing was easy. She heard herself offering an explanation even though he hadn't asked for one. "I work at the food pantry once a week. It's a standing commitment that I won't break."

"Of course." He nodded. "Wouldn't expect anything less." He nodded. Turned away.

"What does that mean?" Tess shoved her hair out of her eyes.

"It just means that I expect something like that from you. You're the responsible type. The help-other-people type. The *good* – "

"You think I'm some sort of good girl?" First of all, she wasn't a girl. She was a woman. And –

"I don't think you're good." He turned to look back at her. "I think you're fucking fantastic. And if I'd met you back when I still had a little part of my soul left, I would never, ever let you go."

Tess sucked in a sharp breath. "What happened to your soul?" He seemed fine to her. He seemed –

"Ah, is that what we're doing now? Sharing? Okay. You did open up to me last night, so I suppose it's my turn." He faced her and put his hands on his hips. "I sold my soul to Uncle Sam because I wanted a shot at a new life. Only that life wasn't sunshine and daisies."

Sunshine and —

"It was blood and death and nightmares that didn't end. *I* was the nightmare, and there was no getting out of it. After a while, I didn't want out. After a while, I didn't want anything but that darkness. Because if you stand in the dark long enough, you start to like it. You like the power and the danger and the rush."

She was holding the bed covers too tightly. "You're trying to scare me right now."

"Actually, I'm not."

It sure didn't seem that way to her.

"You're too trusting, Tess."

Her shoulders stiffened. Now he seemed angry with her.

"You fell asleep in my arms last night. Like I was a guardian angel or some shit."

Or…like he'd been her boyfriend. He wasn't. He *was not.*

"You were unconscious and vulnerable with a man you didn't know. The more I thought about what you didn't know…" He gave a hard, negative shake of his head. "You would never let me touch you again if you *did* know half the shit I've done. Hell, if you only knew one or two of the things I've done, you'd tell me to stay the hell away from you and never come back."

This whole scene seemed out of control. Crazy. A moment ago, he'd been kissing her temple. Calling her sweetheart and now...*what is happening?* Tess rose from the bed and advanced toward him. "Why are you saying all of this?"

He lifted his hand. His knuckles brushed over her cheek. "Because I think I want you too much."

If that was the case, then why was he acting this way? Saying those things? "You're pushing me away."

His hand fell. "You're too trusting. You could have gotten seriously hurt in the hospital. You could have gotten hurt with me in your bed last night."

"You said you'd never hurt me."

"How do you know I'm not a liar? How do you know I'm not some criminal you should never, ever have near you?"

"Are you?"

His lips parted.

Her phone rang. The loud, shrill cry made her jump. Her phone was on the nightstand, and it vibrated again as it rang. "I... have to get that. Could be the hospital." She reached out and curled her fingers around the phone. Tess didn't recognize the number on the screen, but that was nothing new. Different numbers would call all the time. Just part of a doctor's life. "Hello?"

Silence.

Maybe it was a bad connection.

"Hello?"

James took a step back. He turned and headed for her bedroom door.

"Wait," Tess called to him. They needed to finish talking. They needed to—

"*Found you*," a voice rasped on the other end of the line.

"Who is this?" Tess asked. "You've reached Dr. Barrett, and I'm not—"

The call ended. She tightened her hold on the phone and darted a fast glance at James. He'd opened her bedroom door.

He stood there, with his back to her. "I'm not a criminal."

"I didn't say you—"

"But I've done things that would make you have nightmares for the rest of your life. I thought it didn't matter. Thought we could play this game and screw the consequences."

She rocked forward onto the balls of her feet. "James?"

He looked back at her. "You should stay away from me."

Goosebumps rose on her arms.

"Because if you don't, I'm not sure I can let you go. I've lost too fucking much. You don't want me to care about you."

She was rooted to the spot. Clad only in a long t-shirt. Had *he* put her in the shirt? She didn't even remember. She had been dead to the world after they'd made love. He was right. She'd been vulnerable. Too trusting. She was never like that because—

She didn't trust anyone.

But did she trust him?

"You come near me again, and we're going to have to rework our rules. Playtime is over." His jaw hardened. "Be sure you lock the front door after me. And reset that shit security system."

Why did he keep trash talking her security system? And why was he leaving her?

Her phone rang again. Dammit. She clutched the phone tighter as she hurried after James. A glance at her screen showed her Devin's name. Tess knew she had to answer. Could be an emergency at the hospital and —

James was striding out the front door.

"Why?" The question tore from her. "Why are you changing everything this morning?"

He spun toward her. "Because I think things changed for me last night." His lips pressed together and he gritted out, "Answer the call, Tess."

"*Don't* leave." They weren't done. She put the phone to her ear. "Devin, what is it?"

"Your patient has vanished."

"What?"

James glanced heavenward. "Figured it would be that asshole calling you first thing in the morning."

"Is…someone there?" Devin's voice was stilted.

"Yes." That was all she'd say. All he needed to know. "What patient? What are you talking about?"

"The guy who got choke crazy last night. Frederick Waller. He tore out his IVs during the night and rushed away while his nurse was with another patient."

He'd been recovered enough to sneak out of the hospital?

"Security cams caught him staggering out after midnight. He vanished, and the admin put in a call to his brother to let the guy know Frederick would probably be up to his old tricks again soon." A pause. "Not the first time an addict ran away, not the last, either. Just thought you'd want to know."

"I do want to know. Thank you."

He hung up. She lowered the phone. Gazed at James. "Did you catch that?"

"Not enough of it."

"The patient from last night…" The fingers of her left hand brushed over her neck. "He tore out his IV and left the hospital. Slipped past his nurse because she was working with someone else. Security footage caught him, but by then, it was too late."

He lifted a brow. "I'm guessing the guy was clad only in his hospital gown during the big escape?"

She had no idea but probably.

"And that didn't red flag anyone?" His jaw hardened.

"Hospitals get crazy at night." Crazier than most would ever believe. "For all I know, he could have stolen clothes from someone else — or just gotten access to his own clothing. His brother might have brought stuff in for him. And the brother — Devin said Morgan Waller had been alerted."

"Alerted. Right." James nodded. "Well, I've got to go. There's business I need to take care of this morning."

He seemed so cold. He'd never been cold with her before. "James?" She struggled to think of something to say. "Want breakfast?"

He squared his shoulders. "I told you my terms. You think about them." He turned away.

He was leaving. She didn't want him to go. "Everything was fine last night."

His hand gripped the doorknob. "I told you, everything changed last night."

"You want more than I can give." Dammit. She had to blink because her vision had gotten a little blurry. She tossed down the phone onto the entrance table.

"You're right. I do want more. That's the problem, you see, when it comes to you, I'm a greedy bastard." He considered that. "No, I'm a greedy bastard in general. Just a character flaw I have."

She hadn't expected this pain. "You want to collect me? Is that it? Like you do everything else in your life?"

His head turned. His golden eyes burned as they locked on her. "If I could, I would fucking *own* you."

What? She took a step back.

"Because I'm starting to think that you might already own me."

Tess could only shake her head.

"That's why I'm leaving. That's why it's changing. New rules. If you're up for the challenge, you know where to find me." A muscle jerked along the hard line of his jaw. "And lock the friggin' door."

Just like that, he was gone.

She locked the friggin' door.

And tried to figure out what the hell he'd meant when James said…

I'm starting to think that you might already own me.

CHAPTER SIX

"Someone had a late night."

"Do not fuck with me this morning, Barnes. I will kick your ass."

Barnes straightened from his position behind the bar. James had just marched into the club, and he was not in the mood for any shit.

I gave her an ultimatum. What in the hell is wrong with me? He wasn't the ultimatum type. He wasn't the emotional type. And he'd just met the woman.

He hadn't felt like this since…

Had he *ever* really felt like this?

A teenage boy's emotions weren't a freaking thing compared to the chaos surging through his body and mind right then.

"So…the night was bad?" Barnes ventured.

James stopped and glowered. His hands were clenching and unclenching at his sides. "I'm going to need you to find someone for me."

Barnes immediately perked up. "Is this like…a case? Are we working freelance with Wilde Securities again?"

Wilde Securities? Not this time. The elite protection firm wouldn't exactly approve of his plans for the day. "You know how pro ballers have to keep practicing or else their skills get rusty?"

Barnes nodded. "Uh, huh. Sure." Worry flickered in his eyes.

"I mean, if a pitcher doesn't practice his technique, he can't expect to walk onto a mound and strike out the batter, can he?"

"I don't think I like where this is going…"

Too bad. "So if I don't practice my particular skill set, how will I stay sharp?"

"Oh, God." Barnes swallowed. His Adam's apple bobbed.

James smiled. "You're going to find a man who's missing for me, and then I'm going to practice my technique."

***

He got in without much effort at all. The missing patient from Tess's hospital—Frederick Waller—rented an apartment near the river. There were a few locks on the door. Barely took any time to get past them, and the man had no interior security system at all.

Shocker.

What *was* surprising—the apartment was nice. High end. Waller had seemed like a hard drug user the night before, so James was a bit surprised by the place. But then, Barnes *had* discovered that Frederick's brother was loaded. Maybe the brother helped out with rent payments.

Not really his concern at the moment. James had one mission. Only one.

Get in. Get the job done. Get out. Leave no trace.

Be just like a ghost.

Ghost. There was a reason he'd earned that code name during his years working for Uncle Sam. He'd been flawless. No one ever saw him. Not unless he wanted to be seen. No one ever stopped him.

As far as his enemies were concerned, there was no safe place. He could get through locked doors or concrete walls in order to complete his mission.

So it was easy to slip into Frederick's apartment. To search the place but to discover that no, his prey wasn't there. That was okay. James was patient. He could wait.

Ghosts were good at waiting.

But he didn't wait inside the apartment. No sense caging himself in that way. James slipped out of the building. Headed for the alley nearby. The perfect place to blend with the shadows. And...

Well, hello, prey.

The perfect place to find Frederick trying to make a deal for drugs.

Some people didn't learn.

Frederick had better *start* learning.

The dealer — rather, would-be-dealer — suddenly turned and ran away from Frederick.

"Wait, man!" Frederick yelled. "I swear, I'm good for the money! Just come back. Give me a chance, I can —"

James caught Frederick from behind. Slammed him into the brick wall. Then pulled him deeper into the shadows. Frederick struggled, but he wasn't using the strength of an amped up madman this time, so his struggles were bullshit, despite his size.

"Let me go, jerk! Let me —"

James pushed the blade of a knife against the other man's throat. "Do you feel this?"

All struggles stopped. "I-I don't have any money." A pathetic whisper. "If I did...I would've —"

"Scored enough drugs from your dealer to have you attacking another doctor? Gotten enough shit in your system again to have you strangling an innocent woman?" The rage was there, but he was in control.

"I-I don't remember — "

"Remember this," James told him, voice low and hard and promising, "you ever try to hurt Dr. Tess Barrett again, and you are a dead man. I will slice your throat from ear to ear." He let the blade prick his prey.

Frederick whimpered.

"I can find you anywhere, anytime. I can kill you before you ever have the breath to scream."

James caught the stench of urine. *Sonofabitch.* "Get your life together, dumbass. Get in rehab before you wind up dead. Your heart stopped last night. Do you even know that shit?"

"I'm sorry! I'm sorry, I don't —"

"Get your life together. While you still have one."

James yanked back the blade. Slammed Frederick into the wall once more for the hell of it. The guy stumbled and fell, and by the time Frederick rose...

James was gone.

***

"Okay, we're done for the night. Now I want to go somewhere and hear every single detail about what happened between you and your sexy, dangerous hero." Latonya exited the food pantry with Tess. She looped their arms together. Latonya always did that. Looped and laughed and got close. She'd gotten past Tess's guard before Tess had even known what was happening.

They'd met in medical school. Latonya was a few years older than Tess, but Latonya hadn't treated her the way so many of the others had. She'd treated Tess like an equal from day one.

Latonya was blunt, hilarious, and often unfiltered. She was wonderful.

"I heard about it, of course, because our hospital gossip mill goes *crazy* whenever drama goes down. But I like to hear things straight from the source." She paused under a street light and lifted her brows. "Marilyn said he was all kickass and cool. Was he?"

"Yes." James *had* been very kickass. And fast. He'd moved so fast. His punches had been... "He was intense."

"Yes, well, someone was strangling you. Your lover had *better* be intense in response, or you're with the wrong guy." She snorted. "Word is Devin had his scared ass in the hallway, behind a security guard. He saw the shit going down and immediately went for cover."

That sounded like Devin.

"Let's find a diner and a booth, and we can split some crazy delicious food, and I can learn more about your hero."

Tess and Latonya had a routine. After working at the food pantry, they always went to a nearby diner and chatted for an hour or so. The conversation was usually light and easy, and Tess felt good hanging with her friend.

But tonight... "There's nothing to tell." She glanced across the street. Her Jeep waited. "I think we're over."

"Oh, God. If that's the case, we absolutely need the diner. And we're hitting dessert *first*." She turned to fully face Tess. "Did that asshole break up with you?"

"Um, I'm not sure."

Latonya waited.

"I think so?" Tess didn't have a whole lot more to offer.

Latonya shook her head. "Let's get the dessert. We'll eat and figure things out." They headed for the crosswalk. Waited for the light to turn for them. *Right on cue.*

They began walking across the street.

Lights hit them. Bright lights as a souped-up truck thundered toward them.

Latonya and Tess surged forward, their feet rushing frantically over the crosswalk as the vehicle blew by them. They were *inches* away from being hit.

"Hey, dipshit!" Latonya yelled after him. *"Pedestrian right of way!"* She flipped him off. "He could've killed us! Idiot!"

Tess's heart was racing. She could only see the truck's tail-lights. It had happened so fast. The truck had just flashed on its lights and raced right at them.

And for just a moment, she remembered the phone call she'd gotten that morning. She'd been so sure it had only been a wrong number. She'd even convinced herself that *maybe* she'd imagined the words she'd heard...

Found you.

"We need to report that asshole. Did you get his tag number?"

Tess shook her head. "I was too busy running."

Latonya sniffed. "Me, too. Scared the hell out of me."

Me, too. The driver was long gone, and Tess knew there were no street cams in that particular area. Tracking him would be pretty impossible.

"I need to get home." Tess squeezed Latonya's hand. "I want a raincheck on the diner, okay? But I have to go. I-I'm really tired tonight."

"Hey, don't let that jerk ruin your night. He's just an idiot."

Tess forced a smile. "Raincheck?" she pushed again. "Please?"

Latonya nodded.

Tess hurried toward the Jeep. Latonya's car was parked right in front of her ride.

"But one thing…"

Tess paused at Latonya's words.

"How can you not be sure if your man broke up with you? He either said we're done or he said fuck me some more."

Latonya. Yes, she could definitely be blunt. She could also cut right through the bullshit. One of the things Tess admired about her. "James wants more. He just has conditions."

Latonya leaned in close. "Kinky shit?"

"He wants me to…share my life. My past." *Me.*

"Oh." Latonya cleared her throat. "Would that be so bad?" Her gaze darted over Tess's face.

"To actually let a man in? To let a lover get close enough to care?"

But what if he didn't care? What if he found all the dark parts that she kept hidden and he turned away? Her chest ached. "You know how busy my life is. You—of all people—understand how crazy it is to be working in the ER. It takes up so much time and—"

"You can always make time for the things that matter." Latonya pointed across the street. "You've made time for this place as long as I've known you."

Yes.

"If he matters, you'd make time for him."

Tess didn't speak.

"But we both know what this is really about."

"We do?"

"I love you, Tess, but you're scared. You've always been so scared that people won't like the real you."

"No...no, I don't care what people—"

"You don't care what *most* people think. You couldn't give a damn what God Complex thinks. But people who get past your guard, those lucky few, you care about them."

Tess pressed her lips together.

"You care about me," Latonya continued in her easy, no-nonsense voice. "Hell, you love me."

"I do."

Latonya blinked, as if Tess's quick agreement surprised her. "Well, you should. I'm fabulous."

The ache in Tess's chest eased a little.

"But you need more than a fabulous best friend, and I think you know that. Maybe the hero is the one for you. Maybe he's not. But if you keep hiding from him, if you keep closing yourself off, you'll never know for sure, will you?"

"What if he doesn't like who I really am?"

"Then fuck him. He wasn't worth your time, anyway."

***

"Did you kill him?"

James sighed as he lifted a beer bottle to his mouth. Barnes had been skulking behind him as James stood in the VIP area of the club, staring down at the crowd. Another packed night. Bodies were gyrating on the dance floor. The band was pumping. And *she* wasn't there.

"Did you?" Barnes repeated, voice breaking a little bit.

James turned toward him. Offered a cold smile. "See…when you ask questions like that, it makes me suspicious."

Sweat covered the younger guy's brow. He had on his glasses again. Clark Kent, in full effect.

"I get suspicious and I think to myself…Barnes was once an informant for the FBI. How do I know he's not still working for the government?"

The sweating seemed to get worse. "But you worked for the government, too."

"Not the FBI."

Barnes licked his lower lip. "You think I'd rat you out?"

"I think you once made a living doing that very thing. And I think you're crazy if you believe I'd make any kind of confession to you." He didn't like the suspicion, but there had been a few red flags waving lately.

Barnes straightened his spine, surprising James as he confessed, "I asked because I'm worried about you."

"That is so freaking sweet. But I'm not your mama. Don't worry about me."

Barnes gave a little growl. Or a hum. Kinda hard to tell the difference. "I thought you were starting a new life here. I thought we both were. If you're going back to the old business…" A hard nod. "I can't go with you."

This was interesting. And, for a moment, it distracted James from the not-so-little matter of Tess. Or the fact that he hadn't heard from her all damn day. *I pushed her too hard.*

"Let me correct that statement." Another nod from Barnes as his cheeks reddened. His breath seemed to be coming awfully fast. "I *won't* go with you. I'm going to do things right from here on out. I won't be involved with—"

"Barnes, before you pass out, the guy was breathing when I left him, okay?"

Barnes expelled a loud sigh. "Thank God."

James turned away and let his gaze sweep over the crowd once more. "Though if he ever hurts Tess again, he won't keep breathing for long."

Silence.

There were plenty of women downstairs. Women in short skirts. Women in tight jeans. Gorgeous. Tall. Short. Curved. But...

"She got to you, huh, boss?"

James squeezed his eyes shut. "Why are you still here, Barnes?"

"Uh, because there's someone who wants to see you. I was supposed to announce the visitor."

And the guy hadn't *led* with that? James opened his eyes and craned his head toward Barnes. "Who?"

"Didn't give a name. Just said he was with Wilde Securities. I've got him waiting at the bar." Barnes moved to stand beside James. They both looked down at the bar. "He's the one in the white t-shirt, the one with all the tats. Don't know if I buy his story about being with Wilde. Guy looks more like a criminal than a security agent."

James studied the muscled, dark-haired man with the tattoo sleeves. He grunted. "We've crossed paths before."

"Oh. So he is with Wilde Securities?"

"Yeah."

"Do you want me to bring him upstairs?"

Maybe a case with Wilde would be exactly what James needed to clear his head. Or, rather, to get a certain lady *out* of his head. "Sure. Why the hell not?" He drained his beer. "Maybe he needs me to kill someone."

Barnes staggered and nearly fell.

James caught the younger man's arm. "I was *kidding*. Jesus. Lighten up, would you? And tell Cole to come up here."

"Cole?"

Now it was James's turn to sigh. "The jackass at the bar with all the tats. Send him up."

***

Her condo was dark when Tess shoved open the front door. Her alarm beeped, and she hurriedly shut her door, locked it, and then reached to disarm the system. Her fingers swiped over the pad that was lit with a soft, green light, then she flipped on her overhead lights and—

Oh, God.

Her place was trashed. The couch cushions appeared to have been cut open. Stuffing littered the floor. Her TV had been smashed. In the kitchen, she could see plates on the floor. Broken glasses. Destruction.

Destruction everywhere.

She stumbled back. Her shoulders hit the closed front door. And that was when she realized…

He could still be here.

That stupid phone call earlier that day hadn't been a wrong number.

Found you.

Her time was up.

CHAPTER SEVEN

"Welcome to the big leagues," Cole Vincent said as he lifted his bottle of beer and saluted James. "I'm here with an official job offer from Wilde Securities."

James turned his back on the floor-to-ceiling windows of his special VIP room, and he raked his new visitor with a fast, assessing sweep of his gaze. "Didn't realize I wasn't already playing in the big leagues."

Of all the Wilde agents that he'd met, Cole was the one that he couldn't quite figure out. Ex-Delta Force, the man was obviously a badass, or, at least, Cole thought that he was one. James did like the swirling tats that the fellow sported, but when he'd dug into Cole's background, he'd found a few...discrepancies.

A few little slides into the dark.

"Hmm..." Cole lowered his drink. His eyes locked on James. "Here I thought you'd be jumping for joy."

"I *never* jump for joy."

"Noted. Neither do I. But you *were* the one who appeared in *my* boss's office a while back, correct? You were the one asking Eric Wilde for a job because you were looking to, ahem, clean up your image?"

"My image is spotless, thanks for asking. Though I do have to wonder about yours." Because he was watching so closely, he caught the faint hardening of Cole's jaw.

"I'm here to tell you that your probationary period is over."

"Probation, huh? Thought I was a freelancer. You know, the kind of freelancer who gets shit done that the Wilde agents can't. Like on that last case...the woman in New York who went missing. I mean, *you* were supposed to find her, weren't you?" James tapped his chin as he pretended to think about things. "But then you got caught up in all that pesky red tape so I swooped in and saved her for you." Now James winced. "I hate to tell you — and this is awkward — but I believe my thank you package must have gotten lost during delivery. I never got the bouquet of cookies or flowers or whatever it was that you sent to me."

"You're an asshole."

"Of course, I am."

Cole's lips quirked, just a little. "Do you want the job or not?"

"I want more details on the job. In case you missed it, I'm kinda busy being a mega awesome club owner at the moment. Maybe I don't want to end my non-stop partying merely to act as a bodyguard for some bored, too rich society princess. I mean, that *is* what happens at Wilde, isn't it? You watch the rich and pampered?" He yawned. "I do like more action."

"You know we do more than that. There's what the world sees, and then there is everything else."

Yes, he'd rather suspected as much. "Again, I want more details. Specifics are always appreciated."

A frustrated growl. "You are such a—"

A knock sounded at the door.

James frowned. He'd told Barnes to make himself scarce because James didn't want the guy overhearing this chat.

The knock sounded again. James marched forward and yanked open the door. "What in the hell? I told you I didn't want to be disturbed, Barnes."

"But this is different." Barnes was almost vibrating.

"Is the club on fire?"

Barnes shook his head. "No."

"Are we being robbed?"

"No."

"Then what do you—"

"She's here," Barnes announced, all dramatic-like.

James actually felt his heart lurch in his chest. "If you're shitting me, you're fired."

Barnes opened his mouth. Closed it. "I'm not shitting you." He pointed behind James. "Go look through the window. She's downstairs, near the bar."

He whirled and stalked right back to the window.

"Is everything okay?" Cole asked, his voice tense. "There a problem here?"

James ignored him and glanced down below. Sure enough, she was there. Standing close to the seat that Cole had abandoned just a little while ago. Tess's hair was pulled up into her signature bun, and she wore faded jeans that hugged her like a second skin. Paired with the jeans, she was wearing a black tunic, one that flowed loosely around her though it sure did dip to reveal a gorgeous expanse of her cleavage, and—

She glanced up.

Even though the windows were tinted so she couldn't see through the glass, James felt like Tess was staring straight at him.

"Bring her," James growled. "Bring her up here, *now*."

He'd told her his terms. Thought that he'd blown everything to hell and back, but she was there.

She was ready to agree to his new deal?

He heard Barnes scramble from the room and slam the door shut. James didn't move. He kept staring down at her. She didn't look away, still gazing up as if she could see him, too.

But something was off. Her expression wasn't—

Cole coughed. Loudly. "Yes, so…we were kind of in the middle of something."

"The meeting is over. Feel free to hit the bar. Whatever you get will be on the house."

There was no sound of retreating footsteps. "I came to offer you a job. You told me you wanted to know more. Now you want to kick my ass out?"

"Glad you get the picture. Thanks so much." Barnes was making his way through the crowd, carefully navigating his way between the crush of bodies in order to reach Tess.

Her gaze had dropped. Her body was tense. Her movements a bit jerky as she turned and looked through the crowd—

I'm right here, baby.

"What's going on?"

Cole was certainly a nosey one. "Our meeting is over, and you're leaving." James motioned behind him with a vague roll of his hand, but didn't look at Cole. "Don't let the door hit you in the ass."

"Does that mean you're rejecting the job offer?"

Barnes had reached Tess. He spoke quickly to her, then they both headed for the stairs. James realized he'd tensed.

"To be clear…is that no or a yes?"

The man was still there? "It's a fuck off for now. I have something more important to deal with."

Ah, *finally*, James heard footsteps. But they weren't retreating. They were coming closer. And then Cole was at his side and peering down below. "What is so fascinating down there?"

The thing that fascinated him wasn't downstairs any longer. She was on her way to him.

Cole grunted. "I don't get you, man. You move heaven and hell so that Eric will give you a shot at being a Wilde agent. I mean, I understand that part — redemption quest, am I right? Brother, I have been there."

"We're not brothers." He didn't have time for Cole's crap. "Get the hell out."

"Your people skills need work." A long sigh. "You said you wanted specifics, but now you're kicking me out. That makes zero sense."

"You are far more astute than I initially suspected. Good for you." His hands had fisted. He couldn't see Tess in the crowd any longer. She *had* to be on the stairs. Getting closer and closer. And if Cole wasn't going to take his none-too-subtle hint, James would just force the guy out.

James spun and marched for the door. "We'll talk later. After I attend to some other business that's waiting for me." He opened the door. "Go get your ass drunk downstairs—" He broke off because Tess was there. Tess stood in the open doorway, and there were shadows under her eyes. She looked too pale. Her lower lip trembled, and when he stared into the darkness of her eyes, James saw fear.

"What happened?" He didn't wait for her response but immediately curled his fingers around her shoulders and hauled her across the threshold and closer to him. God, he needed her close. As soon as he touched her, a weight seemed to lift from his shoulders. Her warmth surrounded him, and he could pull in a deep breath but…

Something is wrong.

She hadn't come to him in order to renegotiate their terms. Fear had brought her to his door.

And a sick, twisted part of him thought…*I'll take Tess however I can get her.*

No, no, he fucking wouldn't. He was better than that. He *would* be better for her.

"You were right." Even her voice was *wrong.* Too hollow. Dazed. "My alarm system was shit."

"Tess?"

"Someone broke in." She blinked a few times. Seemed to focus on him. "My place is wrecked. The cops came by. They wrote down some notes. Told me to take inventory and see what was missing and—and that's it."

No, sweetheart, it's not.

"Why am I here?" Tess shook her head. "I shouldn't be bothering you with this. We're over. You left, and I don't know what I—"

"We're not over." Guttural. "Slow down. Tell me *everything*."

The tremble in her lower lip got worse. "Whoever it was...he cut up my couch cushions. Broke my picture frames. Shattered my TV. I swear, I don't even think anything *is* gone, so there won't be a list for me to give the cops, but the place is wrecked. And after the phone call this morning, I had to—"

"*Ahem.*"

Cole.

James had forgotten about the SOB for a moment. Hell, how was that for losing his edge? He'd been so focused on Tess that he'd ignored the Wilde agent in the room.

"You're with someone." Tess pulled back. Broke his hold on her. "I didn't mean to interrupt. Barnes just—he came up to me at the bar, introduced himself, and said that you were waiting." She looked over her shoulder. "Where did he go?"

Barnes had made himself scarce because he was smart.

Tess gave a shake of her head. "Doesn't matter." She pushed back a lock of her hair. Most of her hair was in her sexy bun, but tendrils had escaped. They always did. "I shouldn't have come here. But I was scared, and I thought of you."

"You thought of *him*?" Cole laughed. "Oh, God, that is good. That has got to be the first time that anyone has thought of —"

"Excuse me, sweetheart," James told Tess tenderly as he spoke over Cole's words. "I need to deal with one thing." He turned, shielding her with his body. He locked his eyes on Cole. "This doesn't concern you. I asked you politely to leave. I will not be asking again."

Cole gave a little salute. "On my way out…" He sauntered forward, but then stopped near James. "Though, I have to say, it certainly sounds as if your friend has a problem. You know, the type of problem that Wilde agents know how to handle properly." He angled his head around James so that he could see Tess. "Hi, there." He flashed a grin. "I'm Cole Vincent, security professional. Did I hear that you have a little bit of a situation, Miss —"

"*Doctor*," James snapped. "She's Dr. Barrett to you, not that you need to be talking to her again. I can handle her problem."

"But you don't have to do it alone." Cole shifted his attention back to James. "That's what being part of Wilde means. You're on a team. You have help. If you want to learn more about that team, then you know how to reach me. Of course, I'm assuming you have my number. If you don't, I figure your hacker guy Barnes can get it." He rolled back his shoulders and shifted his focus to Tess once more. "Very sorry about your break-in. Bet I could get a security team there by morning to install a system that would blow your mind."

Actually, Wilde did have the best security systems. Mostly because Eric Wilde designed them himself, and the guy was constantly tweaking and updating his tech.

Eric owed him, so James would be calling in that favor. "She wants a new system," James muttered. "Get it for her. Top of the line. The best you have."

Cole flashed him a smile. "See, look at that! We're already working together."

James growled.

"Ah…excuse me." Tess's voice was stiff. "I didn't say I was buying any new system. I just—I want to talk to James, all right? It was, um, nice to meet you, Cole—"

"Don't lie, you know it wasn't," James rasped.

Cole's eyes gleamed. "It was an absolute pleasure to meet you, Dr. Barrett. Very, very enlightening for me. In so many ways."

Dude was a total prick.

"Though I am sorry about your break-in," Cole added quickly.

"Tess," she blurted. "Just call me Tess. We're not in the ER so you don't need to call me doctor. I mean—I'm Tess."

James locked his back teeth.

"Tess." Cole's smile stretched. "I *will* be seeing you soon."

Finally, he sauntered out, and did that asshole's arm brush against Tess's as he exited? It freaking did. James stepped after him.

Tess put her hand on his chest. "Please, I need to talk to you."

He focused on her. Only her. He hated the fear in her eyes. Quickly, James shut and secured the door. "Do you want to sit down?"

Tess shook her head. "I...I didn't feel safe there. In my own home."

If an asshole had broken in, she damn well, *wasn't* safe. "Did he break your locks?"

"No, and he didn't set off the alarm system. I didn't even know anything was wrong, not until I was inside. I had closed the door, turned off the alarm, and I had just flipped on the lights. That was when I realized what was happening. Or what *had* happened."

"He could have still been in your home." Rage burned through James. He took a quick step toward her.

"I know." She swallowed. "That was my first thought, and I got out of there as fast as I could."

The intruder could have been there — or he could have been waiting outside, anticipating that she would run. But, no, someone looking for a fast score wouldn't stay around and wait...

Tess said she wasn't sure anything had been taken.

The perp would stay around and wait...only if he wanted to hurt Tess.

"The lock looked fine, but if he got in once, he could get in again." She wrapped her arms around her stomach. "I have to get new locks. I'll call someone first thing tomorrow."

"I'll take care of it."

"I can take care of my own life!" She blinked rapidly.

Oh, no. Oh, hell, no. Were those tears in her eyes? "Tess?"

"I shouldn't be here." She rocked forward. "*Why* am I here? Why did I run to you? I don't do that. I take care of myself. That's the way it's been since I was thirteen."

"You don't have to take care of yourself. Let me help you."

"I'll stay in a hotel room tonight." A nod. She didn't even seem to be seeing him any longer. It seemed as if she was mostly just talking to herself as Tess doggedly continued, "I'll be safe in a hotel. And tomorrow, I can get a new security system and new locks, and I'll start the cleanup at my place. I'll be fine." Her chin notched up. "Sorry to bother you."

Sorry to *bother* him?

The woman then had the nerve to march back for the door, all determined like, as if she was about to leave him. Like she was going to appear, decimate his world, and then vanish once more.

Pure Tess. Unpredictable. Maddening. Determined. Was it any wonder he was hooked on her?

He moved to the side, stepping into her path. "No."

"No, what?" Her brow scrunched. "You don't think I can get a new system tomorrow?"

"A new system will definitely be installed tomorrow. You'll let me and my Wilde contacts take care of that because security is truly an area in which I excel."

"It is?" Her doubting glance was semi-insulting.

"Let me do this for you because if you don't, then I'll worry and obsess and probably wind up sleeping outside your door."

Her lips parted. "Why would you do that?"

"Because you matter. Because I want to make absolutely sure that nothing bad happens to you." Bad things had happened to far too many people in his life. She was different. She had to be different.

He needed Tess to be okay. No, better than okay. He wanted her life to be perfect. Was that so much to ask? He didn't think so. And if it was too much, he didn't care.

"I'm paying for the system, James. I pay my own way, always."

"The system is going to be free. Wilde Securities owes me, so there isn't a price for it."

"Then I will owe *you*."

He didn't look away from her. "Fine. You owe me. And you can pay me right now."

"What?"

"Pay me with truth. I get to ask you three questions, and you answer me—absolutely honestly each time—and we'll consider this deal paid in full."

She shook her head. "That's not how payment works."

"That's how it works for me. Now stop being adorable and answer my questions."

Her jaw sagged open. Some of the worry *finally* eased from her face. "What?"

"You heard me. Stop being fucking adorable. It's distracting. And you do it all the time. I'm starting to think you do it deliberately just to throw me off my game."

She shook her head. "Are you crazy?"

"Some nights. And I think tonight is one of those nights." He released a hard breath. "Question one. Why did you come to me? And don't say that you don't know. That's not an option. Because you do know. Deep inside, you do, and I want to hear you tell me why."

Silence. Hell. Had he pushed her too far? Time *tick-tick-ticked* on by, and he was about to tell her to forget it, that he was handling the security system and she could—

"Because I don't feel scared when I'm with you. You have this weird way of making me feel safe." The faintest hint of humor appeared in the darkness of her eyes. "Probably because of your superhero routine at the hospital. I feel like nothing can hurt me when I'm with you. And my first instinct—even before I called the police—I wanted to call you."

"Next time, do that." He cleared his throat. "You call me *anytime*, and I'll immediately come to your side. Always know that." She'd answered him honestly. That was a big freaking step. Tess might not realize it, but she'd just revealed that she trusted him.

Sure, she didn't know who he really was, and if she did, her trust would vanish, but it was nice, having her trust him for the moment. Being the lover that she could count on.

"What's the second question?" Another tendril escaped her bun.

"Where do you really want to stay tonight?" If she said a hotel, fine, he'd get her a hotel room. The best one in town. With the best security.

Her gaze lowered. He didn't like that. He liked to stare into her dark, deep eyes and see—

She released a soft exhale. "With you." Her gaze lifted. Her eyes locked on his. "I want to stay with you, and it goes back to answer one. You make me feel safe. I'm a little jittery because of the phone call and having you with me—not being alone—would make me feel better tonight."

His temples throbbed. "What phone call?" She'd mentioned something about that before, but he'd gotten distracted by Cole's asshole self.

"This morning, the call that came through while you were with me—"

"Yeah, it was that jackass Devin." What had he done to set her off? "If he said *anything* wrong to you, I'll take care of him. You don't have to worry."

Her tongue swiped over her lower lip. Delectable.

"No," Tess answered slowly. "Before him."

He blinked. His mind flashed back to her bedroom, that morning. She had gotten a quick call that morning. She'd had the phone to her ear for mere seconds before she'd put it down. But then the phone had immediately rung again, so he'd figured it was the same caller. "Who was it?"

"I don't know." Her gaze darted away, then back to him.

Uh, sweetheart. Why the hell did you just lie to me? Hadn't he told her that he wanted honesty?

"Technically, that was question four," she murmured.

"What?"

"When you asked me, 'what phone call?'— that was question three. And then when you asked, 'Who was it?'—that was question number four. Just so we're both following along correctly."

Oh. So she thought it was okay to *lie* to him because he'd asked more than his allotted number of questions? That wasn't how things worked. "Why did the call rattle you?"

Her delicate throat moved as she swallowed. "Because he said… 'Found you.'"

James felt his muscles lock down. "Someone's been looking for you?"

"I didn't think anyone was." Fear flickered in her eyes. "I didn't think I had to worry about that, but the phone call came today, I almost got run down outside of the pantry, and now my place is trashed. It's been a terrible day, and I'm scared."

His hands had fisted. "*Someone nearly ran you down?*" She'd been in danger while he'd just been standing in his freaking club, pouting because she hadn't called him? His vision bled to red.

"That…I don't know exactly what happened. I mean, this big truck came out of nowhere when Latonya and I were on the crosswalk. He came right toward us, and we had to run." She sniffed. "But we weren't hurt. It scared me. *That's* the reason I went home early. Normally, I go out and eat with Latonya after we work at the pantry. But I was rattled, and I wanted to go home."

When she'd gotten home, the night had gotten even worse.

"I'm scared," she confessed again. "When I'm scared, you make it better."

He had to do it. James closed the distance between them. Wrapped his arms around her, and pulled her against him. "You don't need to be afraid, baby." *Because I'm here. If someone comes at you…the fool will be a fucking dead man.*

***

Cole Vincent strolled out of the club. He looked to the left, to the right, and inclined his head toward the bouncer who gave him a suspicious glance. Cole whistled softly as he walked away from the club, taking his time until he made it to the dark SUV that waited around the corner.

He opened the left rear door and jumped into the back seat.

"Jeez, man, you were in there for-freaking-ever." The driver, Linc Dalton turned toward him. "I mean, if you are gonna have a sleepover with the guy, give us a head's up next time. Don't just leave our asses in the car. I got hungry out here. No, I got *hangry.*"

"*Linc.*" The woman in the passenger seat let out a frustrated sigh. "It wasn't that long." Blair Kincaid always seemed to have way more patience than her partner did. But even as Cole had that thought, Blair swiveled in her seat to face him and demanded, "What's the verdict? Is James in?"

"Did you get a new partner?" Linc pushed. "Because I have got to tell you, I am getting real tired of sharing *my* partner with you."

"Screw off, Linc," Cole muttered as he ran a hand over his face. "I think we have a problem."

Silence. He was pretty sure Linc and Blair exchanged one of their intense, partner-stares. Then Blair asked, "What kind of problem?"

"A problem who is about five-foot-five, with dark hair and chocolate eyes." His hand dropped. "James Smith kicked me out before even hearing all of the details on Wilde's offer because his lady burst in on our little chit-chat. I know fear when I see it, and the woman was terrified."

"Uh, huh." Linc drummed his fingers on the steering wheel. "You're telling me this lady went to James for help? She turned to an assassin? Jesus, what does she want...for him to kill someone for her?"

"I don't know, but my gut was in knots even before I left." Mostly because of the way James had acted around her. *Focused.* No, more than that. *Obsessed?* And it wouldn't be a good idea for a guy like James to get hooked on anyone. "You know I had reservations about him."

"You have reservations about everyone," Blair pointed out. But she wasn't being mean. He got that. He *did* have reservations about most folks. He'd been screwed over in the past. Lied to. Betrayed.

So he had some issues. Whatever. He was working on them.

"He kicked me out," Cole admitted flatly. "Didn't want me anywhere near the woman. Dr. Barrett. Dr. Tess Barrett."

"How does an assassin hook up with a doctor?" Linc wanted to know.

"Maybe she likes bad boys," Blair offered. "James totally qualifies in that category."

"Seriously?" Linc's fingers drummed again. "Is that what you like? Because I thought you were all about the military guys. But if it's the bad boys who charm—"

"We are *not* talking about me. I was just saying—perhaps—this woman likes guys with an edge. I mean, come on, if you're looking for bad, then look no further than James Smith."

Cole's eyes had adjusted to the dimness of the vehicle's interior. He looked between Linc and Blair. "Yeah, okay. Maybe the doctor likes her guys bad, and in that case, well, she may have bit off more than she can handle."

Blair nodded. "Does that mean that James isn't interested in joining Wilde any longer? Because his freelance work was top-notch, and it's going to be a major loss if he's not coming on board for the case that's waiting."

Yes, they did need his skills. And his connections. But first… "He didn't say no. He just told me to get my ass out." Cole considered options. Angles. "Maybe *you* should approach him tomorrow, Blair. From what I've seen, the man has a soft spot for brunettes."

"Fuck off," Linc fired before Blair could respond. "She's not flirting with the guy to get him to take the job."

"Thanks, Linc." She touched his shoulder. Then, even in the darkness, Cole caught her cold smile. "Fuck off, Cole. I'm not flirting with the guy. *You're* the point of contact on this. You're the one who was supposed to offer him the job. You're the one who was supposed to convince him to come on—full-time—with us. And you're the one who can go in tomorrow and talk with him again."

"Damn straight," Linc growled. "And, hey, I have an idea. You're a brunette. From what I've heard, Ghost has a soft spot for brunettes. Maybe try flirting with him—"

"Fuck off. God, I hate it when I get paired up with you two." They always teamed up against him.

"And *that*," Linc announced triumphantly, "is why you need your own partner. Tomorrow, get him to cooperate. Get him to join the team, and we can be out of this town by sunset."

"Yeah." Cole squeezed his eyes shut. "Unfortunately, I don't think things are going to be that easy." Linc and Blair hadn't seen the way James stared at his pretty doctor. They'd missed the look in the fellow's eyes. "For the record, I didn't say Blair should flirt with the guy."

"I'm glad you didn't," Linc fired back.

"I just said she should *talk* to him. He kicked my ass out. Thought he might treat her better. We need him, and I'm trying not to screw this up." Because without his particular connections and skill set, the next case at Wilde would be a clusterfuck. "Hell. I'm gonna have to play nice with the assassin," he groused as he opened his eyes. "Right?"

"Right," Linc told him, all cheerful. "But don't worry, we'll have your back."

"Now I feel so very reassured." No, he fucking didn't. But before he could rage about that—Linc always brought out his raging side—Cole saw two familiar figures exiting the club.

"Speak of the devil," Blair said, voice a bit husky. "I'm guessing that's the doctor cuddled so close to his side?"

Cole leaned forward. Sure enough, that was James, with his arm wrapped around the doctor's shoulders. They were heading for a waiting limo. "That's her."

James let her slide in first, then he looked to the left and the right.

"Shit. Did he just make us?" Linc demanded.

James was staring at them a bit too long. Then he lifted his hand and flipped them off.

"I'd call that a yes," Blair replied.

James followed his doctor into the car. The driver slammed the door shut behind him. A moment later, the limo was taking off.

"Should we follow them?" Linc cranked the SUV.

"No." Blair reached out a hand and touched his wrist. "We know where he'll be tomorrow. Give the man his time with her. If he comes with us, this could be the last night they have together. Let them have that."

"You are such a romantic," he teased her.

She just sighed.

And Cole was about to agree. He was about to say that they should get the hell out of there and leave but…

Then a black car slid away from the curve. It wasn't moving too fast. Not too slow, either. And it slid away without turning on its lights. Yeah, like that wasn't suspicious. The car went to the intersection and turned right. Exactly the way the limo had just gone.

The tension that Cole felt in his gut coiled tighter. "Follow that car."

"Already on it," Linc muttered as he got their SUV moving. They hurried after the car, trailed it for a few turns, long enough to let them know that, hell, yes, the jerk *was* following James but then—

The mystery car sped up. Shot forward with a burst of speed as it ran right through a red light. Linc floored it to follow, but then a big rig's blasting horn had him slamming on the brakes.

They all lurched forward against their seatbelts. By the time the big rig was gone…

The mystery car was gone, too. *This is not good.* "Get to James's place," Cole said. "*Now.*"

But when they got there, when they searched the block, there was no sign of the vehicle that had been tailing the limo.

CHAPTER EIGHT

"Thanks for bringing me here. I appreciate it." Tess rocked forward onto the balls of her feet. "I have a shift that starts at seven a.m. tomorrow, and if I'd been at a hotel, I don't think I would have slept well." *Try...at all.*

"You don't have anything to worry about here. No one will get past my security system."

That was good to know. But... "Are you sure?" It was certainly easy enough to say only —

"Sweetheart, I'm not bluffing. I know my security." He moved toward the windows. Tapped on the glass. "Bulletproof. Just in case you were wondering."

"I had *not* been wondering that." Not at all. They were on the second floor. She hadn't even thought about... "Wait, *why* do you have bulletproof windows? Do people shoot at you a lot?"

His hand curled into a fist. "More than you might expect."

She rushed toward him. "What kind of answer is that?" Now she was afraid again, but not for herself. For him.

His head cocked. "An honest one?"

"Club owners get shot at often?"

"I try *not* to get shot at. But things can happen, and I like to be prepared." Now his hand lifted toward her. His knuckles caressed her cheek.

She flinched. Not because he'd hurt or scared her, but because when he touched her, a bolt of heat slid over her skin.

But, immediately, he stopped touching her. He moved around her. Put some space between them. "You can take the guest room. You don't have to worry about me bothering you tonight. You'll be safe. You can get your rest." He marched away from her as she turned to stare after him. "Tomorrow, my driver can take you to work. While you're at the hospital, I'll make sure your security system is up and running."

His back was to her as he walked away. Since he wasn't staring straight at her, it was easier for her to say, "I wasn't sure you'd want to see me again."

He stopped. Tess caught the stiffening of his shoulders.

"You told me we were done. Then I showed up at your club. This is really going above and beyond for an ex-lover."

He turned on his heel. A crisp, almost military-like move. "I didn't say we were done."

"No?" It had felt that way. When he walked out and the door closed.

"I told you the rules were changing. If you came to me again, I'd want more. That playtime would be over."

Goosebumps rose on her skin. "Is that what you think I was doing with you? Playing?"

He gazed back at her.

"I wasn't playing with you."

"Good."

He didn't say anything else. "What do you want from me?"

Now he stalked forward.

She sucked in a quick, nervous breath as he stopped right before her.

"Sweetheart, isn't it obvious?" His smile made her heart race. "I want everything."

***

If he wanted everything, why was she sleeping alone?

Tess tossed and turned in the guest bedroom, and her fist pounded at the pillow. Not because it wasn't comfortable. The whole bed felt like some kind of perfect dang cloud. No, she was punching her pillow because...

Why am I punching the pillow?

After he'd told her that he wanted everything, James had escorted her to the guest room.

First, she hadn't needed an escort. She knew where the room was.

And, second, he'd *left* her? They touched, and they went full-on inferno mode. But he'd left her.

So much for rules changing.

She flopped onto her back. Maybe she should have said something. She knew—deep down—what he wanted. And hadn't Latonya told her that she'd have to do this? But she'd been afraid. *What if he doesn't like the real me?*

Whatever. She was going to face him. Tess tossed aside her covers and jumped out of the bed. She marched straight out of the guest room and headed for his bedroom. She lifted her fist, squared her shoulders, and knocked as hard as she—

The door was instantly yanked open. "What's wrong?" James stood before her. His chest was bare—wonderfully muscled and bare as he wore what appeared to be a pair of silk, black pajama bottoms. His hair was tousled and sexy, and he was...

Scars.

She blinked. Her eyes widened.

He swore. "Give me a second. Let me grab a shirt—"

He turned away from her and she saw his back. More scars.

"Oh, God." Her hand reached out to touch him.

But James spun and grabbed her wrist. "Don't." His hold was tight. Not painful. He'd never had a painful hold with her. Their eyes locked.

She realized right then—during all the wild times that they'd been together—she'd never actually seen him without his shirt on. And when he had taken off the shirt, they'd been in the dark. He'd caught her hands any time that she'd tried to touch him on his chest or back. In her head, she remembered him catching her wrists and anchoring them with his hold. Now she realized he'd stopped her before she could feel the scars that marked him in so many places.

He'd let her touch his shoulders. His arms.

Not his chest. Not his back.

He'd been so careful, and she hadn't even realized it.

A tear leaked from her eye.

"Don't," James snarled. His hold tightened. "Do not cry because of them."

"There are so many marks."

"Yeah, well, they don't hurt." He let her go. Whirled away. Paced toward the bed.

Tess didn't move from her position in the doorway. She was rooted to the spot. "You hid them from me."

He laughed. A bitter sound. "Did I?"

"You know you did."

His head cocked toward her. "Maybe I thought if you saw them, you'd run."

"I'm not running."

Another bitter laugh. "No, but you're scared to death, aren't you? Because you're looking at them and you're trying to figure out...how the hell did he get all of those marks? You're a doctor. I bet you even know what most of them are, don't you?"

"James—"

He touched a slash near his belly button. "Knife wound." A puckered indention near his ribcage. "Gunshot." He moved his hand to a third scar, one above his right hip. "Barely a graze from the bullet there, but enough to leave a reminder of—"

"Stop." Her head was pounding. There were so many scars. Knife wounds. Bullet wounds. How had a club owner gotten—

"I guess it's only fair that you see my secrets when I wanted to know yours. But, actually, sweetheart, I've been honest with you from the start."

A former assassin turned nightclub owner. No, no, that wasn't possible. "No."

"I even told you that I worked for Uncle Sam."

When he'd told her that his soul was dark and damaged.

"You're the only person I've been that honest with. Because something about you—you were different. I told you the truth, but you didn't believe me."

Her hand rose to press over her racing heart. She was wearing one of his t-shirts — he'd given it to her after escorting her to the guest room. The shirt was soft and huge, and it fell to the middle of her thighs. As she stood there before him, wearing it, smelling of him, Tess felt vulnerable. And very, very —

"Scared of me now?" His voice was rougher. "Why? I'm the same man, Tess. The same man I was when I was fucking you. The same man I was when you were screaming as you came for me."

She took a step back.

He took a step forward. "The same man I was when you came to me because you were afraid."

"James…" No, no, there was no way that he was really some kind of assassin, right? "You're not —"

An alarm began to beep. A fast, furious beep. He swore and hurried past her. Tess shook her head, swiped at the tear on her cheek, and rushed after him. He turned to the right and entered his office. He went to the computer and typed in a quick code. A moment later, she could see a crystal-clear image on one of the two, giant monitors.

"Isn't that the guy we met at your club?" Tess asked as she frowned at the image. "His name was —"

"Cole Vincent. And he shouldn't be here." He yanked out his phone and tapped on the screen. A moment later, he ordered, "Cole, get your ass off my doorstep. I'm not talking about the offer tonight."

Offer?

"Go crash at your hotel and leave me alone."

Cole leaned toward the door, and when he spoke, his voice filled the room. "I'm not here about Wilde." He looked over his shoulder and then back at the door. "I'm here about the asshole who tried to tail you home from the club. Now how about you play nicely and open the door?"

James was typing on the computer's keyboard and pulling up more images on both of the computer monitors. She hadn't even noticed the cameras outside, but Tess could have sworn it looked like James was accessing about three different street view cameras.

"Who's the backup with you?" James demanded.

She squinted at the screen and at the dark SUV that was idling about half a block away.

"Wilde agents," Cole answered.

"All of you—get in here, now." James ended the connection. On the screen, though, she saw Cole pull out his phone.

Then James rose and turned toward her.

She hadn't backed up, so when he turned, their bodies brushed. His nostrils flared, as if he was pulling in her scent. Then he sidestepped. Moved away from her.

"You should go back to the guest room. I'll deal with Cole."

"Seriously. You're trying to dismiss me? We were kind of in the middle of an important discussion. A discussion about you being—"

"A former assassin. Yeah, that's what I am. Or was. I told you that already. There's not much else to say. The work I did for Uncle Sam was classified. I don't get to share. Hell, I'm not the sharing sort, anyway."

Neither was she, but his words still made her ache.

"So that's who has been touching you, sweetheart. The hands that have been on you? They are a killer's hands. But then, you realized that, didn't you? I could see it in your eyes, as soon as you found my scars. I could see the understanding of what I was in the way you pulled back from me. You're scared as hell now, and you know what? Maybe you should be. Maybe you—"

She grabbed him. Locked her hands around his shoulders and stood on her toes as she glared at him. "How about you don't tell me how I feel? How about that?"

His eyes widened. "I didn't mean—baby, dammit, I don't want you afraid of me. I know what I am. I know how the world sees me. I'm a monster, straight to my core."

"That really what you think you are?"

"It's what I know I am."

"That's not what I see." Tess yanked his head down toward her. Her mouth slammed into his as she kissed him with a wild fury. Frustration. Desire. Need. But not fear.

Because he's not the only killer in the room.

Even as that thought registered, Tess shoved against his chest.

He let her go, but watched her with blazing, golden eyes.

"I'm not afraid of you." Her voice came out too husky.

"No? Because I think you're a—"

"Don't you dare call me a liar." Now she was ice cold.

A pounding knock came, seeming to echo through the whole place.

His head jerked at the sound. "You don't need to be here when we talk. This is just about Wilde and I—"

"I don't know who Wilde is, but I do know that if you were followed tonight—if *we* were followed—then I am definitely listening to the conversation. Someone broke into my house. What if that person followed me to your club? And then what if I just brought the jerk to your home?"

His jaw hardened.

"I'm not hiding in the guest room."

His gaze dipped over her. "How about you at least put on some pants? Because if Cole is staring at your legs, I'll have to kick his ass, and that will slow down the whole 'conversation' as you called it."

Fine. She spun and stormed for the guest room.

"Tess, why'd you kiss me?"

"Because you fucking needed kissing," she snapped back. *And I needed to kiss you.*

***

"This is Wilde Agent Lincoln Dalton." Cole waved to the guy in battered jeans, a black t-shirt, and a bomber jacket.

Lincoln inclined his head. "Friends call me Linc."

"Do I look like your friend?" James wanted to know. Yeah, he was in a real pisser of a mood and taking out his rage on everyone.

Instead of appearing annoyed or offended, Lincoln's lips twitched.

"What in the hell are you even doing at my place?" *I need to calm down. Dial this way back.*

Cole cleared his throat. "I'm currently introducing you to the team." He waved his hand toward the brunette in the black dress pants and green sweater. A woman with a classical, sophisticated beauty. "This is Blair Kincaid."

The name clicked. So did the woman's face. James offered his hand to her. "Heard about the work you did down in Mexico. Ballsy as hell of you to go in there and get those women out with the full force of the cartel surrounding you."

"I didn't think it was ballsy. It was desperate." She shook his hand, then let go. "If I hadn't gone in, they would have never come out." Her gaze swept over him. "But just how did you hear about that? Because that case was before Wilde, and it was supposed to be a classified job."

He shrugged. He'd actually been in Mexico at the time, scheduled for a hit under Uncle Sam's orders. He'd had an up-close view of Blair Kincaid because she'd slipped under his scope's view. That was why he knew her face. She'd once been in his cross-hairs. Not his target, she was one of the good ones.

Even as she'd rushed those women to safety, he'd taken out the leader of the cartel.

"Okay, so now that the names are out of the way…" Cole squared his shoulders. "Where can we talk privately? Without your guest interrupting and—"

Footsteps padded toward them, cutting right through Cole's words.

James didn't glance over his shoulder. He waited for Tess to join the group. When she walked past him, he saw that she was wearing her jeans and loose top again. Her hair was still down, all tousled and sexy. She hadn't paused to put on shoes. His eyes narrowed when he saw the blue polish gleaming on her cute little toes. The polish was new. The last time he'd seen her, Tess's toes had been painted red.

"I don't think *I'm* the one interrupting," Tess clarified crisply. "I mean, I was here first." Her gaze swept them all. "I think I missed the introductions. I'm Tess."

Cole cleared his throat. "Well, I'm Cole. Though you already knew that." He pointed to his left. "This is—"

"Linc." The guy flashed her a slow smile. "At your service."

"And I'm Blair." Blair walked forward and offered her hand to Tess. They shook. "Nice to meet you. Though I am terribly sorry that we crashed in during the night."

Lincoln—hell, *Linc*—frowned. "We *always* crash on people during the night. That's like our thing."

"Ignore him," Blair instructed. "Or, try to."

James could feel his temples throbbing. "Could we just cut to the chase? You're all interrupting. Tess and I were busy."

"I bet," Cole muttered.

James looked at him. Just looked.

"Fuck. Sorry. Was that out loud?"

"Well, it wasn't silent," Linc assured him. "That's for certain."

He did not have the time for these assholes. "The tail. Who was it?" *And how had I missed him?*

Tess moved closer to him. Her arm brushed his.

Awareness surged through James.

Ah, right. That would be how. He'd be extra freaking vigilant from now on. When Tess was near, she occupied too much of his attention.

"We don't know who he was. After you, ah, waved good-bye to our group here…" Cole lifted his hand and waved…with his middle finger extended a bit. "We watched you drive away. We figured you were good for the night, but then a black car —"

"With no plates," Blair added.

" — took off after you. We tailed the car, but the driver made us. And ditched us."

James lifted a brow. "You were ditched? I expected more from Wilde."

A shrug from Cole. "I wasn't driving."

"Oh, for shit's sake." Linc narrowed his eyes. "Let's not point fingers. I mean, the jerk *ran* through the light. A big rig was coming right at me. I'm sorry I stopped to save everyone. My bad. And, can we not overlook the fact that this fellow here — Mr. Big and Bad — didn't even notice the tail? I mean, I thought you were this legend. I thought you were this unstoppable machine of —"

"Does he always talk so freaking much?" James asked. He cut in deliberately because he didn't want Linc to finish his rant.

"Sorry," Linc said before one of the others could respond. He straightened his shoulders. "Had a whole lot of caffeine tonight. Makes me crazy. And I'm hangry. I talk more when I'm hangry."

Good to know. James pinched the bridge of his nose. "So you're all here because someone tailed me a few blocks, ditched you all, and escaped into the night?"

"Yes, basically," Cole confirmed. "We thought you'd want to know."

"I did." James blew out a breath as his hand dropped his side. "Any identifying information that I can use?"

"Black sedan. Older model. The driver didn't turn on head-lights. He was parked right outside of the club, so he was waiting for you to come out."

"Um…" Tess rocked forward onto the balls of her feet. He hated that she was nervous, and he knew the others would also notice her telling movement. They were like him—they noticed tells from everyone and stored them for future reference. "Are you sure he was waiting specifically for James? Did you *see* when the sedan arrived at the club?"

The agents shared a quick look. A look he understood. No. Hell, they hadn't seen it arrive.

"Maybe the driver wasn't waiting for you, James. Maybe he was waiting for me." Tess's eyes turned darker with her worry. "I was in the limo with you. He could have been following me."

"Why would someone want to follow you?" Linc asked. "There trouble happening in your life?"

Like the guy didn't know. James was sure Cole had briefed both Blair and Linc on everything that Tess had said in the club.

But…

As he stared at Blair and Linc, James realized they seemed truly concerned. And curious. *Huh. Maybe he didn't tell them.*

James caught Tess's hand in his. Then he moved in front of her. A deliberate move so that the others would understand that she was off limits. "There's nothing else you need to know about Tess."

He knew her secrets. Only because he'd dug deep and hard in her life. And, yes, he probably shouldn't have fucking done that. Tess didn't know that he'd ripped into her past the first night they'd met. But, when you'd been burned as many times as he had, you stopped being trusting. You looked for threats. You eliminated the threats before they could hurt you.

He knew her secrets, and he didn't want the Wilde agents to know about them. He wanted to protect her. *From every threat.*

"Well, one of you was the target," Linc noted. "So we thought you should get the heads-up."

"Appreciate it." He did. "Now, good night." He kept up his position in front of Tess.

She nudged him. "Are they the Wilde people who will be putting in my new security system?"

Hell.

Cole's brows climbed up.

Tess nudged James again—and he realized that, shit, he'd forgotten to put on his shirt. He'd had the whole damn conversation in his jammies. Fucking figured. No wonder Linc was all smirky. *Yeah, I'm a badass assassin, and I like silk pajamas. So screw off.*

"I'll be talking to their boss," James muttered. "He'll make sure the system is installed. I already told you, Tess," he glanced back at her, "it's a done deal. I've got it covered."

"But if they are going to be involved, I would really like to pay them—"

"Why does she need a security system?" Blair asked, her voice very careful.

"Because there was a break-in at my place," Tess explained. "That's why James is letting me stay here tonight."

Cole flashed a shark's grin. "He is such a sweetheart like that. A real hero."

I will kick your ass. "Thanks again for the info. It's late."

Cole made no move toward the door. "You still considering my offer? Because you know, in situations like this, it pays to have friends and not to pull the lone wolf routine."

"I have plenty of friends." He didn't. Whatever.

"Fine, but we're friends with special skills. Keep that in mind."

"I also have plenty of skills, thanks." Why were they lingering? What did they think he wanted, a friggin' slumber party?

"We'll be in town a bit longer, if you need us." With that, Cole *finally* headed for the door. About time.

James followed because he wanted to make one hundred percent sure the Wilde agents left his property. Tess moved with him, but he turned. There were some things that she couldn't hear. *Or maybe I'm afraid for her to hear them all.* "Baby, if someone is watching the building, I need you on the second floor. It's the most secure space. I'll be right back. I swear."

She nodded. Grudgingly.

He made quick time of heading downstairs with the others. And when they were on the ground floor, clear of Tess, he knew that Cole would ask—

"So, what's your take, Ghost?"

He didn't stiffen at the use of his code name. He knew Cole's use of the name had been deliberate. It was the name for a man who'd retired. He wasn't Ghost, not anymore.

"Was the guy tailing you tonight after your lady upstairs?"

If the sonofabitch was, he'll be sorry.

"Or was he after you?" Cole's gaze held no emotion. "Did someone from your past just track you down?"

He hoped to hell not. Because if this was about his past — shit, no, he could not bring that kind of nightmare to Tess. "I don't know." A true answer. An honest one. "But I will find out."

Linc and Blair stood by, silent and watchful.

Cole exhaled. "We can help. You get that, don't you? I mean, it's what Wilde does."

"I'm not Wilde."

"But you wanted to be. You busted ass, proving yourself on freelance missions, and I am here with the job offer." For just a moment, Cole's expression showed his confusion. "What's changed? You wanted this so badly before."

I want something else more now. Not just something else. Someone. And if he went with Wilde, that would mean he had to leave town. Leave Tess.

He wasn't ready to do that.

"Priorities." James shrugged. "They've shifted. For now, I'm not taking the job."

"But you want your lady safe."

He would do anything to keep her safe.

"So tell us what you need and let us help. Wilde owes you. Hell, you don't need to call Eric. You can tell me right now, and we'll give you whatever you need." Cole's voice was low. "You want a new system at her place? Consider it done. You want an extra protection detail? Done."

"For now, let's start with the security system." As for everything else… "I have some digging to do. When I learn more, I'll be in contact."

"We're not leaving town, not for a few days." Cole didn't move. The guy sure liked to linger. "If you need more from us, if you want help, we're here."

He wasn't used to accepting help from anyone. Wasn't used to needing it. But this was a different world. A different life.

"Just one more thing." Blair's voice was low. "Who put those marks on her neck?"

"A patient who got out of control. He's been handled." Flat.

"You sure?" Linc prompted.

"Damn sure." With that, he got them out of his building. Was about to slam the door shut, when Linc threw up a hand and pushed it against the metal. "What now?"

"You obviously think this isn't some random break-in situation. I can tell by the way you're acting." His gaze raked James. "So why is someone after that gorgeous lady upstairs?"

"That's the big question, isn't it?" James replied. "Don't worry, I'm on it."

"Good to know." Linc's smirk flashed once more. "By the way, love the jammies."

"I will kick your ass."

Linc snatched his hand back from the door. "Jeez, you need to lighten up."

"You need to fuck off." He slammed the door. But James didn't immediately turn away.

He breathed slowly. Deeply.

Could just be a break-in. Could be something random. Or…

Hell. If her past had come back to attack her, he would fight as dirty as necessary to protect her. Tess wasn't alone this time. She wasn't easy prey.

She had him.

And he wasn't going anywhere.

Wilde could fuck off. The rest of the world could fuck off.

He would stay with Tess, no matter what.

***

The new guy in her life had money and power. A swanky limo. A driver.

Protection.

Tess had run straight to him. She probably thought he would keep her safe. Probably thought she had nothing to fear when she hid behind that guy and his money.

She was wrong.

So wrong.

She had everything to fear because Tess had everything to lose. The new boyfriend didn't know her. Not the real woman. He saw the pretty mask she wore. Saw the perfect woman that she pretended to be.

Tess wasn't perfect. She was as far from perfect as it was possible to be.

When the new lover found out the truth, he'd kick her aside. Then Tess would have no one. She'd be all alone and vulnerable.

And I'll be waiting.

***

"I thought he'd be scarier." Linc slid behind the steering wheel.

Blair buckled up in the passenger seat.

In the back, Cole tried to figure out what in the hell his next move should be. *Security system. Tess's place.*

"I mean, I read the dude's bio. He was supposed to be this infamous hit man—the big, bad Ghost. He was the boogeyman. If he was after you, you were as good as dead."

You weren't as *good* as dead. You were dead.

"Wilde didn't even know Ghost was working for the US government, hell, everyone thought he was working for himself, and in some circles, that's still what people believe."

In *most* circles. Because Ghost was a legend. He was a code name to most people. The Wilde agents knew the flesh and blood man, but few others did.

"I thought he seemed intense," Blair said, speaking slowly. "He's a man who has seen his fair share of hell. And you have to admit—just looking at the freelance work he's done for Wilde — the guy can get the job done."

Cole sighed. "Blair's right. His resume speaks for itself." It also gave him a few nightmares. "So we're going to bide our time in Savannah for a bit. We're going to find out exactly what's happening with Dr. Barrett. You know Wilde agents stick together. We always have each other's back."

Linc angled toward him. "He's not Wilde."

"Not yet," Cole agreed. "But we have to give the man time to think over our offer. Let's show him how useful a team can be. He's spent his whole life being a lone wolf. And you know what happens when you do that?"

"I'm not much for the lone lifestyle," Linc replied, deadpan. "Though I do think of myself as more of an alpha."

"In your dreams," Blair muttered.

Cole ignored them and glanced through the window back out at the dark street. They didn't get it — he knew that Linc and Blair, despite their bickering, had a deep bond. Partners, through and through. They didn't know what it was like to have no one to depend on when the darkness closed in on you.

Cole understood. He'd been there before, and that was why he could relate to James.

When you were alone too long, you lost faith in the world. You lost hope.

If you weren't careful, with the kind of work that they did, you could lose your soul, too.

CHAPTER NINE

"You still have bruises on your neck."

Tess's fingers fluttered over her throat. She'd been waiting in the kitchen for James to return, and he'd entered with silent steps.

"Do they hurt?" He headed toward her. His eyes were narrowed and locked on her neck. When he reached her, he lifted a hand, and his fingers feathered over her throat.

Her pulse immediately sped up like crazy beneath his touch. "N-no," she stammered. "They don't. Barely feel them."

He caressed her again. "Why do you lie to me?"

"They don't hurt. They—"

"If Frederick Waller ever puts a hand on you again, he's dead."

Now a chill blew over her. He'd learned her attacker's name. *Must have gotten the info from someone at the hospital.* "I doubt our paths are ever going to cross again. I talked to his brother Morgan at the hospital. Frederick has had a problem for a while, and Morgan is trying to get him help. But sometimes, people don't want to take the help that's given to them."

"No, they don't." He stared straight at her. "Are you going to accept my help?"

"I'm here, aren't I? By the way, thank you for giving me a place to stay. I mean, I know we broke up and—"

"That's the second time you said that shit. Let's be clear. We didn't break up."

Oh? She sucked in a breath.

"We weren't ever fucking together."

Her heart squeezed at the surge of brutal pain that pierced right through her.

"No, correction." His hand pulled away. "We *were* fucking, but that was all." He turned away. Took a few steps—

"Stop." Okay, she was almost shaking.

James stopped. His powerful shoulders flexed, but he didn't look back at her.

"Why are you acting this way? You were the one who was fine with the arrangement. You were the one who first proposed it to me in your club. Now you're trying to change up everything on me. What's the new deal? You help me out with my security if I bare my soul to you? I have to tell you all of my secrets or there is no help to—"

"No." He spun toward her. His eyes blazed with a barely banked fury. "There's no price on my help. You're in trouble? You need me? I'm there. *Always.* Simple as that."

"Nothing seems simple with you." She shook her head. "No, it was simple before. When we were meeting for sex, and it wasn't anything else and it—"

"That's the problem. I want something else."

What if I don't have anything else to give?

"With you, I found out that I was a possessive bastard. I don't want secret moments from your life. I want everything. I want you moaning and screaming as you come for me. I want your dreams in the middle of the night. I want the fears that you try so hard to hold back, but that I can see creeping into your eyes when you think no one is watching."

She took a step back.

"And I want your hopes. I want to know what you long for in the future." He rolled back his shoulders. "That way, I can give it to you."

Safety. That was what she wanted most. Safety and security. But she was coming to realize... "You're not a safe man, are you?" He'd told her from the beginning, but she hadn't believed him. That was on her. Well, kind of on her. Who would have believed the whole assassin turned club owner story?

Maybe she should have run from him the first night.

Wait, I did.

But then she'd run back to him. At the first sign of trouble, of pain, he'd been in her head. She'd gone to him. "I never did that before."

His brow furrowed. "Okay, sweetheart, what the hell are you talking about?"

But she took another step back because her mind was spinning. She'd gone to him when she'd been in pain. After she'd lost her patient, she'd gone straight to him.

Then when someone had broken into her home, James had been the first person she'd thought about. She hadn't been able to get to him fast enough.

What did that mean?

"You're scared of me, Tess. Dammit, I told you, you don't ever need to be afraid of me."

He was an assassin. An *assassin*. "You killed people."

A mask slid over his face. "Yes."

She shuddered.

"And you save people. You use your hands to help, and I use mine…" He stared down at his hands. "For an entirely different purpose." He looked up at her. "That why you're backing away? Because you realize the hands that touched you have blood all over them? I warned you, I told you from the beginning, I—" James stopped. Shook his head. "No, I fucking didn't."

She couldn't move.

"I'm sorry." His powerful shoulders sagged. "I knew you didn't believe me when I told you what I used to do. Hell, who would believe me? And there was freedom in that. I got to tell myself that I'd been honest with you, but the truth was…I knew you wouldn't want me touching you, not once you knew who I really was." His hands fisted. "I knew this moment would come. Knew all along you were too good for me. I was tasting heaven when I should have just kept my ass in hell." A hard nod. "You will stay safe. I guarantee that. There is no one who can protect you better than I can. I'll find out what's happening. I'll find out and I'll keep you safe, and then I'll get out of your life, and you will never have to see me again." His nostrils flared. "Go to bed, all right, Tess? I need you to go to bed now. I need to put space between us. I need — *screw it*. I could really use a damn drink."

He strode away from her. Headed toward the bar.

She was still rooted to the spot. His words played in her head over and over again. He thought she was too good for him? That his hands were the only ones stained with blood?

She took a few halting steps toward him. "What about what I need?"

He whirled toward her.

She advanced a bit more. "Don't you want to know what I need?"

"God, yes." He waited, seemingly holding his breath.

A dam broke inside of her. A dam, a wall, whatever the hell internal protection she'd given herself. He'd told her about his past. All the dirty, dark parts.

Now it was her turn. Her head tilted forward, and her hair slid over her face. "I was thirteen when I killed him." She didn't look at James. Couldn't. "I was…my parents were gone. My mom had tried to take care of me, but she got sick and she died, and my dad—he…" She swallowed. "He didn't want me. He left me in the street, and, after that, I was afraid, I was so desperate. I was hiding from everyone, and I didn't think anyone ever saw me. I didn't think anyone noticed me until…" She wasn't sure she could say this.

Silence.

Tess risked a quick glance at James. He stood a few feet away, his hand curved around a clear glass. A whiskey bottle was on a shelf near him. He hadn't reached for the bottle. Not yet.

It was gutting her, but she made herself keep talking. "One day, this fancy black car pulled up next to me. I…I was walking. I used to go to the library as often as I could. You know—the libraries let anyone in, and I could read as long as I wanted, and there was a bathroom there, and I—" She pulled in a breath. This story wasn't about the library. Though, it had been such a haven for her. "The guy driving the car only looked a few years older than me. He rolled down his window and asked if I went to his high school. I went closer to the car because I didn't think anything was wrong, and—" She just stopped.

She hadn't told anyone this story. Not ever.

"Tess."

She was staring at James, but she hadn't *seen* him. Not until he said her name. She blinked, and her gaze focused on him.

"You don't have to tell me another damn thing. I'm an asshole. This is hurting you. *Please.* Forget I said—"

"He grabbed my arm and shoved a needle in me. I felt the prick, and he was smiling, and then everything went all gray and black. When I opened my eyes again, I was in an alley. The car was on one side of us, a brick wall on the other. He told me that he was going to do anything he wanted to me, just like he'd done before, and when he was done, he'd make sure I went on the best trip of my life." Her voice sounded so flat. "I knew he'd drugged me. That was how he'd gotten me to the alley. I don't think anyone ever saw him put me in the car. Or, if they did, they didn't care."

James growled.

"He was yanking at my shirt and my pants, and I was trying to scream, but it was like I was dreaming. Have you ever tried to scream when you dream? I mean, when you have a nightmare? You can't make your lips and mouth move in reality, and all that comes out is a little gasp, if you can even manage that. And in that alley, all I could do was gasp and choke and hope it was a dream, but then he grabbed another needle, and I knew he was going to pump me full of whatever the hell was in it and I — I grabbed it from him."

"Good."

There had been nothing good in that alley. "I couldn't scream, but I could move my hands plenty, and I grabbed that syringe. I plunged the needle into his neck."

Everything about that day — about that man — was still blurry. *A gray and black fog.* Tess couldn't even clearly remember his face. She just had the vague memory that he'd been good-looking. *A handsome face to hide the devil inside.* "He screamed and stumbled back. I jumped up — or I tried to — but my body slammed into him, and he fell."

Thud.

That sound. That sound haunted her still. "His head hit the back of the bumper. We were that close to the car. His head slammed into the bumper, and there was so much blood, and he didn't move. He just…he was slumped there, and I was swaying, and I knew I had to get help. I didn't know what he'd given me. I didn't know…" *If I'd killed him.* She exhaled. "I made it out of the alley, but I was confused." Freaking understatement. She'd barely been walking. More like crawling. "I went straight into traffic. It was night. There were lights everywhere and one of the cars barreled toward me. I thought I was dying. Actually, I thought I *did* die. Because the bright light was the last thing I remembered."

Breathe. In. Out. It can't hurt you anymore. "Until I opened my eyes in the hospital's ER. A doctor was there, and she was shining a light in my eyes and asking me what I was on."

"What did you take? You have to tell me what you took so I can help you!" That voice thundered through her head even now. So desperate. So determined.

James grabbed the whiskey. Did his hand tremble a little? Surely not. He poured whiskey into the glass. The liquid sloshed over the edge.

"James—"

He downed it. Squared his shoulders. Shoved the whiskey bottle back on the shelf. "You didn't know what you were on. You were a thirteen-year-old kid who'd been attacked." He walked toward her. Slow. Careful. Like he was afraid a sudden movement would spook her.

"I couldn't talk. I started seizing. Later, I was told that I'd been given some dangerous mix of street drugs and that I was lucky to be alive. I'd never felt particularly lucky, but when I looked around and saw the white hospital walls and the clean sheets and the social worker who wanted to help me—I felt lucky then. For the first time in my life, I did."

He was right in front of her again, but he wasn't touching her. She wanted him to touch her. She wanted him to pull her into his arms and tell her that...

Hell, what? That everything was okay?

She wasn't that scared girl. She didn't need fake words or promises.

"I told the social worker that someone had grabbed me from the street. Put the needle in me. And that things had gotten foggy after that." Mostly truth. A truth that hid so much.

"Why didn't you tell her everything?"

"I was afraid I'd killed him. I didn't..." She rubbed her chest. "I was being told I could have a new life. That I was going to be placed with a foster family. I could go to school. I could have a home. I was so afraid that if I told the social worker and the cops about the man, then all of that would go away." A bitter laugh escaped her. "He wasn't a man. He was a boy. Like I said, I thought he was close to my age, but I could have been wrong about that. The truth is, when I try to picture his face, I can't. It's just fog."

"His body wasn't ever found?"

"As far as I know, nothing was ever found. I didn't ask the cops about him back then. I just moved forward." That had been her mantra. "One step at a time. The female doctor from the ER? She came to see me. She helped me. Made sure I got better. And the social worker—when I was with her, she got me tested so that I could be placed in the right grade. She was so excited when she saw some of my scores relating to school and IQ. She couldn't believe that I hadn't been inside a school classroom for over a year." Shame burned through her. "I was being given a second chance, and I was determined to take it. My social worker kept telling me that I was special. I didn't feel special. I've never felt special. Special people don't wind up on the street. They don't wind up pinned in an alley. They don't—"

"I want to put my arms around you," he paused. "I need to touch you." A tense pause. "May I?"

She threw her arms around him. Held on tight. Tears leaked from her eyes because this story was gutting her. She'd shoved the past as far back in her mind as she could possibly shove it. She'd wanted to forget. She'd wanted that thirteen-year-old girl to be someone else.

Tess had worked hard to *become* someone else. She'd never told her friends about her past. Not Latonya. Not Marilyn.

She'd never told lovers.

She'd told him.

Because…

"Are you happy?" Tess whispered. "Because now you have my secrets."

He stiffened against her. Then he bent and his mouth feathered over her cheek. It took her a stunned moment to realize that he was kissing away her tears.

That just made her cry more.

James lifted her into his arms. Held her easily. Cradled her against his chest. "No, baby, I'm not happy. I hate myself. I hate that you hurt yourself because you thought you had to do that for me."

She hadn't—

"When you went back to that dark place, it hurt. I can damn well see it." He carried her out of the kitchen. Down the hallway. To the guest room. He put her down on the bed.

No, no, he wasn't just going to leave her, was he?

But James climbed into the bed with her. He pulled her into his arms and held her there. "You don't have to ever go back to the past again, understand? Not for me. Not for the selfish sonofabitch that I am. You don't have to hurt because of me."

"I wanted you to know that I'm not better than anyone." Her voice was thick. Choked with tears. "I had nothing. I lived on the scraps of life. I may have killed a man. Then I lied and I—"

"You survived. You pulled yourself up from a nightmare. You're a doctor. You save lives. You help people every single day. Hell, that's why you go to the food pantry once a week, isn't it? Paying it forward because you visited pantries when you were a kid, didn't you?"

"I had nothing. Other people helped me. I want to do the same."

He pulled her even closer against him. "That why you became a doctor? To help?"

"That ER doctor shined a light in my eyes. She didn't care that I was homeless, she thought I was an addict, and she was still fighting like hell to keep me alive. That's what doctors are supposed to do. They're supposed to help, and I wanted to become someone who would help."

"You are someone like that, baby." He pressed a kiss to her temple. "Now, I'm going to need you to stop crying before you break my heart."

"I didn't think you had a heart. I thought you said—"

"I say a lot of stupid shit. A whole lot. Asking you to tell me your secrets, not realizing how much they hurt you? That's probably going on my top five of all-time stupid comments. You don't ever have to tell me another thing, got it?"

She wasn't crying any longer. The tears had dried up. He was holding her close, and her hand was over his heart. It beat so fast beneath her touch. "I wanted you to like me." Soft. A little slurred because suddenly, she was feeling exhausted. What time was it? She had no clue.

"I do like you."

"Didn't want you to pity who I'd been. Wanted you to like me. Didn't think you needed to know…that girl is gone. I think she died in that alley."

"That girl is freaking still alive, and she's beautiful and strong. And I like her. I like *you*. That's why I pushed. Why I'm an idiot. Because I like you too much." He was stroking her hair. "Now go to sleep. Rest. Tomorrow, we will deal with everything else."

"You...aren't going to judge me." It was hard to stay awake. His touch was soothing, and Tess felt hollowed out.

"How the hell could I judge you for anything? I spent my life following orders. Hunting for Uncle Sam. You spent your life trying to help others even though you didn't have to do it. Like I said before, you're too good for me."

No, no she wasn't. She wasn't—

"But I don't think I can give you up. That's gonna be a problem, isn't it?" His voice turned almost tender. "We'll have to see what we can work out."

"No." Unease pushed through her.

"Tess?"

"I don't want to give you up." The words pulled from her. They were the truth. The whole reason she'd bared her soul and opened up the pain of her past was because he wanted her secrets. "I accepted your new deal." She licked her lips. "Playtime is over." Wasn't that what he'd told her?

His hand slid under her chin. He tipped her head back on the pillow so that she had to look at him. "Know one thing with total certainty."

She waited. A faint glow spilled from the open doorway, letting her see the intensity etched into his handsome face.

"I'm not playing with you. I never was."

Good. "I'm not playing with you, either," she whispered back.

Where did that leave them? Tess wasn't sure. She thought he might kiss her. All right. She *wanted* him to kiss her. Or — or something.

And he did do something. He pulled the covers over her. He held her in his arms.

They didn't speak again.

She fell asleep with him holding her.

***

Her phone vibrated.

Tess was on her way to the cafeteria, but at the vibration, she paused in the hospital corridor and pulled out her phone. The text was from James. Short and to the point.

New security system will be installed by the time you are off your shift.

That was great news. She could go back to her place or —

I'm getting new furniture delivered for you. Sorry the sonofabitch wrecked your place. I'll fix it.

She frowned at the phone. She didn't need him to buy her new furniture. When he offered to buy her stuff, it made her stomach knot. She didn't want to be anyone's charity case. That stirred up too many painful memories. She typed out a quick response to him. *I'll buy new furniture.*

She saw the little dots appear that meant he was about to send a response to her and —

"You okay?"

Her head snapped up.

God Complex was in front of her. Only he didn't look superior. Devin appeared worried. His gaze was on her throat.

"Jeez, Tess. Those look terrible. I can see the bastard's fingerprints on you." He lifted his hand and moved toward her.

She instantly backed up. "I'm fine."

His jaw hardened, and his fingers clenched into a fist. "I'm sorry, all right? I get why you're mad. I was supposed to be the one attending him and you got attacked while I—" He stopped. The words hung between them.

While you—what? Ducked for cover? Because that's what I heard you did.

"Good thing your boyfriend was there to rush in," Devin added grimly. "I thought I heard someone say that he was originally here because he was stabbed?"

"Not a stab wound." She tightened her hold on the phone. "You must have heard wrong." It had been a slice, not a stab.

She took a step forward.

He moved into her path. Why was he always doing that?

"I have somewhere to be, Devin."

"Don't you think he's a little rough?"

"He's not rough at all with me." *Except when I want him to be.*

"He's dangerous. The guy came in with a stab wound—"

"Told you, the wound wasn't from a stabbing." A slice was different from a stab. James had been right on that score.

Devin sighed. "I'm just worried about you."

"You don't need to be."

His lips thinned. "You had a break-in at your place last night."

When it came to gossip, hospitals were the worst.

"You're having one hell of a week, Tess, and if you need some help, I want you to know that I'm here."

Her phone vibrated. She glanced down.

And Tess heard her name being paged at the exact same moment. She rushed forward because it was a code—

She bumped into Devin. He'd moved closer just as she'd tried to hurry past him. The phone slid from her fingers and hit the floor. He bent and scooped it up, frowning at the screen.

"*My guy*?" Devin's voice had turned stilted.

Her cheeks burned. She'd forgotten that was the way she'd listed James in her contacts. Or, rather, the way he'd listed himself. *My guy.*

"Huh. Your guy says he'll be here to pick you up when your shift ends." Devin handed the phone back to her. "Is he taking over your life now? Seems like everywhere you go, he's there."

"No, he's not taking over." She squared her shoulders. "But when I need help, he's the one I turn to. So thanks for the offer, Devin, but I'm very good. Now I have a patient waiting." She shouldered past him.

Her name was paged again. Her steps picked up speed. She was being paged to a location on the other side of the hospital. The location barely gave her pause. It wasn't unusual for her to be called to another unit. While she was supposed to be working in the ER, sometimes, a doctor's special skills were needed with different patients, and she'd done lots of rotations during her training.

She rushed past Latonya, giving a quick wave as her steps picked up even more. Tess shoved through double doors that would take her down a long, winding corridor. This wing was actually under construction, so it would save her a few minutes as she cut through to get to her—

Someone slammed into her. Hit her hard, and Tess didn't even have the chance to scream as she was thrown to the floor. Her head hit the tile.

CHAPTER TEN

James stalked through the ER's doors. He'd texted Tess twice, but she hadn't responded to him, and that shit was making him nervous. He glanced down at his phone. Yes, he got that she could have been called away for a patient, but so much time had passed since he'd first tried to reach her. *Too much time.* With the break-in and that damn near hit by the mystery truck, he was on edge. He'd stay that way, until he could make certain everything was okay. He knew her shift should have ended, and that was another reason why he was so twitchy.

I'm not twitchy. I'm worried.

The ER was filled with people, no big surprise there. Tess had said the place was always packed. He paused a moment inside, glancing around with narrowed eyes. Maybe Tess had needed to extend her shift. She could've gotten so busy that she had to stay late.

But tension was thick in his gut. He needed to see her. Once he made certain she was okay, he'd get the hell out of her way.

He caught sight of a familiar figure. Marilyn bustled down the hallway, wearing blue scrubs. James locked on her and closed in. "Marilyn!"

She turned. Her eyes widened. "Oh, thank God!"

Wait…thank God?

"She's okay." Marilyn grabbed his arm and hauled him closer. "But it scared the hell out of me, you know?"

His heart slammed into his ribs. "What scared the hell out of you?"

"Tess's attack. Damn, that woman has some serious bad luck happening right now. Two attacks so close together and —"

"Stop." She'd been trying to haul him toward a swinging door.

Marilyn frowned at him. "Why? Don't you want to see Tess? She's out of the exam area now and she's okay, a slight concussion, but —"

His entire body iced. "What the fuck are you talking about?"

A throat cleared behind him. "Marilyn, you have patients waiting. I'll explain things to Dr. Barrett's…friend."

He knew that prick voice. Devin Goddard.

Marilyn didn't move. Her eyes narrowed on James. "You didn't get a call about her? But you were supposed to be notified. I thought…" Her voice trailed away as she glanced back at Devin, then over at James.

His teeth clenched. "Something happened to Tess?"

Marilyn gave a quick nod. "She was attacked earlier. Someone knocked her out when she was cutting through the corridor under renovation, but—"

"But, luckily, I found her," Devin cut in. "I chased off the bastard in there, and I carried Tess to safety. She's quite all right now."

He didn't look at the guy, not yet. James pulled in a slow breath. Released it.

"You were supposed to be notified," Marilyn mumbled. "Tess asked for you to be called."

Yet he hadn't been. When Tess needed him, he hadn't been there.

Fucking hell.

"You have patients waiting, Marilyn. Are you going to neglect them all night?"

Marilyn's gaze snapped toward Devin. She gave a little growl then stomped off.

James faced off with Devin. "Where is she?"

"Come this way." Devin headed to the right, not even looking back to see if James was following him. He pushed open a door marked STAFF and his tennis shoes squeaked over the tile as he strode past two nurses and then took a left.

James followed right on his heels. Rage and adrenaline spiked through him. Tess had been attacked. Again? No way, no freaking way, was he going to buy that as coincidence. It just wasn't going to happen.

When he took the left after Devin, James found himself in what looked like some kind of small break room. There was even a narrow bed—more like a cot with some folded covers—on the side of the room. James figured that must be where the staff crashed on long shifts, but there was no sign of Tess.

"We need to talk." Devin crossed his arms over his chest. Tried to look tough.

He failed.

"The only thing you need to do is take me to Tess."

Devin's lips thinned. "She doesn't need someone like you in her life."

"You have no clue who I am." With the danger stalking her, Tess needed someone exactly like him. No, not *like* him. *She needs me.*

"You're a shady club owner who thinks he's a badass. I've seen your type. The big, tough guys who strut around town like they can handle any shit that comes their way."

"You're wasting my time. Where is Tess?" He still had his phone gripped in his hand.

"She's out of your league."

Tell me some shit I don't know.

"So you saved her once. Big deal. Anyone can be a hero once." Devin's chest puffed out. "You weren't here today, and I was. I was the one who ran off the jerk who'd knocked her down. I was the one who picked her up. Who carried her to the exam room. I was the one who checked her for a concussion, and I was the one—"

James stood toe-to-toe with the asshole. "You are the one in my way right now. You don't want to be between me and Tess." *Tess was hurt.* That was all he could think about. She'd been hurt, and he hadn't been notified. He should have been there and—

Suspicion slithered through him. "You attended her after she was hurt."

Devin's chin notched up. "Damn right I did."

"And did you tell the staff not to notify me?"

Devin swallowed. "You're not family. You're just some guy she met at a club. She didn't want you to come and—"

James felt his phone vibrate. A little ping filled the air. He looked down and a surge of relief rolled through him when he saw the text.

I need you.

He needed her, too.

Can you come to the hospital?

He fired out a fast response. *Baby, I am already here. Where are you?*

Devin cleared his throat. "You're not the right person for Tess. You two have nothing in common. There is no possible reason for the two of you to continue—"

His phone pinged and vibrated. "Hold the thought," James told him with a cold smile. *"My best sex ever* is texting me right now."

"Your—what?"

James flipped the phone around so the dick could see. *"Best sex ever."* Had he stuttered? James didn't think so. "She's looking for me. Seems she needs me. So this bullshit talk between us? It's over." He was done wasting time. Tess had texted back and said she was making her way to the ER waiting room. He exited the break area and strode back toward—

Devin grabbed his arm and spun him around. "It's just sex to you. That's all she is." His voice was low and mean. "That will get old. She'll stop getting off on the thrill that comes from screwing someone like you."

Did it look like he had time for this crap? James leaned toward him. "Let's be clear on one very important thing." He smiled. Coldly. Lethally. "I'll make sure she never stops getting off with me."

Devin's face mottled. He opened his mouth to reply.

"James!"

Tess. He forgot the asshole and whirled to see her coming toward him. Her hair was loose, sliding around her shoulders. She was too pale. And the smile she gave him didn't reach her eyes.

She was the most fucking beautiful thing he'd ever seen in his life. James lunged toward her and pulled her into his arms. He lifted her up—

"Easy, dumbass," Devin snarled. "She was attacked. She has a concussion. She lost consciousness for a moment, and the last thing she needs is to be manhandled by—"

"I need him," Tess said flatly. Her arms curled around James. "I told them to call you, but I know you were busy and you couldn't get here—"

He tightened his hold on her. "No one called me." He tucked her against his side. Held her there. Wanted to keep her there forever. His head turned and his gaze pinned Devin with dark promise. "That's a mistake that won't happen again."

"I told you." Devin straightened to his full height. Sniffed. Looked all pompous and spoke with an arrogant edge as he continued, "You aren't family, so I saw no need to notify you since you were not—"

"Tess is mine. I'm hers. You come between us again, and you'll wish you hadn't."

Devin's eyes turned to slits. "I was the one who picked her up off the floor. I was the one who took care of her!"

And that's why you don't have my fist hitting your face right now. Because I know what you are doing, asshole. You want her and you're trying to cut me out of her life. Not happening. I'm not going anywhere.

"Thank you, Devin," Tess said quietly. An edge of exhaustion had turned her voice husky. "I appreciate what you did for me."

Over her head, James mouthed *Fuck off* at Devin.

Devin sniffed. "Anything for you, Tess. We are friends, you know that."

They were? Since when?

"You can always count on me."

The guy was going to be a problem. Good thing James was used to handling problems.

"Can we go home?" Tess asked as she leaned into James. "I really want to go home."

"Absolutely." He picked her up into his arms.

"No, James, I—"

"Baby, I just found out you were attacked." *Again.* "I want details. I want to know how the hell this happened, and I want to carry you. Okay? I need to feel you in my arms." He headed toward the exit, leaving Devin behind.

They passed Marilyn. She smiled.

Tess had her arm behind his head. "I am completely capable of walking."

"Yeah, so are most people who leave the hospital, but I still see you docs always making people exit in wheelchairs. They have to stay in the chairs until they get to their cars—"

"That's a liability issue, just something hospitals require—"

"And carrying you is something *I* require. Because I'm barely holding onto my control. I just found out that you were hurt. I wasn't close. I couldn't help you, and I need to feel you in my arms to make sure that you're okay." Did she get that? Just touching her, holding her, calmed the savagery that was raging inside of him.

The exit doors slid open. His limo waited, with the driver at the ready.

"I need to feel you, too," Tess whispered. "I asked for you as soon as I could, just because I wanted you close."

And Devin hadn't called him.

Sonofabitch. The guy was going to pay for that.

He eased her into the limo. "Take us home," he told Ryley.

"Is she okay?"

Ryley wasn't one for much conversation. The retired marine was usually a wall of silence. The fact that he'd asked about Tess showed that she'd managed to slip under his skin, too.

"I'm fine," Tess called out softly. "Thank you, Ryley."

He nodded.

James held his gaze. "If you notice any cars tailing us, alert me immediately."

"Absolutely."

The door slammed behind him as James slid in next to Tess. The car started a moment later, and they were on their way. He caught her hand in his. Threaded his fingers with hers. "Tell me everything."

"There isn't a whole lot to tell." Her voice sounded so tired. Too weak. Tess wasn't weak. "I was paged, and the patient was on the other side of the hospital. I knew I could cut through the renovation area to get there faster, and when I did, I was hit by someone. I remember the person slamming into me, and then…I think my head hit the floor." Her free hand rose and slid under her hair. She gave a little wince.

He shoved down his fury. The car eased to a stop and sped up a moment later.

"When I opened my eyes—I swear, I don't think I was out long at all, barely seemed a minute—Devin was crouched over me. He said he saw someone running away." She swallowed. "He, um, thought it looked like Frederick Waller."

Bastard. James had warned him to stay away.

"Frederick might have come back to the hospital looking to steal drugs. There is a storage area in that unit, and it's possible I interrupted him. He slammed into me when he was trying to run away. I mean, maybe that's what happened. It's what Devin thought, what he told the detective who came to investigate—"

"If it was Frederick, he's a dead man."

"*Don't.*" Her fingers jerked in his. "You don't get to say things like that, understand? It's not a joke."

"It's definitely not. It's your life. I don't joke about your life."

She shivered. "With your past, you *can't* say things like that. You can't say things that you don't mean."

He brought her hand to his lips. Kissed her knuckles. The moment was tense and heavy, but it was time she realized something very important. "Sweetheart…"

Her head turned toward him. The faint glow of illumination in the back of the car let him see her delicate features.

"Do you think I wouldn't kill for you?"

Her lips parted.

"Do you think I would hesitate? If someone was threatening you, I wouldn't. So I'm not saying anything I don't mean. I'm stating a fact. You are my priority. I will do anything to protect you."

Tess shook her head. "I don't want that. I don't want you killing for me! I didn't ask — "

"Something is off." Every instinct James possessed screamed that truth to him. "The attack on you today. The break-in at your place. All of this stuff happening at once…"

"M-maybe…maybe Frederick did that, too. Maybe he broke in to my home." Once more, the car slowed down. Turned. Tess cleared her throat. "Devin suspected he might have. That he could be locked on me, or something. That Frederick went to my place looking for cash. Or looking for *me*. The detective who came to the hospital thought Devin might be right."

If they were right, and Frederick was targeting her…*dead man*. But James didn't say those words again. Tess wasn't ready for the darkness that he carried. Maybe she never would be.

But he wasn't kidding. If someone threatened her, he'd do anything necessary to keep her safe.

"The detective—his name was Wesley Cade—he's going to call me after he talks to Frederick."

Once more, James kissed her knuckles. "I'm sorry I wasn't there."

"You can't be with me twenty-four hours a day." Her brow furrowed. "Devin handled it for me. He said he took care of the patient and that everything was fine. I guess I'll owe him for that, too."

"You don't owe him a damn thing." Wasn't it so very convenient, all of these things that Devin was suddenly doing?

Or maybe I'm just a jealous bastard who needs to calm the hell down. He sucked in a breath. Smelled her sweet vanilla cream. Tess had told him that she used that lotion because her hands got dry. Since she washed her hands so often at the hospital, she always kept her lotion close. Anytime he smelled vanilla now, he thought of Tess.

I need to make things better for Tess. And he needed to smother his jealousy. "Tell me how to help you." He wanted to help. "You have a concussion. What all do I need to do? What can I do?"

"I'm okay. No vomiting. No blurred vision. And I'm carrying on a normal conversation." For the first time, humor slid into her voice. "So I'll count all of those as wins."

He wanted to hold her tight. To never let her go.

They drove in silence for a while, then Tess said, "You didn't make love to me last night."

Make love.

"Is it because of the way things ended? Our new, um, rules? I'm ready for the new agreement. I shared my past with you. I shared everything I had and—"

He kissed her. James leaned forward and pressed his lips to hers. The kiss was slow and easy because that was what she needed. Tenderness. He savored her lips. Caressed her. Wanted to give her everything. When his head lifted, he rasped, "Let's be clear about something. I always want you. Every minute. I look at you, and I need."

Her breath caught.

"I want to be *what* you need, too. And last night, I thought you might want a gentleman. I can do that shit, too, you know. I'm not just a killer. Not just some criminal from the street."

"I never thought you were."

She hadn't. Plenty of others had.

He stared into her eyes. "I know my past scares you." It would give anyone nightmares.

"You don't scare me."

Baby, maybe I should. If she knew what all he'd do to protect her…

No, now wasn't the time for that. In another life, he'd gone after the worst of the worst. He'd attacked. He'd hunted. He'd lost every bit of his soul.

But he could swear that Tess was starting to give it back to him.

Or, hell, maybe she is my soul. Because she made him want to do more. To be better.

To not be the bastard in the dark that the whole world feared.

Her phone gave a quick peal of sound.

"I tried to reach you earlier," James heard himself say.

"I…think Devin had my phone. One of the nurses brought it to me, and I saw that I'd missed your texts."

His eyes narrowed.

Her phone rang again.

He eased back. Tess lifted her phone. "It's the detective." She swiped her finger over the screen, turning on the speaker. "Detective Cade?"

"Dr. Barrett, where are you right now?"

"I'm on my way home."

"I'm going to need you to come to the station."

James didn't like the guy's tone.

"Why?" Tess asked. "Did you find Frederick?"

"Are you alone, doctor?"

"No, I'm not."

A pause. "Who is with you?" There was a murmur of voices in the background. "By any chance, is it James Smith?"

"Yes," James answered bluntly. "It is."

A swift inhale. "Dr. Barrett, I need you at the station, now. Can you come to me or do I need to come to you?"

"I don't understand," Tess said. "What's happening?"

"Come to the station—you and Mr. Smith—and I will tell you everything."

***

It wasn't his first time in a police station. Not even close. All the stations generally seemed to look the same, though. Not as clean and tidy as you saw on the cop shows that lit TV screens. More cramped. Filled with tired cops and detectives. And always noisy. Phones ringing. Voices rising.

James and Tess had been met by the detective as soon as they'd arrived. The detective—and a few uniformed cops—had been waiting on the steps. Hardly a good sign.

Another not-so-good sign? Detective Wesley Cade, a guy in his mid-fifties with a military haircut and a faded, brown suit, kept eyeing James with suspicion.

They were currently in a small interrogation room. Just like thousands of other interrogation rooms in the world. A one-way mirror was to the right. A wobbly table was in the middle of the space, and some crappy coffee had been poured into two mugs for James and Tess.

Tess didn't drink the coffee. Neither did James.

And the detective *still* hadn't told them why they were there.

James tapped his fingers against the table top. He'd pulled his chair close to Tess. The closer he was to her, the better he felt. The detective had lifted his brows at the movement but hadn't commented.

The game of silence was getting way old.

James sighed. He wasn't in the mood for this crap. "You gonna tell us why you demanded we appear here? Or do we sit in silence all night?" He inclined his head toward Tess. "She needs rest, not this BS, so I think—"

"I wanted her here so that I could be certain she was safe," Detective Cade cut in. "How are you, doctor? Is there anything that you need?"

"I'm fine," Tess responded. Her pale lips trembled. "Please, just tell me what's happening. Did you find Frederick Waller?"

He nodded. "We did."

"And was he the one at the hospital? Dr. Goddard thought it was him but—"

"There is no way that Frederick Waller attacked you at the hospital tonight." He held a manila file in his hand. One he'd just been holding like it was something precious.

"Oh." Tess sagged against her chair. "He has an alibi then?"

"You could say that." Detective Cade put the manila file in the middle of the table. "He's dead."

"What?" Tess leaned forward.

The detective flipped open the file. "He was killed last night. Didn't even realize he was in the morgue, not until I went looking for the bastard."

James glanced at the photo. Hell.

"As you can see, his throat was cut. From ear to ear. A brutal attack. He bled out in the alley."

James grabbed the file and slammed it closed. "She didn't need to see that."

The detective blinked. "She's a doctor. I assume she is used to seeing all manner of gore."

"I am," Tess agreed softly.

"Screw that. She doesn't have to see a murder." That was exactly what they'd seen. And what *he'd* seen...dammit, Frederick had been in the same alley—the same place where James had confronted the man. He'd recognized the dumpster behind Frederick's sprawled form. The dumpster had been tagged with bright red spray paint that was very distinct.

"Could've been a drug deal gone wrong," the detective murmured. "That's certainly the theory from narcotics. But, in light of everything that seems to be happening with you right now, Dr. Barrett, I find the timing suspicious."

It was suspicious as hell.

James rose. "I'm taking her home."

Detective Cade's gaze swung to him. "Who are you?"

What? "You know my name already. James Smith. You know—"

"I know that Dr. Goddard told me you were dangerous. He told me that you attacked Frederick Waller and that you had to be pulled off the man in the hospital."

"Yeah, I did." James gave him a cold smile. "So you'll probably find my DNA on the guy's body." *Thanks for giving me that out, detective.* "I fought him at the hospital when he tried to choke Tess. Those are his fingerprints on her throat."

"And it pissed you off when he hurt her."

Seriously? "Pissed doesn't begin to describe how I felt."

Tess's chair scraped over the floor as she stood. "James—"

The detective didn't look away from James. "You attacked him, you had to be pulled off him, and Dr. Goddard said you were furious."

James knew where this was going.

"Now the man who hurt Dr. Barrett is dead." Detective Cade rose to his feet. Nodded. "You understand, of course, why I insisted that you come to the station. I wanted to speak with you both."

James understood, all right. The detective had wanted to see how James reacted to learning Frederick was dead. He'd wanted—

"Enough." Tess slammed her hands down on the table.

The detective's eyes widened.

"Don't attack James." She huffed out a breath. "He saved me when Frederick was choking me in the hospital. Don't throw around accusations at him because he didn't do anything wrong. He's been protecting me, nothing else." A crisp nod. "Let's get out of here, James. I want to go home."

He took her hand in his. Hated that her fingers shook. "Okay, sweetheart." They headed for the door. Were almost at it when—

"One more thing," Detective Cade called out. "By any chance, have you recently been to Frederick Waller's apartment, Mr. Smith?"

Fucking hell.

James glanced over his shoulder.

"Because a witness reported seeing a man who matches your description in the area. So I couldn't help but wonder…seeing as how you were so pissed—I mean, furious—at Frederick. Perhaps you went to pay him a little visit?"

Had he been seen? James didn't let his expression alter. In the past, no one had ever caught sight of him on a job, not unless he'd wanted to be seen. He'd been cold, calculating, and completely controlled. In the past—

Tess wasn't in my past. She was in his present, and everything was different because of her.

Cold, calculating, and controlled—no, he didn't feel any of those things. He was burning hot. Rage pulsed through him, and as far as his control was concerned, it had splintered the minute Frederick put his hands on Tess.

"Mr. Smith?" Detective Cade took a step toward him. Frowned a little. "That name of yours, if I didn't know better, I'd swear it was a bad alias. Might as well call yourself John Doe. Pretty much the same as James Smith, isn't it?"

James sent him a tight smile. "If you have additional questions for me, those questions should go through my attorney."

"There will be more. Count on it."

James turned his head. Found Tess staring at him. Her eyes were so deep and dark. He *hated* the shadows that slipped under them. As she stared at him, he saw the flicker of uncertainty in her gaze.

She was worried that he'd gone to pay a visit to Frederick.

She was worried…that he'd killed the man?

He tightened his hold on her. Got her out of there. They didn't speak as they exited the station. His driver scrambled to open the limo's back door. Tess slid inside.

James hesitated by the open door. He glanced to the left. To the right.

He'd been off his game before. He'd thought he was dealing with some amateur, but that wasn't the case. Frederick Waller was dead, and someone had pointed the cops at James. A witness? Really?

Had he lost his edge that much?

James saw the dark SUV down the road. Waiting.

James gave an almost imperceptible nod toward the vehicle. He knew the Wilde agents were inside. Dodging his steps. He should have been angry at them. Hadn't he told the crew to back the hell off?

But maybe he needed them. So he gave them the nod and knew they'd get his message. They'd come in for a chat.

The team could help him on this one. Maybe it was time to stop being a lone wolf. Maybe.

He climbed into the limo.

The door slammed behind him.

Tess still didn't speak. Not until Ryley had the limo on the road. Not until they were away from the police station. Then, voice trembling, she asked him, "Did you kill Frederick Waller?"

CHAPTER ELEVEN

She'd insisted on going back to her home. Chill bumps covered Tess's skin, and she couldn't seem to shake the cold that clung to her. In her mind, she kept seeing the dead man. His throat had been sliced open from ear to ear.

James had just sat there, no expression on his face while the cop accused him of —

An alarm was beeping.

Tess stopped, blinked. They'd just entered her place, and the new alarm system was beeping. James headed straight to the control panel and reset it. He told her the code, and she blinked again, feeling dazed.

Then she glanced around *her* place. When she'd last been there, her home had been utter destruction. But now…

Everything was back in place.

The furniture — it was perfect. It was *her* furniture. The same white, oversize couch. The same brand and size TV. Her broken photo frames had been replaced with new ones — ones that looked exactly as they had before.

Everything was in the position she'd placed it in before the intruder destroyed her house.

James had repaired everything for her. Her hand pressed to her chest. "Thank you for doing this, but I told you, I was going to pay for the furniture myself." Her voice sounded hollow to her own ears. "Give me the bill." She tore her gaze from the couch. *Her couch?* Tess locked her stare on him. "For the furniture and the security and —"

"No."

Her brows shot up. "I pay my own way. Always. I'm not the girl who had nothing any longer. I can pay for anything I need."

"I know you can. I know you can do any damn thing in this world." He ran a hand through his hair. "I wasn't saying no on the repayment. Though I really don't want it. I want you to think of this furniture as a gift. I *wanted* to do something good for you. You deserve something good." He lowered his hand. "When I said no, I was answering your question from the car."

Her chin jerked up. The car.

When they'd left the station and her gut had been twisting in knots, she'd asked him one thing. *Did you kill Frederick Waller?*

He hadn't answered her. He'd just sat in silence.

She'd lowered the privacy screen and asked the driver to take her home. Her address. Her place.

When they'd arrived, James had followed her up. He'd shadowed her steps, and she'd seen him searching the area for any would-be threats. Now he was inside with her and saying that he hadn't killed Frederick.

Relief surged through her. Right, right, of course, he hadn't killed Frederick. "He was wrong." Her breath shuddered out. She smiled. "The detective was wrong. The witness was wrong. You were not anywhere near—"

"I went to his apartment."

Her arms moved to wrap around her stomach.

"I went *inside* his apartment."

"He let you in?" she croaked.

"No, sweetheart. I let myself in."

He'd just confessed to breaking and entering. She hugged herself even tighter.

"He wasn't there. But I did a quick survey of the area. Waited because I wanted to talk to the bastard."

"Why?"

His head cocked to the left. "Because the sonofabitch put his hands on your throat and tried to kill you. Because I wanted to be very, very clear with him. If he ever went near you again, he was a dead man."

He is a dead man.

"I found him in an alley."

Oh, God. In the picture that Detective Cade had shown her, hadn't Frederick been in an alley?

"He was trying to make another drug deal. The dealer ran off, though, didn't give Frederick anything, and when he was alone, that's when I had my little chat with the bastard."

She couldn't move. Her legs had turned to stone. "You didn't kill him."

"No, baby, I didn't." His eyes didn't leave her face. "I made my intentions clear. When I left that alley, Frederick was still breathing."

"You threatened him."

"Yes. I wanted him to get my message and to keep his ass away from you."

He'd definitely be away from her now.

"You think I don't see it?" His voice was low. Rough.

"See what?"

"You're terrified of me right now. You look at me, and you see a monster."

"I don't know what I see." That was a lie. She saw him. *James.* But… "Is that an alias?"

He blinked.

"Your name. Is it really James Smith?"

"My first name is James, yes. When I was growing up, most people called me Jimmy or Jamie. So I've gone by lots of different versions of that name."

He hadn't said if Smith was really his last name. "There is so much I don't know about you."

He nodded. "And a whole lot that you do." James glanced at his watch. "They'll be here soon, so we don't have long left to talk without them hearing us."

Her heart jerked. "Who will be here?"

"The security team who will be watching you while I hunt the perp out there."

She shook her head. "What? I don't have a security team."

"You do now. A man is dead. Some asshole is trying to pin his murder on me. This mess has gone lethal, and I can't risk your safety."

He couldn't risk it? Heat finally began to build inside of her, pushing past the ice that had numbed her ever since she'd seen the photo inside the manila file at the police station.

"I thought this was about you, Tess. That someone from your past had caught up with you. That maybe that bastard who'd drugged you so long ago had resurfaced and was coming for his pound of flesh. I've had Barnes looking for him, just as a precaution, digging into the case ever since—" He stopped.

But it was too late. Far too late. She stopped hugging herself. Her hands fell to her sides and fisted. Tess stalked forward. "You knew my secrets." It was there. She could see it in his eyes. "Even before I told you about my past, you knew."

"The security team will be here soon. We need to go over—"

"Screw them," she said flatly. Everything was out of control and crazy. "You knew, didn't you?

Even before I told you one word about my life on the streets, you knew." Why did that hurt? Why did that make the fire inside of her burn even hotter?

She waited for a denial. There was a big, big part of her hoping for—

"I knew."

Her lips parted.

"I knew right after we met. I had my assistant dig up your past even before you came back to find me at the club. But I didn't know that someone had drugged you. I didn't know that you'd been attacked, not until you told me about that mystery bastard. That's when I directed my attention to—"

No. No. "*Why?*"

His brows flew down. "Why did I want to find him? Because I don't want him to ever—"

"Why did you dig into my past when we were just strangers?" He'd better answer her. She wanted the truth, and she wasn't budging until she got it.

He swallowed. "Because I have a line of enemies that stretch from here to the end of the world. Because I can't trust anyone. Because I looked at you, and I forgot to breathe. Because the way I wanted you so suddenly and completely was dangerous, and before I got lost in you, I needed to know you were safe."

"You thought I was some kind of threat to you?"

His hand lifted. He cupped her cheek. "I took one look at you, and I couldn't see anyone else. If you were the enemy, if you were bait, then I was screwed."

She backed away from his touch. "You lied to me."

"No, I told you from the beginning exactly what I—"

"Stop! You know what I'm talking about. You let me believe that you didn't know about my life. About my past." The fire inside grew hotter with every word. "If you knew, then why didn't you tell me? Why didn't you say something? You let me pour my heart out to you when all along, you had already dug into every little dirty secret I had."

"Because if you told me on your own, it meant you trusted me!"

Maybe…maybe she *had* trusted him. "I was wrong."

His jaw hardened.

"I was insane." Pain—that was all she felt in that instance. "You broke into Frederick's apartment. You threatened him. Who are you? I don't even know your real name!"

"I told you, James is my real—"

"You knew everything about me! I knew *nothing* about you!"

"You know more than most of the world."

"It's not enough. You know every secret I have. If you want me to stay with you, if you want us, then you tell me everything." She was done with pain. Done with secrets. They were going to be together? Then they'd be equals.

A sharp rap sounded at the door.

She jumped.

He didn't move.

"Who the hell is that?" Tess muttered.

"Your security team."

"I didn't ask for a security—"

"I was an assassin for the government. I killed and I lied, and was very, very good at both jobs."

She sucked in a sharp breath. He was giving her...everything?

"I made enemies, and I burned bridges, and I didn't look back. There was no reason to look back. You want to know about my past? Fine. That's only fair. When the Wilde agents are gone, you can ask me as many questions as you want, and I will tell you everything. Because I choose you, Tess. I want to be with you, and I'll agree to any terms that you set."

Her heart raced faster and faster.

"Let's start with one of the worst times in my life. I can give you that before Wilde pushes in here. When I was a teen, I thought I was in love. Beautiful girl. Beautiful dreams. Only her dad was one of the bad guys. One of the most evil assholes in the world. I thought I could get her away from him. I thought we could be safe. Stupid fucking kid, that's what I was."

The rapping came again.

"Her dad found out about us. He and his men beat the shit out of me. He was going to kill me, but she risked her life to save me. The bastard threw me to the wolves after that. He put a price on my head—hell, I guess he thought if he didn't actually pull the trigger, his daughter would never know that he was responsible for my death. So he got every criminal in the area to hunt me down. A teen who was lost and scared as fuck. They kept coming after me. And you know what? I learned to survive. I learned to kill before I was killed. My skills caught the attention of good old Uncle Sam. I was taking out his trash, you see. So the government decided to use me."

Tess stared into his eyes. Saw the pain swirling there. Talking about his past hurt him just as much as talking about her past had hurt her. But he was doing it, for her. Just as she'd shared, for him.

"I was no one. US agents took me in, trained me, gave me a new life—dozens of new lives—and I did my job. I had nothing else. I didn't want anything else. There were no dreams for me. No freaking happy ending fantasies. I didn't care about that shit. I didn't care about anything. Not really. Not until I turned around in my club, and I saw you staring at me."

He could *not* be saying—

The rapping came again.

He sucked in a breath. "Everything changed. *You* changed it." Then he spun around. He tapped something new in the alarm code, checked through her peephole, and swung open the door.

Two men and a woman were in the doorway. She recognized them instantly. There was Cole, Blair, and —

"I need another freaking minute!" James blasted. He slammed the door shut and whirled back toward her.

Her mouth was still hanging open.

"Where the hell was I?" He scraped a hand over the thick stubble that lined his hard jaw.

"Everything changed," Tess prompted.

"Right." His hand returned to his side. Fisted. "Standard operating procedure for me before I get involved with any lover is to do a background check. You're at your most vulnerable when you're fucking."

Her throat was bone dry. "That's nice to know."

His eyes narrowed. "See. It's that kind of shit that screwed with me."

"I have zero clue what you're talking about."

"*You.* I can't predict you. Not what you'll say or what you'll do. You surprise me, and it makes me smile, even when I'm mad as hell like I am right now. Everything you do — even when you are driving me crazy — just seems damn adorable. No, more than that. Sexy. Feisty. Fierce. Hell, I don't think I can ever describe it all." James shook his head. "That's the shit that sealed my fate.

That's the shit that made me obsessed with you."
He reached for her hand. Lifted it up. "And that
wrapped me around your little finger."

"You don't look wrapped around it to me."
Her voice was so low.

"Baby, I am ready to kill for you. Fight for
you. Die for you. Trust me, I'm yours."

Her heart was racing out of control. The
thunder of the beat seemed to shake her whole
body.

He squeezed her fingers, then let her go. "But
I get it."

Her fingers felt warm now.

"You're scared of me. Of what I've done.
What I'm capable of doing. And you're right to
be. Because if you're threatened, I stop
pretending I'm nice. I let the darkness out."

She could see the hardness in his eyes.

"You don't want the real me." Now he was
halting. Wooden. "You wanted the excitement.
The rush. But when you see the monster in front
of you, you don't want that guy."

She shook her head.

"So I'm going."

Had he just said *going?*

"I'll make sure you get protection. Wilde
agents will stay with you until I track down the
bastard who is doing this. Because — hell, I can't
be sure this is even about you. Maybe someone
from my past is trying to hurt me by coming after
you, and I can't let that happen. I won't." He

squared his shoulders. Turned once more. Opened the door.

The three agents on the threshold made no move to enter Tess's place.

After a tense moment, Linc cleared his throat. "Is this a trick? If I step forward, are you going to slam the door on me?"

"Get your ass inside," James ordered as he stepped back.

They got their asses inside. The door was locked. The place secured once more. No one sat. Everyone just stood, all uncomfortable-like.

Linc glanced at Blair. She raised her brows. Once more, he cleared his throat. "Place looks great. Can't even tell that it was ravaged to hell and back twenty-four hours ago."

"*Linc.*" Blair winced. "We have talked about tact. Over and over again."

"Why be tactful? She knows her place was trashed." He pointed at James. "Ghost worked a serious miracle getting it fixed for her. I'm impressed."

"*Ghost?* Is that like your code name or something?"

His lips pressed together, but he nodded.

She turned to a silent Cole. "Why is that his code name?"

"Because he could get in and out of any location without alerting anyone. Without leaving a trace of evidence behind. Because he could get right next to his victims…" Cole moved to stand beside Tess. "And they would never know. By the time they realized what was happening…" His words trailed away.

James lifted his chin. "They were the ghosts by that time."

Silence.

Linc tossed his body onto the couch. "Nice. Soft." He settled in comfortably. "I need a badass code name. Something that tells people who I am. What I can do. Something like—"

"Asshole?" Blair offered with an innocent smile. "Wanna-be?"

"Stud." He pointed toward her. "Superman."

Blair rolled her eyes.

Why were these people in her home? "No."

Everyone stared at her. Actually, she thought that James had been staring at her the entire time.

Cole coughed. "Want to go over your new security system? I was here with James and Linc during the installation and—"

She waved that away, for the moment. Her gaze raked over James. "You think you're leaving me with these people?"

"Is that why you signaled us to follow you when you left the police station, Ghost?" Linc asked. "You wanted some protection help? Got it."

They'd been at the police station? Her brow scrunched. "You all know that Frederick is dead?"

"We figured it out," Blair told her carefully. "Once you two were in the station, we did some digging. Wilde has access to a lot of very useful technology."

Her head was pounding. "How long have you been following me?"

"Technically, we were following him." Blair pointed to James. "He tore out of your place like a bat out of hell, and we knew there was trouble."

Cole nodded. "Wilde sticks together when there is trouble." His gaze lingered on her. "You okay? You look really pale."

James took a quick step forward. His hands rose, as if he'd reach out to her, but he caught himself and froze. "No. She's not okay. She was attacked at the hospital. That's why I want bodyguards for her. Until I can stop the bastard, Tess has to be safe."

Okay, now it was her cue once more. "*No.*"

When she said that, why did everyone look at her like she was the crazy one?

"You don't understand," James growled. "If this is someone from my past, if you're being targeted because of me —"

"I understand perfectly. Thanks. You're not dumping me on them."

"Tess —"

"This is my life, and I choose what happens. Right now, I say you don't get to just drop your little bombshells and walk away while you leave a fire in your wake."

His eyes widened.

"Oh, God," Linc muttered. "What I would not give for some popcorn right now. This is some serious drama."

Tess swung her gaze toward him.

Blair sat on the couch next to Linc. Elbowed him hard.

"We need to talk," Tess huffed as she focused on James once more. "Without an audience."

"I thought you'd want me gone." He seemed…lost. "I told you what you wanted to hear, but I thought, after you learned that, you'd tell me to go."

"I haven't told you to go anywhere."

Did hope light his eyes?

She stormed right on because Tess was pissed. "You don't know what I think. You want to know what's going on in my head? Try asking me."

"This feels really personal." Cole coughed. "Should we go back outside?"

James eliminated the space between him and Tess. Stopped right in front of her and she tipped back her head to stare up at him.

"You're scared of me," he accused.

"Uh, yeah," Linc called. "Because she's smart. I'm scared of you, bro, and I barely know you. Are you scared of him, Blair?"

"Not at the moment."

"Yeah." Linc seemed to consider that. "He does look a bit whipped."

Screw them. She wasn't in the mood for an audience. She was only in the mood for James.

Tess grabbed James's hand and hauled him toward her bedroom. As soon as he was inside, she slammed the door shut behind him.

"Tess, listen, I just want—"

She grabbed his shirt-front and hauled him down toward her. Her lips crashed into his. The kiss was wild, rough, and it made her knees quake. His arms rose and curled around her shoulders as he pulled her closer.

Tess tore her mouth from his just long enough to pant, "Why don't you let me tell you what I want?"

***

"Well, this is awkward." Linc stretched his left arm out along the back of the couch, effectively moving it behind Blair's head.

She shot him a glare and jumped off the couch.

Cole could only shake his head. "It's not awkward. It's dangerous as hell." He glanced toward the closed bedroom door. "Her attacker from the hospital is dead. One of the most infamous assassins in the country was just in the local police station being questioned by a detective."

Blair tapped her lower lip. "You think his cover might be blown? You really think this attack is about him and not her?"

"I think James suspects it could be or he would never have let us walk inside tonight. He wants our help because he's worried things are going bad, fast."

"Uh, yeah." Linc was still reclining comfortably on the couch. "A man is dead. I'd say we're already in the 'bad, fast' category."

Yes, they were. Cole pulled out his phone. "I'm calling Eric." He needed to check in with the big boss. "You two stay here and wait for James. We can't make a plan of attack until we know what—who—we're up against." He was hoping that the Wilde tech team could ferret out useful information for them.

A few moments later, he exited Tess's place. The door clicked closed behind Cole even as Eric came on the line. "Have you gotten anything on Tess Barrett that I can use?" Cole asked.

"Yes, but it's not pretty."

In his world, nothing ever was.

***

"I'm going to need you to do me a big favor." Blair put her hands on her hips and looked down at Linc. "So take a deep breath and just do it, okay?"

His brow furrowed, and, for a moment, he actually appeared worried. "You know I'd do anything for you." His voice had even gone serious. "You're my partner. There is no one closer to me in this world than—"

"Stop being an asshole."

His lips twisted. "Well, sorry. Some talents just come naturally to me."

"No, I mean it, stop. This case is making me nervous. Heck, there wasn't even supposed to be a case. We were here on a recruitment assignment. Eric sent us down here to offer James a job and—" She stopped.

Stared at Linc.

His eyebrows lowered. Lifted. Lowered again. "B?"

"Why did he send all three of us down here to offer James a job? That's hardly a three-person deal."

Linc shrugged. "I figured Eric was still pissed at me because I, um, went off book on the last case and got a little personally involved."

A little? Blair locked her back teeth. Linc had gone straight-up crazy, and, worse, he'd lied to her. Linc had been after his sister's killer—a sister he hadn't even told Blair about—and he'd broken every rule in the book to get his justice.

Blair's trust in him had been shaken. Linc seemed to think that they were back to normal. That everything was fine and dandy again.

He was wrong. As he was so often wrong about her.

"Look, B, the way I see it, Eric was angry with me, and he was benching me by giving me some grunt work." He waved toward her. "Thought maybe you'd done something to make the boss mad, too."

"Eric isn't mad at me," she snapped. "Hell, quite the opposite. He offered me a promotion and a new partner."

Linc straightened, suddenly — finally — at full attention. "You're leaving me?"

Was it her imagination or did the mask that he wore — every single day — finally crack? He acted like the world was a joke, but she knew the truth — it was an act. Linc felt far more deeply than he wanted anyone to realize.

She turned away from him and marched for the door. Suspicions were burning in her head, and she did not like walking in the dark.

She reached for the doorknob.

Linc's hand closed over her shoulder and he gently tugged her around to face him, trapping her between his body and the door. "You're ditching me?"

"Linc, we can talk about this later."

He shook his head. The mask was completely gone. His eyes blazed at her. His jaw was rock hard, and his face was twisted with worry. "I'm sorry I hurt you."

Linc? He'd just said he was sorry?

"You are the one person in the world I would never, ever want to hurt."

"Then maybe you shouldn't have lied to me." The words spilled out because the pain was still there, even when she tried to deny it.

His chin notched up. "I didn't want to bring you into my hell. I knew I was breaking rules. If I was going down in flames, the last thing I wanted was for you to burn with me."

"So you were protecting me." She'd heard this story before. "News flash, I don't need anyone to keep me safe. I can do that just fine by myself." She turned her head. Stared at the hand that gripped her shoulder. "Remove it."

His hand fell away.

She could suck in a breath again. Wonderful. What Linc didn't know—what she'd never told him and never would—was that his touch made her feel...weird. Not bad. Just too aware. Too warm. Too many things.

"I didn't want that part of my life touching you, B. I didn't want the bastard who'd hurt my sister getting close to you. I didn't want you in his sights."

"Well, he's dead now, so I don't think we have to worry about that. You got your justice."

If anything, his eyes blazed brighter. "I got that, but I'm going to lose you? Is that how it works? You're the price I have to pay?" Each word sounded ragged.

"I can't talk about this now. There is something I have to check on with Eric." Once more, she spun away from him.

"Blair—"

She wrenched open the door. The security had been disengaged when Cole stepped out a moment before.

Cole spun toward her. His brows lifted in surprise as he gripped the phone in his hand.

"That Eric on the line?" Blair demanded.

He nodded.

"I'm gonna need to take that call." She plucked the phone from his grasp. "Thanks." A calming breath then, "Eric."

"Hello, Blair." His voice drifted to her. All casual and easy, as if he didn't have a care in the world. Bullshit. He had about a million cares.

"Why am I in Savannah right now?" Blair asked him.

"Because you're recruiting a new agent?"

"Try again, and this time, leave the bullshit at the door. If I can't trust my boss, then I'm leaving Wilde."

"Dammit. Blair, look, I don't have any proof yet, I just have my gut and I—"

"He's compromised, isn't he?" It was the only thing that made sense. "You found some intel that indicated Ghost's true identity had been discovered, and you wanted us here to protect his ass."

Eric's sigh drifted over the phone even as she heard Cole swear behind her.

She felt like swearing, too, as Eric finally replied, "Possibly."

"Possibly? Come on, you've got three of your best agents here. You must think this is worse than just *possibly*."

"Yes. Dammit. The fact that you've got a dead body in the morgue makes me think this scene is going exactly as I feared."

"Then cut the sugar coating and tell me what we're up against."

"That's the problem. I don't know. I heard whispers of intel. Got an informant who swears that one of Ghost's old handlers was selling out his agents. Only when I tracked that trail, I found out that the handler was dead. So, no, he's not selling anyone out now. But maybe he leaked information before his heart attack hit. Or, hell, maybe it wasn't a heart attack. His body is in the ground, though, his widow buried him, and I can't exactly exhume the body to the find out what happened. I can just try to cover my new agent, and the best way to do that was to send you three over there. To bring James back to Wilde and to move the hell on." He wasn't sounding so calm and easy now. "Didn't know James would get obsessed with some doctor up there. Didn't know she'd suddenly be in danger. But now—more than ever—I need to make sure you and the others are there with him. Contain the situation.

Provide James with whatever backup he needs. Keep him alive."

"I thought you didn't even like the guy," she groused.

"I don't. Fine, I do. He's proven himself useful on more cases than you know. He's got connections and talents that Wilde can use, but he's also—beneath the cold bastard exterior—a damn fine man. He got a shit hand in life, and he deserves more. *That's* why you're there. I could be wrong. My informant could be wrong. But I don't take chances. When danger comes, Wilde agents stick together. Whether he accepted the job offer officially or not, we stick together."

Yes, they did stick together. Wasn't that why she was still with Linc, even after he'd kept his secrets from her?

"James has got enemies for days," Eric continued gruffly. "What he doesn't have—what he needs—are friends. A team. We can give him that." A pause. "Can't we?"

It looked like they'd be staying in Savannah for a while. "You know we can. But there won't be any more secrets. Everything will be put on the table." She hated secrets. Mostly because secrets had a way of biting you in the ass and destroying the carefully ordered life that you had planned. She slanted a glance to the left and found Linc staring at her. She'd caught him off guard with her quick glance, and for an instant, Blair could have sworn that she'd found him looking at her with—

Longing.

He blinked and whatever had been in his gaze was gone.

"Keep me updated," Eric urged her. "The last thing I want is any of my agents getting hurt. Watch each other and bring down the bad guy."

Well, some people would say they were there to protect the bad guy. Ghost didn't exactly have a legion of fans. But sometimes, things weren't always as they seemed. "Who gets to be the one to break the news to James?" *The lucky one to tell him that, hey, buddy, your cover may have been blown and you're marked for death.*

"Why not let his new partner do the honors?" Eric suggested.

Sounded like a stellar plan to her. She offered the phone back to a watchful Cole with a shrug. "Looks like you're up, slugger."

CHAPTER TWELVE

She was the most beautiful woman he'd ever seen, and he'd brought her straight into his hell.

"I want you," Tess told him. Her husky voice was music to his ears, and for her to say — despite everything — that she wanted him?

James knew he didn't deserve her. But he'd be damned if he'd give her up without a fight.

"I don't want you walking away. I don't want you hiding parts of yourself from me. You're the first person that I've let into my life — really *in* — and I don't want to lose you." She licked her lower lip.

Fuck, he wanted to lick that lip, too. Wanted to lick, to suck, to bite. To pretty much devour her.

Concussion, jackass. Don't forget about her injury!

"I don't want lies. No secrets or half-truths. You give me everything, and I'll give you the same."

Sounded like a good deal to him. But, before anything else happened, he should start with the most basic truth. The one that would probably drive them apart. "You shouldn't let me touch you." His shame. "I've got more blood on my hands than you can ever imagine. The last thing you should do is let me put my hands on you." He let her go. "I'm trying to do the right thing with you. I'm not following someone else's orders. Not being a freaking puppet. It's my life, and I'm trying to do what's right because *you* matter." He needed her to understand. "You're too good. I knew it from the start. But I wanted you, and when I want something, I take it. *I'm* not good. Or decent. To live the life I have, I needed to be dark. I needed to lose my conscience. Hell, my soul, and I did. I can't offer you the life that others can. I can't even offer you what that dick Devin can — the nice, easy life with a safe husband and a home with a dog and —"

"Who said I wanted easy?"

"Baby…" He shook his head. "I know you. Far better than you realize. When you came into my club that night, you were out of your element." Yet, somehow, she'd wound up with the most dangerous bastard in the room eating from the palm of her hand.

And I'd die for her in an instant.

The thought settled heavily around his shoulders. So he just straightened under the weight and continued, "You want safe because you weren't safe growing up. You want security — the nice house, the picket fence, the settled life — because you grew up without it. You need a boring dick like Devin because he can give you all of that — "

"I know what I need. I'm not going to lie and say I haven't been confused before. I have been. You get hooked on one thing and think it's the best. Think it's what you *should* have. Screw that."

He blinked.

"I walked into the club, and I wanted you. I couldn't take my eyes off you."

His muscles tensed.

"I went back to that club because I couldn't get you out of my head. Anytime something bad happened, I turned to you." She stepped toward him. Closed the space until their bodies brushed. "I know what I need and what I want. No one else has to tell me."

It took every bit of his willpower not to grab on to her, to hold tight, and *never* let go.

"Safety. Yes, I do crave it. Because I was scared and alone and vulnerable and you never forget what that's like. So I gave myself a good job and a good home and then — then some bastard came and he tried to take those things away from me."

I will make him pay.

"My home was wrecked. I was attacked tonight by someone who left me unconscious on the floor of the hospital. Each time something bad happens, do you know what I do?"

A sharp knock sounded at the door.

"They are always rapping at my door. I am not Edgar Allan Poe," Tess muttered. "I'm saying this, dammit. I'm saying this!" she shouted out. Tess stiffened her spine. "I turn to you."

He couldn't speak. The lump in his throat was too thick.

"You think you're the bad guy? To me, you aren't. To me, you're the guy that I run to when I'm scared. You're the guy I want at my side when my life is wrecked. You're the guy who makes me feel stronger." A faint smile curved her lips, and, for a moment, even lit her eyes. "You're my guy."

He'd put that on her phone, done it as a joke at the beginning but—

"I think you were my guy from the moment we met, and you still are. So don't walk away from me. Don't turn away." She reached for his hand. Curled her fingers with his. "And don't stop touching me." She lifted his hand to her lips and pressed a kiss to his knuckles. "I can be mad as hell at you—you should have *told* me that you dug into my past—but I don't want to lose you. I'm not ready to lose you."

"You won't." She wanted him? She needed him? He could barely believe what she'd told him, but if Tess was choosing him, there would be no way in hell he'd walk away from her.

"Yes, ahem." Cole cleared his throat very, very loudly from the other side of the door. "I need to talk with my partner. And it's pretty damn important."

Tess's brow furrowed. "Who is his partner?"

"Yeah, about that…" She was still holding his hand. It was nice. He liked holding hands with Tess. "Seems I was offered the job. Wilde Securities wants me to come on board as an agent."

Her lashes flickered. "That means…you'll be leaving Savannah?" He'd told her a bit more about Wilde, including the fact that the company had headquarters in Atlanta.

"That means I haven't taken the job, and Cole isn't my partner." Once, he'd thought working with Wilde would be exactly what he needed. A way to atone for the sins from his past. But taking what Wilde offered would mean leaving Tess.

Not even a contest.

"I have news from Eric," Cole continued grimly. Loudly. "It's news you'll want to hear, man. Trust me."

He didn't trust him, though. That was the problem. In this world, he pretty much trusted…

Tess.

"Eric is the one in charge of Wilde," Tess said.

He nodded.

He'd told her that, too. Given her some brief details about the fellow.

"Then we'd better hear what he has to say." She let go of his hand and opened the bedroom door.

Cole tugged at his collar. The tattoos that peaked beneath the sleeve of his shirt twisted and coiled, moving a bit like a snake that wanted to strike. "Sorry to interrupt, but there is news you need to hear, James."

Blair and Linc stood a few feet behind him.

Cole motioned James forward. "We should talk privately."

Privately was code for without Tess. That shit wasn't happening. "She hears everything. No secrets. Not anymore."

Blair let out a little sigh. "Glad we all got the memo on that one." Her gaze slanted toward Linc. "Some people understand how dangerous secrets can be. Downright toxic to a relationship. I mean, a partnership."

"I am fucking *sorry*," Linc rumbled.

James didn't have time for their drama.

Tess squeezed his hand. They left the bedroom.

Cole drew in a few deep, seemingly time-wasting breaths and then announced, "Eric thinks your cover may be blown. He received a tip from an informant that one of your old bosses sold out some agents. It's possible your name was included. The former handler is dead and buried, so not like we can get him to tell us for certain, but Eric was concerned enough that he sent us down here because he wanted to make sure you had backup if trouble came knocking at your door."

James waited.

Cole looked intense…and that was all.

Oh, right. James figured the others were waiting for his response. "I already knew this."

"You did?" Cole squinted at him.

Of course, he did. "Three Wilde agents showed up at my club. Only takes one to offer me a job. Hell, it takes a phone call to do that shit. I know how Eric works. The guy takes caution to an extreme. He wanted backup here for me, so he got it." James shrugged.

"Well, damn. Steal my thunder, why don't you?" Cole rubbed the bridge of his nose. "Okay, fine, we're all on the same page now. It's time for a battle plan. Because I'm really not the type to just sit around while the bad guys close in. Makes me twitchy."

"Probably something from your Delta Force days."

Cole stopped rubbing his nose. "How'd you know about that?"

"The same way I know Linc over there is a former Atlanta detective and Blair...well..." His gaze raked her. "Blair, you're an all-together different manner of agent, aren't you? I have to admit, I was impressed by your resume, and I'm not easily impressed."

"*Don't.*" The one word seemed torn from Blair.

Tess poked him in the side. Hard. "Sorry. I've just discovered that's one of his things. He's a prier."

Linc had moved protectively closer Blair. Though from what James had learned about the woman, she didn't need anyone's protection.

"You dug into our pasts?" Linc demanded.

"Guilty."

Linc's lips parted, but before he could reply, Cole pointed at Tess. "He dug into your life, too, didn't he? That why the two of you were fighting when we first arrived?"

She gave a curt nod.

"Women don't like that shit, man." Cole whistled. "It's like dating 101. You don't dig up the past. People share what they want to share. The rest you leave the hell alone. If it's buried, it's in the ground for a reason."

"Sorry. I missed dating 101 and went straight to kill-the-bad-guy 201."

Cole flipped him off.

"I had to know who was around me." All right, dammit, now he felt bad about investigating them, too. He'd never felt badly before, not until Tess. The woman was becoming his freaking conscience. "If my past was catching up to me, I had to be sure one of you wasn't here to sell me out."

"Not us." Linc's brows climbed. "Looks like the handler from your past might be the one who did that."

"Cameron Queen." He knew exactly which handler was to blame. "And, yes, the bastard sold out others. I worked with him — only briefly — so

I thought he'd lost the trail on me. Maybe I was wrong." He looked at Tess. Hated to tell her, but, "And if I was wrong, if the people who want to hurt me are in this town, then I'm the reason you've been targeted. They think they can hurt me by going after you."

"Are they right?" Linc asked, voice quiet.

"Yeah." James leaned forward and pressed his forehead to Tess's. "They are."

***

James stalked out of Tess's bedroom and headed for the kitchen.

"Are we going to talk now?" Cole demanded as he sprawled on the couch.

James stilled. He'd known the guy was still out there, of course. Linc and Blair had left hours ago, but Cole was sticking close. Cole kept claiming he was James's new partner and that meant they were supposed to stick together like glue.

James wasn't exactly in the mood to be glue.

"She asleep?" Cole asked, glancing toward the closed bedroom door.

"I think so." He wanted her like hell on fire, but with Cole just beyond the door—and Tess sporting a concussion—he hadn't been about to take things to the next level. So he'd held her. Funny thing. He liked holding her almost as much as making love to her. She was soft and warm in his arms, and he enjoyed the way she snuggled against him.

She felt right. She felt good. She felt like the woman he never, ever wanted to let go.

"Good. Then we can drop the BS."

James walked toward him. "I wasn't aware that I was bullshitting you."

"No. Maybe you were bullshitting her." Another glance at the closed door. "Because we both know the bastard could be from her past. Hell, seeing as how the attacks are focused on her, that's where my money is, too. I mean, I get it, you're trying to take the heat. Maybe you think that by acting like it's your past rearing its God-awful head, you give her some kind of comfort or something." His lips twisted. "Whatever. You're obsessed with her, you're in love with her, and you want to do anything to keep her safe."

"I'm not."

Cole blinked. "You're not willing to do anything to keep her safe?"

Of course, he would do anything to keep her safe. "I'm...not in love with her."

Cole stared at him. Hard.

CHAPTER THIRTEEN

No good ever came from eavesdropping. She knew this, yet Tess had still tip-toed out of the bed as soon as she'd realized that James wasn't there. She'd missed him. Had actually felt his warmth slip away from her. So she'd gotten up. She'd headed for the door. She'd heard voices.

And she'd eavesdropped. Her choice.

That meant she had no one else to blame for the pain spiraling through her.

I'm…not in love with her.

Crap. That hurt. It pierced straight to her heart, and the impact of that pain took her breath.

While she was struggling to pull air into her lungs, she heard James say—

"You don't need to be concerned with how I feel about Tess."

"Yeah, well, how you *feel* about her is messing with your head. You're locked on her so hard that you screwed up."

James had screwed up? When? She pressed closer to the door.

"You were seen at Frederick Waller's place. Don't look surprised. I got the full four-one-one on that with a little digging while you were tucking your lady in tonight."

Tucking her in? Seriously? *Jerk.*

"The big, bad Ghost is never seen. You slip in and you slip out, and you just leave death in your wake. I mean, you are your own freaking urban legend, man."

"I like to think of myself as a superhero, thanks."

"Uh, you mean super villain, don't you?"

Tess pressed her ear to the wood of the door. If only there was a drinking glass nearby that she could use. Their words were mostly clear, but she didn't want to miss anything.

"You slipped up because you're too involved with her. She's in your head, and you're not thinking clearly. That's why you were spotted at Waller's."

"I'm not so sure I was spotted. The detective didn't give me the witness's name or any other identifying info. For all I know, he was bluffing. Trying to push some kind of confession out of me because he thought it was amateur hour."

"Sure, okay. That could be one option. Option two is that you got sloppy and you were seen."

"And option three is that I'm being framed. Because, you see, I did put a knife to Frederick's throat in that alley."

Oh, God. Tess put a hand to her throat and accidentally rammed her elbow into the door.

Silence.

Maybe she should tip-toe back to the bed. Really, really quickly.

"I put the knife to his throat, and I told him that if he came near Tess again, if he tried to hurt her, he was dead."

"This stuff? This craziness right here? It's why I said you were more villain than hero. You can't go up to someone in a dark alley, put a knife to the person's throat, and make threats! That is not normal human behavior. That's not what the good guy does."

"It wasn't a threat. He wasn't going to hurt her again."

Cole coughed. "No, he clearly will not hurt her again."

"If someone from my past is stalking me now, that SOB could have seen me with Frederick in the alley. Decided to finish what I started in order to make me look like Frederick's killer."

"Okay, sorry, excuse my confusion, but how does framing you help someone from your past who wants you dead? Not connecting the dots there, partner."

She wasn't, either.

"You're right. It doesn't help anyone from my past." James's voice was lower as he delivered this conclusion, and Tess had to strain to hear him.

"That's what I was thinking." Cole, however, was blessedly clear with his loud voice. So clear that Tess began to wonder...

Does he know I'm listening?

"But if a frame job gets you out of the way, if it gets you shoved into a cell some place," Cole continued doggedly, "then, suddenly, the lovely Dr. Barrett is all alone. Seems to me that it would make more sense if the perp was someone from her past. Someone who wanted to separate her from you."

"Good thing I'm not Tess's only protection."

"Yeah, it's a good thing." A beat of silence. "You know that I had to dig into the good doctor's history."

Her control snapped. Tess yanked open the bedroom door. "Does everyone need to know every dark secret that I have? Does everyone—"

James was a few steps in front of her. Waiting, with his arms crossed over his chest.

She stopped. "You knew I was listening."

"Not the whole time. Only caught on at the end."

"I knew," Cole offered up, seemingly helpful. "I mean, I suspected."

So he'd deliberately been asking his questions to mess with her?

"And we all have dirty secrets. Some of us are just better at hiding them than others." Sympathy softened Cole's expression. "When you were thirteen, you were attacked. Pumped full of a drug cocktail mix."

"Yes." Goosebumps were on her skin.

"You weren't the only one."

Her lips parted. Her gaze jumped between him and James. "What?"

"Once we started digging, Wilde Securities found a few connections. The victims were in other cities, that's what made them hard to spot initially. Young girls, mostly runaways. They were found, typically tossed in alleys, with a mix of drugs in their systems that would have made them incapable of fighting off an attacker. Four dead girls were recovered."

She felt sick.

"After your attack, the MO stopped. No more twelve and thirteen-year-old girls found in alleys like broken dolls, with their bodies pumped full of a mix of street drugs. Wilde is still digging, and trust me, our techs can put together profiles on killers and vics like you wouldn't believe, but this perp's victims ended with you."

Her spine straightened. "Because I killed him."

James didn't look away from her. "No body, Tess. I dug, too, with Barnes helping me. If you'd killed the SOB in that alley, he would have been found there."

"Maybe he managed to drive away from the alley. Maybe he died somewhere else." That was what she'd always told herself, even as she kept looking over her shoulder.

"That's possible." Cole was pacing. "In fact, I think it's the most likely scenario. He got away from the alley. And he died somewhere else. Because guys like him—guys who prey on victims, guys who are sick and twisted on the inside and driven by their compulsions—they don't just stop. This bastard did. After you, he stopped. No more vics who fit the profile. As far as Wilde is concerned, he disappeared from the radar."

She pulled in a breath that seemed to chill her lungs.

"But even sick freaks have families. They have people who are attached to them. Who might want vengeance." Cole stopped pacing. "It's possible that's what we're looking at here."

"How would the person even know it was me? How would he know what I did?"

Face grim, Cole replied, "He'd know because he knew your attacker's MO, too. Because he dug, just like Wilde did. Just like James did. Because he found a thirteen-year-old girl who entered a hospital with so many street drugs in her system it was a miracle that she survived."

James wasn't talking. Just watching her with his intense gaze. And she was scared. "Why wait this long? If he knew the truth, why not come after me sooner?"

"Yeah." Cole winced. "On that one, I have no fucking clue. Haven't worked that part out yet. Give me some additional time."

This was crazy.

"Unless there was a trigger." Cole tilted his head. "Something that set the bastard off. Something that made him attack and stop the waiting game."

"You're saying he's known about me for years? But that he only came after me now?"

"I'm just telling you my suspicions. If I'm right, a man like that—someone who has waited and watched you so long—" But Cole stopped and clamped his lips together.

"Oh, seriously? Now you're going to stop?" She marched forward.

James caught her wrist. His fingers feathered over her pulse. "He would have watched you and gotten attached."

Her head turned. The gold of his gaze was burning.

A muscle flexed in his jaw as James carefully stroked her inner wrist. "He would have watched and waited, and he could have stayed very, very close. So close that he was in your life. Part of your life, and you didn't know it."

"You think he could be someone I know?" *Oh, God.* "A friend?"

"Doesn't have to be a friend. Could be someone on your periphery. But he'd be close enough that he could watch you. Close enough to study you. Close enough to feel like you belonged to him."

"I don't belong to anyone."

"He thinks you do." James's mouth tightened. "And if we're looking for a trigger, something that might have set off the bastard, then I know what it could have been."

Her heart shoved into her chest. "What?"

"Me."

Cole closed in. "That's a definite option."

James focused only on her. "I came into your life. I took you away from him. *I took you.* And he acted. He tried to get me out of the way. He tried to punish you for being with me."

"This is sick. This is out of control."

A bitter laugh came from Cole. "This is the kind of shit that Wilde Securities handles. We take care of the stalkers, the nut jobs, the madness. We've got this. You don't need to worry."

Easy to say, when it wasn't his life on the line. "So we have two big choices. The guy doing this is from my past. A freak who is obsessed with me and wants both vengeance for what I did and—"

"You," Cole supplied darkly. "I think he wants you."

"Not happening." James's face had darkened with fury.

"Yes, I don't want that to happen. Let's put that very much in the no column." Tess tried to take lots of deep breaths. "Our second choice is that the bad guy is from James's past. Probably some super criminal who kills for fun and is used to hurting people."

Cole inclined his head toward her. "Good job. I'd say that sums up our villain choices nicely."

There was nothing nice about the situation. It was a mess. A nightmare. Only there wasn't going to be any waking up from this bad dream.

***

"Why is there a hot guy on your couch?" Marilyn stood inside of Tess's kitchen, her body practically vibrating with curiosity and her eyebrows doing a very meaningful wiggle. "As if I didn't know, you sneaky new sex kitten—"

James strolled out of the bathroom, a towel around his hips and his muscled chest deliciously bare.

Marilyn gave a little moan. "Ohmygosh. You have two men here? *Two?* When Latonya and I told you to do some bad things, we had no idea that you were going to let this wild side out." She bounced. "I am so proud of you. When you go bad, you go *bad.*"

James stopped. Narrowed his eyes. "She is not sleeping with Cole."

Cole waved from the couch. "Hi! No, she's not sleeping with me, though, of course, if Tess was interested, I'd be happy to oblige—"

James jerked his head toward Cole. "Don't make me kick your ass first thing in the morning. I haven't even had my coffee yet."

Cole slumped back down. "No ass kicking required."

James growled and stalked down the hallway.

Tess lifted her hair and twisted it into a messy bun. "I'm not sleeping with both of them."

Marilyn hopped onto the counter stool. "I can see that James isn't the sharing sort."

"Definitely not." And she didn't want anyone else. Just him.

"So what is going on here?" Marilyn motioned toward Cole. "And, damn, but this place looks great. When you told me there was a break-in, I was expecting chaos. That's why I stopped by this morning. To try and help you clean up." She tucked a lock of blonde hair behind her ear. Her gold hoop ear-ring swayed with the movement. "But everything looks just as spotless as always. I guess the thief didn't break anything, huh?"

"The place was a wreck." She reached for a mug of coffee. Enjoyed the warmth from the mug against her fingers. "James just fixed it up for me."

"Isn't he handy?" A light laugh from Marilyn. "Makes me wish I'd seen him before you did. Then I could have called dibs."

Her gaze cut up to her friend.

Marilyn smiled. "I guess you're not the sharing sort, either, huh?"

"No. I guess I'm not."

Marilyn leaned toward her. "What if you hadn't gone to the club that night? Do you ever think about that? I'm the one who dragged you there, so I guess you need to be thanking me, don't you?"

If she hadn't gone to the club...

She wouldn't have met James. Wouldn't have taken one look at him and not been able to look away.

And what would everything else be like? No break-in? No attack? Some crazy guy still stalking her in silence?

Without James, there would be no passion. No sense of safety. No soft smiles. No—

"Are you in love with him?"

She heard a door open behind her. She should keep her mouth shut. Or she could offer a denial. James had done that last night. She didn't have to say anything. But...

But she was tired of not saying what she really felt. Tired of being afraid to feel. That was how she'd been, before him. Tess had been walking along, moving in some kind of void, then she'd found him and everything had sort of exploded. "Yes."

Marilyn blinked. "Say that again?"

Behind Tess, there was the quick sound of a breath being sucked in—very, very sharply.

"I said…" Tess made her voice nice and loud. "I'm in love with James."

Marilyn's face went slack with shock. "You're kidding me."

"No."

"But I was only teasing when I asked you that question! You just met him—"

Tess shrugged. "Sometimes, you know the truth quickly."

"Do you *know* him?" Marilyn leaned forward a bit more. "Really, really know him? Because I've been hearing some shady whispers at his club." Her voice was low. "That assistant of his, Barnes, he's been telling me some things that make me nervous as all hell." She was whispering now as she added, "Look, I get that the sex must be good but good sex isn't love, and if you'd had more good sex before in your life, you'd realize the difference—"

"He doesn't love me." Now her voice was low, too, and her cheeks stung. So much for her big moment of bravery. James was hearing *all* of this, and she got that Marilyn was trying to look out for her, just as she'd done before, but this time was different. Tess didn't need anyone looking out for her. "And it's okay. I know what I'm doing with him."

"Do you?" Marilyn didn't look convinced. She slanted an angry glance over Tess's shoulder. "And why the hell doesn't he love you?" Now her voice was raised. Belligerent. "You're freaking lovable! One of the most lovable people I've ever met!"

"Thanks for visiting today, Marilyn." Uh, oh. James sounded all curt. "But I need to talk with Tess right now."

Marilyn hopped off the stool and headed for him with the determination of an attack dog. She put her hands on her hips and glared at James. "You just using my friend? You just want her for sex?"

Tess moved to stand between them. "We're using each other."

"Bull!" Marilyn didn't seem to be buying that line. "You told me that you loved him." Her right hand flew up as she pointed around Tess and at James. "But you don't love my best friend? Why the hell not?"

Tess wasn't in the mood to hear the reasons why not. "It's okay, Marilyn. I know what I'm doing."

"It's not okay!" She shook her head. "He doesn't deserve you. I hear he's little more than a criminal. Some guy who collects things because his life is empty. What do you think you're doing now, James? Collecting her? Collecting something good? Because you are not going to—"

"*Enough.*" Tess kept her voice flat as she added, "You don't need to protect me. James isn't here to hurt me. I went into our relationship with my eyes wide open, and they are still open. I love him, but I'm not looking for him to love me back."

"You should be, though. We all deserve love." Marilyn sniffed. Slanted another glare at James. "Well, maybe not *all* of us." She peered at Tess once more. "When I dragged you to his club, I wanted you to have a night of fun. To see what being wild could feel like." For a moment, it seemed that tears gleamed in her eyes. "I didn't want this. I never wanted this."

"I want this," Tess told her. "I want him."

Marilyn backed up a step. "Then I hope you're happy with what you want." A nod. "And if you need me, you know where I am." She straightened her shoulders. "I'm already late for my shift. I have to go. Just watch yourself, all right?"

Tess nodded.

"Because you're too trusting. You believe in the wrong people." Marilyn's gaze lingered on James. "I think that's going to get you hurt in the end."

CHAPTER FOURTEEN

She didn't love him. Of course, she didn't love him. James had just walked Cole out — okay, he'd thrown Cole out because he wanted to be alone with Tess so they could clear the air. *Without* an audience.

She didn't love him. Couldn't love him. She wanted him. The sex was good. No, great. It was fucking awesome. But that wasn't love. Tess was probably confused because of all that had happened. Adrenaline rushes could be major bitches. They'd mess with your mind and make you think you were feeling something that you weren't. Intense emotions led to confusion, and there was no way —

He spun toward her. She still stood in the kitchen, near the gleaming counter. "When you said you were in love with me, you — you didn't mean it." A stark pause. "Did you?" His voice was strained.

She'd put her hair in the bun that drove him crazy. The one that exposed the slender column of her throat, and, thank Christ, the bruising there had finally started to fade.

He stalked toward her. "Tess?" She hadn't answered him. Of course, maybe that was an answer. No, no, there was no way she loved him. "I get it."

"I don't think you do." Her brows lowered.

His heart thundered in his ears. "Why did you tell her that you loved me?"

She tilted her head to the side. Tapped her cute chin right in the dimple he adored. "Let me think. Oh, yes, because I love you."

He stopped. Frowned. Shook his head. Couldn't dare to hope—*no.*

"I said it because I meant the words. I didn't see a point in lying."

James could barely hear because his heart thundered so freaking loudly. "The sex is great."

"Yes, yes, it is. Appreciate you noticing."

"There's been a lot of danger."

"Again. True point."

"Danger leads to adrenaline. Adrenaline leads to confusion. When you're experiencing an adrenaline rush, you feel things that you don't always interpret the right way."

Her expression shifted. Became curious. "Why are you afraid?"

"I'm not." An instant denial.

She was the one to close the last of the distance between them before she lifted her hand and placed it over his racing heart. "Yes, you are."

Her gaze searched his. "I think you're afraid for me to love you."

If possible, his heart thundered even faster beneath her touch.

"I'm not asking you for anything," she continued in her careful, husky voice. "I was simply stating a fact to Marilyn. I love you. I didn't mean for it to happen, it just did."

James gave a hard, negative shake of his head. "You should ask me for something." Anger burned in his gut. Anger directed at himself. "You should ask me for the whole world." Because she deserved it. He wanted to give her everything —

But Tess was asking him for absolutely nothing.

A faint line appeared between her eyebrows. "Why would I ask for something? I heard you last night. You don't love me."

His heart stopped. Just stopped.

For a moment, all he could hear was silence. Thick and consuming. Then his heart was racing again. *Bam. Bam. Bam.* "Lie," he forced out that one word.

Her lashes fluttered. "I'm not lying to you."

No, no, she wasn't the liar. She wasn't the dangerous one. She wasn't the one with secrets and pain and a life of deceit. That was him. He closed his hands around her waist and lifted her up, carrying her back toward the counter.

"James?"

He sat her on the counter. Stood between her legs. Kept his hands around her waist. And tried to breathe.

But with every breath, he pulled in her scent. Sweet vanilla cream.

She was all he could see.

All he could feel.

All he could ever want.

"I hurt you," he muttered.

Tess shook her head.

"You heard what I said last night, and it hurt you."

"It did. Yes."

She was *gutting* him. "I'm so fucking sorry, baby." He'd promised he wouldn't hurt her. And he hadn't just been talking about physical pain. There were so many ways to hurt in this world. He'd never wanted Tess hurt. Never.

"You can't make someone love you." She was all serious. So solemn. "It doesn't work that way. I understand that. I'm not asking for anything, I told you that, I just want—"

"I want you to ask me for something." His voice had turned savage. "I want you to ask me for everything in this world, and then I want to give it to you. I want you to have everything."

Tess's eyes widened.

"I lied. Not like it's the first time. And it won't be the last. Since I've been a teen, my life has been a lie. I've been a hundred different people. Sometimes, I'm not even sure who I really am anymore." No, that wasn't completely true either. "I know when I'm with you." His hold tightened on her waist. "I know who I am and who I want to be." He kissed her. His mouth took hers in a firestorm of need and desire. No control. No finesse. Just desperate, starving hunger. A lust that would never be sated. A craving that would never end.

Her hands rose and pushed between them. Her breath came in pants as she stared at him. "What are you saying?"

She thought he didn't love her? "I wanted you from the first moment I saw you."

"Lust has been easy for us."

She didn't understand because he was making a mess of things. He was trying to explain that he could control his lust with anyone, but her. There was no control with her. "How's your head?"

The little line between her brows grew deeper. "It's fine."

"The concussion? You're okay? You're sure—"

"I'm fine."

He kissed her again. Dipped his tongue into the sweetness of her mouth. "I want you, but only if the sex won't hurt you."

"Trust me. I'm a doctor. I'm *fine*." She grabbed the bottom of his t-shirt and shoved it over his head. "I want you. Like I said, lust is easy for us."

"No." His shirt hit the floor. "This isn't lust."

"Sure feels that way to me."

"You're more. We are more." They were alone now. It was safe. "I trust you. Only you."

"James…"

"No one else can be used against me. I don't care enough about anyone else. You are different. You got past my guard. You got to me when no one else could. I want you. I need you." Dammit, *say it*. He had to man the hell up and say—"I love you."

Her dark eyes widened. "But you told Cole—"

"I don't trust him. You don't give people weapons when you don't trust them not to turn around and fire a bullet right into your heart." She was the bullet. She was his weakness. One he'd never expected to have. When Cole had asked if he loved her, James had responded instinctively, wanting to protect her. A denial should have brought her protection.

But, dammit, it had brought her pain. "I'm so sorry, baby." He feathered kisses along her jaw. "I didn't trust him, and I lied. I was trying to keep you safe, but I fucked up. *You* are the only one I trust." He couldn't afford to trust anyone else. Hell, even Barnes had apparently turned on him. The guy had shared secrets with Marilyn? Since when? Sure, Barnes was young, impetuous, but…

He turned on me?

James would deal with Barnes soon enough. For the moment, he had to focus on what mattered most. Tess. Tess thought he didn't love her. Shit. He knew she'd been eavesdropping the night before, but he'd been so certain she'd missed overhearing that part. When he'd gone into the bedroom with her, she hadn't said a word about that stupid denial.

He'd thought he was safe. James had been planning a big, romantic confession for her. One that involved lots of candlelight. A bubble bath. And her precious chocolate fudge. So much for that plan.

Not love her? Seriously?

She was the only thing he did love in this world.

"I want you so much, Tess, because I do love you. Because it's not just sex and hasn't been. Hell, baby, why do you think I wanted to change the rules?"

Her fingertips smoothed over his chest.

He stared into her deep, dark gaze. "I didn't just want stolen moments with you. I wanted everything. I wanted all that you would give to me."

Were there tears in her eyes? No, no, he didn't want that. He didn't want Tess to cry. He wanted to make her happy, but he didn't know how. He didn't have any experience making a lover happy. Giving pleasure, sure, he had that covered. But pleasure wasn't happiness, and he wanted to make her happy and he wanted—

"I want to give you everything I have," he told Tess. "I don't want to be a ghost anymore." Drifting through life. Not bound to anyone or anything. He wanted to be with her. "When this mess is over, when I've stopped the bastard out there, I want to be with you. If you'll have me."

"If I'll have you?" She shook her head. "What part of 'I love you' did you miss? I want you, James. All of you."

"Not all of me is so good." He leaned forward. Had to press kisses to the curve of her neck. To the bruises that were faint now but still pissed him off.

"And not all of me is good either." Her hand slid down to the front of his jeans. "Did you see me running when I found out the truth about your past?"

Most women would. His past was scary as hell.

"My past is dark, too. I'm not afraid of darkness. And I know you wouldn't hurt me."

"No." Never.

"You're a good guy, James."

"No, baby, I'm not."

"You didn't hurt innocent people."

He swallowed. That didn't wipe his scorecard clean, not by a long shot. When he'd worked for the government, he'd become a monster in those days. Part of him would always be that monster. Because when he thought of the danger around Tess...

I want to destroy. I want to kill.

"Kiss me again," Tess urged him. "Kiss me."

His mouth took hers. He tried to make the kiss gentle. Tender. He didn't want to hurt her, and James wanted to show Tess how good he could be to her.

Because he *wasn't* a good man. But she brought out the parts of him that wanted to be better.

Her hand unsnapped and unzipped his jeans. Shoved them down and then she was touching his cock. Stroking him with her hot little fingers and his erection thrust eagerly toward her.

"I wanted you last night," she confessed.

I want you always.

He stepped back.

"James!"

"Baby, you keep squeezing my cock, and I'll come long before I have time to do what I want." He drank her in for a moment. So perfect. He would never get tired of the sight of her.

She smiled at him. Then yanked her shirt over her head. Dropped it to the floor near his. She wore a silky bra. One that she tossed aside after sliding her hands behind her back in one of those casual, but sexy moves women did when they unhooked their bras. She kicked away her shoes. And started to unbutton her jeans.

"Let me." He was barely managing speech. Almost drooling. But he wanted to show her how good things could be.

Sex wasn't love. Pleasure wasn't happiness.

But...

Fuck, at the moment, pleasure was all he had to give her.

He pulled off her jeans and tugged her panties with them. She was on the edge of the counter. Tess started to hop down. "We can go to the bedroom," she began.

"No." He pushed her back onto the counter. Spread her legs wider. Stared at her pretty sex. Touched her. Stroked her with his fingers.

Tess stiffened and hissed out a breath.

She was warm and already wet. He slid one finger inside of her. Loved watching the way her sex took him in. Another finger. He sank both fingers in as deep as they could go.

Her hands slapped down on the counter.

He bent. Put his mouth on her clit. Licked and sucked and kept thrusting with his fingers.

"*James!*"

Pleasure wasn't happiness, yes, he got that, but he wanted to give her more pleasure than she'd ever had in her life. Wanted her to desire him more than she'd ever desired anyone.

Was he a greedy bastard?

He lapped at her sex. Hell, yes. He'd told her that in the beginning.

She moaned his name.

Was he a possessive bastard?

He tasted more of her. Got drunk on her. Hell, yes, he was possessive.

He stroked her faster. Harder. Licked and licked.

He was possessive. She was his. He was hers. No one would take him from her. She'd chosen him, said she loved him, and he would give his life for her in an instant.

She came against his mouth. Called out his name. And he didn't want to stop. He wanted to taste her for freaking ever. Wanted to forget the rest of the world.

But he also wanted to sink deep and hard into her.

Another lick and his head lifted. Her hands were pushed down against the counter, and her head tilted back. Red stained her cheeks, and her eyes blazed with dark fire when she looked at him.

Oh, yeah, he needed to fuck her. Right then.

He scooped her into his arms.

"No! Your stitches! Don't forget about—"

He kissed her. James didn't even know if the stitches were still in his arm, and he didn't care. All that mattered was getting in her. He carried her to the bedroom. Put her down long enough to grab a condom and shove his remaining clothes out of the way.

Then she was pushing him down. Straddling him. And taking him all the way inside. His hips surged toward her as her tight, hot sex gripped him. When he was in as deep as he could go, when she surrounded him completely, he smiled up at her.

Her breath came in quick pants.

"I love you, Tess."

Her eyes flew to his.

"I will do anything for you." He wanted to withdraw. Thrust. Pound to a completion for them both. But he needed to say this. For her. "You never need to fear when I'm close. I'd give…" *Ah, Jesus, that felt good.* She'd just tightened her sex around him, and his eyes wanted to roll back into his head. "Give…you…*everything*…"

"Then give me everything now." She pushed her hands down on his chest. Angled her body so that she nearly slid off his cock, only to slam back down again.

He thrust like a man possessed and held her hips as tightly as he could.

She came again, and he was with her. James poured into her, the release going on and on in a seemingly endless stream of pleasure. He roared her name. Distantly, James realized it was a good thing he'd sent Cole away.

There were some things a partner didn't need to hear. And definitely not see.

Tess collapsed on his chest.

James pressed a kiss to her shoulder. His heart pounded, and he could swear he felt the wild beat of Tess's heart matching his. She fit him perfectly, in every single way. James only wished that he'd met her sooner.

Now that he did have her, though, he had no plans to let her go.

"I'm squishing you." Her voice was muffled.

He stroked her back. "Not even a little."

"Liar." She pushed up. Stared down at him. She was smiling, but her smile slowly faded. "Promise me you won't do that."

Her hair had come free and tumbled over her shoulders. Her lips were swollen from his kiss. She was absolute perfection. "Do what?"

"*Anything.* I don't want you doing something crazy like putting yourself between me and a bullet. That's not how this relationship works."

He wanted to kiss her again. "But you're a doctor. If I get shot, then you can patch me up."

"James." She was still straddling him. "I'm serious. Promise that you won't get hurt trying to keep me safe."

He wasn't going to make that promise. But he could compromise. "I'd prefer to attack in order to keep you safe. Not really planning on getting injured. Does that work?"

"James—"

A phone rang. Hers. He turned his head and saw it vibrating on the nearby nightstand. He reached his hand out. Grabbed it. Stared at the screen.

Devin Goddard.

The dumbass.

Tess slid off James. Dammit. He hadn't wanted her to move. But she took the phone and, naked, she backed away from the bed.

"I'm not due at the hospital today." She gripped the phone. "I still need to answer, though, because it could be an emergency."

He sat up in bed. He needed to ditch the condom, so he stalked to the bathroom. But behind him, he heard Tess say…

"Devin, what is it?"

When he passed the mirror, James caught a quick look at his reflection. His stubble appeared to have become a beard. Scars marred his chest. His hair was a rumpled mess. In short, he looked like warm hell.

And Tess still wanted him.

He was a lucky SOB.

"*What?*" Her voice sharpened.

In a flash, James was back at her side. He took the phone from her hand and swiped his finger over the screen and turned on the speaker.

"I lied," Devin was saying. Even on the speaker, his voice was strained. "I need to tell you what I really saw. Jeez, I'm so sorry, Tess!"

She looked from the phone to James. Her expression was confused. Afraid.

"We need to meet," Devin's words tumbled out. "We have to meet. I have to tell you what really happened in that corridor."

"*Tell us right now,*" James ordered.

A sharp inhale. "You...you're not alone," Devin stammered.

"She's never gonna be alone, Devin," James snapped right back. "So if you've got something to say, spit it out." *And if you're trying to lure her to you so that you can hurt her, forget it.* He knew the Wilde agents were investigating everyone in Tess's life. Linc and Blair had left to coordinate and get as much information as they could from their tech agents.

"I can't...Not on the phone."

"Yeah, you want to meet, asshole? Let me guess. You want to meet Tess alone, in some remote location so you can hurt—"

"*No, asshole,*" Devin threw back. "I'm trying to help!"

"Really? Because you *helped* already by saying a dead man was in the corridor at the hospital, that a dead man attacked Tess. Who really did it?" He waited a beat. "Was it you?"

"No! No, I'm being set up! I didn't—"

Join the club.

"I'll come to you," Devin promised frantically. "Tell me when and where. I need to see Tess. I need to—"

"When? Right now. Where? My club. It's closed so we'll have plenty of privacy."

"You'll bring Tess there? I have to see Tess!"

James stared at Tess. He put a finger to his lips. "She'll be there."

Devin hung up.

CHAPTER FIFTEEN

"This is some bullshit." Tess crossed her arms over her chest and glowered at James as he headed for the door. He'd dressed in record time. So had she because she'd thought that she was going with him to face off against Devin.

Only now she was being left behind.

"It's not bullshit." He turned toward her. He gripped his phone in his hand. He'd been quite the busy bee on that phone in the last few minutes. "It's for your safety."

"I thought I was safe with you. But it looks like you're leaving me."

"This place now has the best security system in the city. And I ordered Cole to get his ass in here and stay with you. You'll have a bodyguard and a fool-proof system."

But I won't have you. "I want to come."

He shook his head.

"Okay, let me rephrase. *I'm coming with you.*"

"This is what I do, baby. I go out and I take on trouble."

"We don't know that Devin is trouble." Okay, yes, they did. He'd admitted to lying. But… "He saved me. I woke up and he was there. He was taking care of me. If Devin wanted to hurt me, then he could have killed me in that corridor. We were alone. No one would have stopped him."

She watched as the expression on James's face completely altered. His jaw hardened. His eyes narrowed. His gaze turned cold and brittle even as his nostrils flared and his lips thinned. He stalked back to her.

"You won't be killed," he rumbled.

"It's certainly not on my agenda for the day—"

He kissed her. Hard and deep and long and she grabbed his shoulders. This wasn't the time for some crazy, passionate kiss, but she still just— hell, she just kissed him.

"You call the shots in the hospital," he said against her mouth. "You're the boss in the ER. But dealing with bad guys? This is my world. And I want you to stay here, to *please* stay here, because your safety has to come first."

She stepped back. Her hands fisted at her sides. "He could be luring you away deliberately. We don't know where he called from. Maybe he's outside my building, waiting for you to leave. Maybe he'll attack when you're gone."

"No one can get inside this place. Not once you set the system." He turned away. Glanced through the peephole on her door. A few moments later, he opened the door and Cole stepped inside. "And…" James continued doggedly. "That's why he's here. My safety net." He leveled a hard glare at Cole. "Anything happens to her, and you'll find out what it's like when a ghost breathes down your neck."

"Chill out. You're my partner, man. She's your lady. Nothing will happen. Not on my watch."

Then James was gone. Cole shut the door. Locked it. Reset her alarm.

"I don't like being left behind." Not one bit.

"He's trying to keep you safe."

Her head whipped toward him. Cole had dropped onto her couch.

He winced. "Look at it this way, if a man fell to the ground in front of you and James, and the guy on the ground needed immediate surgery, who would step in to help him?"

"That is a terrible comparison of —"

"Would James be the one to operate on the guy? Or would the doctor handle things?"

She crossed her arms over her chest. "You know I'd handle things."

"Right." A firm nod. "Well, in this case, consider James to be a death doctor, so to speak. This is his thing. He's had years of training to deal with the bad guys—that training is like his medical school. He's equipped for this situation. And if you were to rush after him, if you were to show up at the club with him, then his attention would be divided." His voice deepened. "I've seen it happen before. When emotions get involved, objectivity goes out the window. Even the best agents turn to mush, and they make sloppy mistakes. Mistakes that get people killed. Considering the way James feels about you, if you were to be in a situation where he felt he couldn't keep you safe, the man would pretty much implode."

She tried to keep her poker face in place. "You heard him last night. James told you that he didn't love me."

Cole looked up at her ceiling. "Yeah, right." His gaze slid back to her. "You think I don't know a lie when I hear one? Though to be honest, he used to be way better at lying."

She gaped at him. Cole had known James was lying?

"You should take a breath, Dr. Barrett. I know it's hard, but calming breaths really do help. I started this meditation program last fall—" He grimaced at her glare. "Or not. Ahem."

"I don't want James to be alone. He needs backup."

Cole nodded. "He has it. You think I didn't tell Linc and Blair to haul ass over to his club? I did. Wilde agents protect each other. We've got this."

He sounded so confident.

Why was her stomach in knots?

"By the way, your friend sure left in a hurry. Drove away with a squeal of her tires." He tapped his finger along the couch. "She dating anyone?"

"You're making my temples throb."

"But I'm also keeping you distracted." He offered her a wide smile. "Win, am I right?"

***

"You sold me out." James glared at Barnes.

The young guy was sweating. Sweating and repeatedly wiping over the same spot on the bar top. A constant, nervous move.

"I-I don't know what you're talking about."

James flattened his hands on the bar top. "Did you think I wouldn't find out?"

"Man, look, you've got this all wrong! I didn't! I swear—I didn't tell anyone a word about you! You gave me a second chance. I wouldn't do that shit to you." He gulped. Behind the lenses of his glasses, his eyes were wide. That whole deer-in-the-headlights wide. Wide and twitchy.

"I know your tells, Barnes. When you're lying, your left eye twitches."

"I didn't talk about you—" *Twitch.*

James lifted a brow. "Want to try again? Because, just so you know, when you lie, you also clean. So how about dropping the cloth and dealing straight with me, before I kick your ass?"

"It was nothing. I swear, *nothing.* I was just…she was hot." His eyes squeezed shut as he dropped the cloth. "She was so fucking hot." His eyes opened. "And she was flirting with me. *Me.* Most women like her just look right through me. She didn't. She looked at me. Saw her the first night that you took your lady up to VIP. I mean, they were friends, so I figured what was the harm?"

"What all did you tell her?"

"I am so dead."

"*What* did you tell her?"

Barnes took a step back. "I told her that you'd saved my ass, all right? That you were a cold-blooded bastard, that it was a mistake to be your enemy, but that you were good, deep down. You know, like, way, way deep. Like, if you dig with a shovel and you don't give up, that kind of deep."

James ground his back teeth together.

"I was trying to talk you up because you were so wild for her friend. I thought I was helping." *Twitch.*

"No, you didn't."

"All right, fine. I thought I was kind of helping. I also thought I was getting close to the pretty blonde. She's like, smokin', you know? And I've always had a thing for Marilyn Monroe. You know that. I own all of her movies on—"

"I think I should have left your ass behind when you had killers closing in on you."

Another gulp from Barnes. "Look, I did not tell her anything confidential. I wouldn't do that."

No twitches. No cleaning.

"I wouldn't betray you that way, man. I swear it. I owe my life to you, and I know it."

Again, no twitching. The cloth was in a crumpled heap on the bar top.

"I was just flirting. She was flirting. It was casual talk. But the woman wasn't interested in me. Not really. I learned that truth when I was taking some flowers to her at the hospital, and I saw her leaving one night." He sniffed. "She was making out with some other guy. Right next to his car. I got the hint. Well, I mean, I guess it wasn't a hint so much as—"

"What guy?" James demanded through his clenched teeth.

"Uh, blond guy? He was still wearing scrubs so I knew he worked at the hospital, too. It was dark, and I couldn't see a whole lot, but I did get a solid stare at his ride." A whistle of appreciation. "That Jag was a beauty. When I saw that ride, I knew it was over for me. I have a friggin' scooter. He had a Jag. How was I supposed to compete?"

Devin Goddard owned a Jag. "A visitor will be arriving here any minute." He analyzed options. Considered situations. Realized he didn't like this mess at all. "I want you close. Take a look at him and tell me if he's the same guy you saw with Marilyn."

Sweat soaked Barnes. "What's going on?"

"I think someone is trying to kill me."

"Ah, shit!"

"Exactly."

Trying to kill me because I'm in his way. If he eliminates me, he thinks he can get to Tess. "Don't worry. It's not happening. I won't be dying anytime soon."

***

An hour had passed. Tess glanced at the clock on her phone. Yes, she'd been clutching the phone pretty much the entire time. Worried? Why, yes, yes, she was. The fact that time kept crawling by and she hadn't heard anything...

That just made everything worse.

"Relax," Cole told her. It had to be the tenth time he'd told her that. Each time he said the word, it felt like he'd just run his nails over a chalkboard. "James can handle himself. And I told you, Linc and Blair are there for backup."

"You know, just saying 'relax' doesn't actually make a person relax."

"I have been told that before. Think Blair mentioned it a time or twenty."

"Why haven't we heard from James?"

"He's got this. Seriously. You should just—"

Her gaze cut to him.

He coughed. "Want a drink?"

"No."

The phone vibrated in her hand, right before a quick jingle filled the air. Her gaze snapped back to the phone, but the ID on the screen wasn't for James.

Latonya. Her finger swiped over the screen as she lifted the phone to her ear. "Latonya? I'm sorry, but this isn't the best—"

"Have you seen Marilyn?" The thread of worry in Latonya's voice was unmistakable.

"Yes, she was here this morning. But she said she was late for her shift and she left."

Tess heard the sound of someone being paged in the background. There was a rumble of voices.

"She didn't arrive. I tried calling her cell. I tried her home. I can't find her." More tension. More worry. "There was a massive pileup, and we're getting in wounded left and right. Jesus...you don't think...?"

No, not Marilyn.

"And Goddard is missing, too," Latonya added quickly, angrily. "We're short staffed, this place is exploding with patients, and he's decided to pull a disappearing act on me. Typical."

Tess knew where Devin Goddard was. "Yes, about him—"

"*I'm coming!*" Latonya yelled to someone in the background.

"If you're short staffed, I can help," Tess said immediately.

"You know you can't see patients, not when you got a concussion less than twenty-four hours ago. No way the folks in charge will let you on the floor." Her voice was quieter. "But try to find Marilyn, will you? I'm worried about her. And these pileup victims…God, I just don't want to turn around and see her on my table."

"I'll find her." A promise.

The call ended. Tess immediately dialed Marilyn, even though Latonya had said that she'd attempted to reach her before.

The call went straight to voicemail.

"Marilyn, it's me. Look, Latonya and I are worried about you. Please, please call me as soon as you get this message." She hung up and lowered the phone.

Cole stared straight at her. "What's going on?"

"You saw Marilyn leave, didn't you?"

"I saw her car drive away, yes."

"She didn't make it to the hospital. She never showed up, and my friend Latonya just called because Devin Goddard isn't there, and they've got a lot of victims from a pileup and—" Her lips pressed together. "I didn't tell her that Devin was with James. The hospital needs Devin." Provided he wasn't a freaking killer or crazed stalker. She dialed James. *They need help.*

***

James held his phone to his ear. "There's no sign of him?"

"We've had the street staked out the entire time you've been in the club," Blair assured him. "The guy isn't out here."

He'd been set up. Wasted an entire hour. "Get back to Tess's place."

"Are you sure? He could still show."

"And if he does, I've got him. But I want more protection there for her." Because he was afraid, and James was very, very rarely afraid of anything or anyone.

He ended the call, only to feel the phone vibrate in his hand once more. A glance at the screen had him answering immediately. "Tess? Baby, are you okay?"

"Did he show?"

His gaze swept around the empty club. Barnes was still behind the bar. Waiting. Ready. "No."

"He's not at the hospital, and Marilyn never showed up, either."

Marilyn. His gaze flew back to Barnes.

"She won't answer at home or on her cell. She's okay, isn't she? Latonya told me there was a pileup on the interstate, but Marilyn wouldn't have gone that way. Not from my place. If she'd been heading straight to work from *her* place, yes, then she normally takes that route, but since she came to my house first, I—" Tess stopped. "I'm worried about her."

So was he. "Did you know that she was involved with Devin?"

"What?" A shocked laugh. "Of course, she's not involved with him. Marilyn thinks he's a joke. She's told me over and over again what an arrogant jerk she thinks he is."

He was still staring at Barnes. "I have a witness who saw them making out in the hospital parking lot."'

"That's…are you sure?"

Barnes held his gaze. "I saw it," Barnes announced flatly. "I'm not lying to you, boss."

"I'm sure," James told Tess.

"And they're both missing?"

He didn't like this. If Devin was obsessed with Tess, could the guy be using her friend in some kind of attack against her? Devin and Marilyn were both missing. Not good. Not good at all.

"I'm coming back to you. Get Cole to call in help from Wilde. See if they can track Devin and Marilyn's phones. If we find the phones, maybe we find them."

"Marilyn's phone goes straight to voicemail. If the phone is off, can it be traced?"

"I'll take care of it."

"I don't want something to happen to Marilyn." He could hear the threat of tears in her voice. "Especially because of me."

"We're going to find her, I swear it. Just stay with Cole, okay, baby? I'm coming back to you."

"James?"

"Yeah, sweetheart?"

"I love you."

The words pierced right to his heart. Before he could say the words back to her, she'd hung up. He stood there a moment, still holding tight to the phone. Then he glanced at Barnes.

Barnes swallowed. "What can I do?"

"Get your ass up to my office. Get on my computer. And help me find two missing phones. Marilyn didn't show up for work, and I want to know where she is and where Devin Goddard is right now."

When it came to hacking, Barnes was first class. Between Barnes and the Wilde agents — he knew Cole would get his tech team cracking right away — they would find the phones.

Yes, if a phone was off, it made things trickier.

Barnes rushed upstairs.

If Marilyn's phone was off, then they could find the phone's location history to see where it had been right *before* the phone was powered down. That would be a starting place for them.

One way or another, James would find Marilyn and Devin.

The bastard lured me here. So what's his plan? What does he want? James glanced toward the front of his building.

And he realized that maybe Blair and Linc hadn't seen Devin arrive because he'd been there the whole time. Maybe he'd just been waiting for his moment to strike. Waiting for Blair and Linc to leave?

If so, Devin would be making his attack at any moment. If he came for James, Devin would realize that Ghost wasn't prey.

He was the predator, and it was time to go back to his old habits...

CHAPTER SIXTEEN

"You're not going to like this." Barnes hunched over the computer in the upstairs office. "But I found the last known location for Marilyn's phone."

"Tell me."

He looked up. "Your girlfriend's place. The phone turned off right outside of Tess's building." Barnes rattled off the time.

It roughly matched up with Marilyn's exit from Tess's place.

"And…um, Devin's phone just came back on." Barnes tapped his fingers over the keyboard. "Holy shit! He's right next door! In the building right beside us. He just turned on his phone and he's—"

James's phone rang.

He yanked it to his ear. "Hello, Devin."

Silence.

"I thought you wanted to talk. Thought you wanted to tell me what really went down in that hospital corridor."

Again, Devin didn't speak.

James narrowed his eyes. "I know where you are."

Nothing.

"Am I going to have to come and get you?"

The bastard still didn't respond.

"Where the hell is Marilyn?"

Devin hung up.

Barnes watched James with huge eyes. "You're going to get him, aren't you?" he whispered. "This is just like the old days."

"Not quite." James headed toward the locked closet. The one with the state-of-the-art security system. Not really a closet. More like a safe, a custom designed one. He typed in his code. Used his thumb print for verification, then had the reinforced door swinging open.

He took out a bullet-proof vest. He put it on and covered it up with a jacket. James pulled on his gloves—no sense leaving fingerprints behind. Not like it was amateur hour. He grabbed two guns and two knives.

"Do you need backup?" Barnes asked. His quaking voice said he really hoped James did not need him for backup.

"I need you to lock this place down. Stay inside until I come back for you or until I call."

Barnes nodded.

James headed for the door.

"Ghost!"

He stilled.

"Be careful."

James glanced back at him.

"You're an asshole, but you're the only family I've got."

***

"I don't like this." Blair gripped her phone as she sat in the passenger seat of their rented SUV. "I don't like leaving a team member behind, and this whole set-up reeks to me."

"Yeah, well, the goal is protecting the doctor, right? We need to get back to her." Linc headed straight for the intersection and their green light. "Ghost is a big boy. He can take care of himself."

"Everyone needs help sometimes. I feel like we're leaving him to an ambush. This just doesn't sit well with me." Why hadn't Devin made an appearance? Why leave them hanging for an hour?

"We've got Wilde agents digging into the backgrounds of the people close to the doctor." Linc's voice was reassuring as they left the intersection and turned to the right. He accelerated down the empty side road. The GPS directed them as it gave the fastest route back to Tess's place. The light was green up ahead, so their SUV didn't slow down. "Soon enough, we're going to find the clue we need. We're going to find out exactly who is after—"

She didn't see the other car coming. Blair just felt the impact as it slammed into the side of the

SUV. *Her* side of the SUV. Glass shattered. Air bags deployed.

And, distantly, she heard Linc roaring her name.

***

He didn't leave through the front entrance of his club. James didn't exit via the back, either. He'd done research after he'd started remodeling the club, and like many places in Savannah, he'd discovered his new collection piece had been filled with secrets.

Or, rather, a few secret passages. Because, once upon a time, his club had been an old school speakeasy, a place that needed more than a few fast, secret exits for patrons. While renovating, he'd made sure not to destroy those passages, and he'd also gone ahead and purchased the building next door since it connected in so many ways to his club. He hadn't done anything with that building yet. It simply sat empty and closed up.

Through one of the old speakeasy passages, James was able to make his way out of his club and to get inside the building next door. *Too easy.* Then it was just a matter of slipping toward his prey.

The place was full of dust and the air smelled stale. His steps were silent as he searched the first floor. No sign of Devin. As he continued searching, he took the stairs, but he'd been on those stairs before, so he knew exactly where to step so that he would not make the old wood creak or groan. Soon he was on the second level, and then…

A door was ajar. Faint light spilled from inside, light from one of the big windows there.

Was the sonofabitch in here the whole time? Watching me? Waiting for me to send Linc and Blair away? He eased out a slow breath. For Devin to be this organized, though, hell, it didn't make sense. The guy was a doctor. He wasn't some criminal mastermind. He wasn't—

He's not me. He shouldn't know how to play my games.

But this wasn't a game. This was Tess's life.

James gripped one of the guns in his right hand. The other gun was tucked in the back waistband of his jeans. He lunged inside the room, shoving the door out of his way. "*Freeze!*" James snarled.

Tess. Tess everywhere. The light from the window showed him the photos on the wall. Photo after photo of Tess. At work. At her home. At *his* club.

Tess was smiling.

Tess was walking.

Tess was kissing…*me.*

This was some serious stalker shit, and it made his body vibrate with fury.

"H…here…"

He whirled.

Devin had just staggered out of the closet in that room. He stood there, blinking, with a gun in his hand.

"*Drop it,*" James thundered.

Devin looked down at the gun. Then back up at James. "Wh-where's...Tess?"

"Drop the gun or I will shoot you!"

"M-Marilyn..."

"Yeah, I want to know where the hell she is!"

Devin lurched forward.

Screw this crap. James fired.

***

"Blair! Blair, God, *look* at me!"

Why was Linc screaming at her? Blair cracked open one eye.

And almost vomited. Wow. What was up with that? Pain pounded through her — her head and her side and...jeez, were her ribs broken? She knew that pain, her ribs had been broken before, and it wasn't as if you could forget it when something like that happened.

Only...how had her ribs been broken this time?

"Keep your eyes open!"

Had she closed them?

"I'm going to get you out of here, understand? Baby, you're pinned right now. I'm going to get you out. You don't have to worry. I'm not leaving you. I'm getting you out."

Her temples pounded. "You…called me baby."

He sucked in a breath. "I didn't. I said *Blair*. You're confused."

"You're…bastard."

He squeezed her hand. Tight. "That's right. I am. I'm *your* bastard. So trust me when I say that I'm getting you out. You're going to be all right. An ambulance is on the way. Firefighters will be coming with the Jaws of Life. Everything will be okay."

She forced her eyes to stay open. She was pinned in the SUV. Deflating air bags were around her. Metal shoved into her side. She was pretty sure that she could smell her own blood.

They'd been in a wreck. Someone had hit them. And… "The other…driver?" Her voice was too weak. That wasn't a good sign.

"Ran," he bit out. "Ran and disappeared down the street. I heard an engine growling. Bastard had a second car waiting."

This…wasn't an accident then. "Am…bush?"

He nodded grimly. "Looks that way."

"You…should have…gone after him." It hurt to talk. Actually, everything hurt. "You should…stopped him before he got…to…other…c-car…"

Linc was still holding her hand. "I wasn't leaving you. There is nothing that could make me leave you."

He was staring at her. All intense and hard and with a look in his eyes that she'd never seen before. It was important, and she should say something about it but Blair was pretty sure that she was about to pass out again. "Something…is in my side."

His eyes widened.

"I'm…bad. I think…I'm bad…" A tear leaked down her cheek. She never cried. Well, okay, she cried plenty. But usually in the privacy of her own home when she was watching holiday movies. Everyone did that, though, didn't they?

Her thoughts were scattering. She could definitely smell the coppery scent of her own blood, and now she felt the pain growing.

"You're going to be okay." His voice seemed to shake.

Linc. He usually had some quick one-liner or a sarcastic remark for her. But not this time.

Maybe it was the pain or maybe she was just confused — super disoriented — yet she could swear that cool-as-you please Linc…

Appeared absolutely terrified.

***

"Blair and Linc are coming this way." Cole had been talking into his phone, but now he marched out of the kitchen and headed toward her. "I was just talking to Eric. Our techs are working on your friends—"

The fact that the lives of her friends were being investigated made her stomach roll. "My friends aren't bad people. Latonya is one of the most brilliant doctors I've ever met. She's smart, and she's strong, and she'd go to the mat for me in an instant. She's not some crazy killer. She saves lives."

"I assure you, an investigation like this is standard procedure. In cases like yours, the bad guy often turns out be someone much closer than you'd ever expect."

She wasn't going to turn on her friends. "I'm the one who kept secrets. Not them. They were always open books to me. Hell, I spent every Christmas of my med school days with Latonya's family. She always invited us over to spend the holiday with them."

"Us?" Cole prompted.

"Marilyn and I would be invited. Marilyn didn't always go, though, she had family commitments of her own." But Marilyn hadn't enjoyed her family. She'd said they were too stuffy. Too cold. She liked being with her friends better because they understood her.

We have to find Marilyn.

"When did you meet Marilyn? Was she in med school, too?"

"No, no, she was studying to be a nurse. Um, we met at the library one day. We were both hauling around anatomy books, and Marilyn came up to me. She was smiling and made some joke about our light reading." *God. I was so serious back then.* "Told her it wasn't light reading. That the books were very heavy, and she laughed and she…sat with me. She stayed with me after that. Pushed me to go out. Tried to make me have more fun." Tess swallowed. "Marilyn is always good at seeing the fun parts in life."

Her phone vibrated as a text came through. She didn't recognize the number—but the text said:

It's Marilyn. I'm downstairs. I need you.

Her head whipped up. Relief made her feel a little light-headed. "Marilyn is downstairs. She needs—"

He took the phone from her. Stared at the screen. "No."

"What do you mean, 'no'?" Hadn't he heard her? "Marilyn needs—"

"You don't know that this is Marilyn. This could be the bastard after you."

"Or it could be *Marilyn!* Look, we have to find out. What if she's hurt? She said she needs me. I can't just leave someone who might be hurt down there!" Did he not understand her whole Hippocratic Oath? She had to help people.

And this wasn't just *people.* This was one of her best friends. "I'm going down there."

"No." He shook his head. "I am. I'll check the scene. You stay here *behind the security system.* Blair and Linc will be arriving any minute. I'll get them to help me canvas the scene downstairs. If your friend is there, I'll get her." His lips pressed together. "And if it's not your friend, I'll take care of whoever the hell is down there."

She pushed him toward the door. Someone had to get down there. Fast. "*Go!*"

***

Cole didn't like this setup. Not one damn bit. He'd tried to call Blair and Linc on his way downstairs, but they hadn't answered him. Neither had James.

When he reached the road, he didn't see anyone. Or at least, no one who seemed suspicious.

There was a lady with a stroller across the street, but she was playing with a baby, not even glancing his way. He kept close to the building. His gaze swept the scene for any vehicles that appeared suspicious. For anyone out of place...

A group of school kids walked in a tight line near the red light. Looked like they were on some kind of tour or field trip.

No sign of Marilyn. No sign of anyone who seemed dangerous. The whole scene felt normal.

He whirled and headed back into the building. But as he did, Cole caught a glimpse of blonde hair as a woman inside rushed toward the elevator.

"Marilyn?" Cole called as he hurried after her. His holster — and gun — were hidden beneath his coat.

The elevator doors started to close. He shoved his hand through them, activating the motion sensor so that the doors would open once more. As they flew back, he could see her figure huddled against the rear wall of the elevator.

Her scrubs were wrinkled and torn in a few spots. Her hair hung over her face. Her chest rose and fell with jerky, frantic movements. Her hands were hidden behind her back.

"Marilyn? What happened?"

Her head tilted back. Her big, blue eyes — wide and desperate — met his. There was an angry, red mark on her face. A hand print?

"Did someone hurt you?"

"Yes," she whispered. "He did…"

***

The bullet slammed into Devin's right leg. He screamed and immediately dropped his gun as he fell to the floor. Then the doctor was clutching his bleeding leg, rocking back and forth, and continuing to scream.

I don't have time for this shit. James crossed the room in an instant and put the gun to Devin's head. "Stop screaming."

Devin stopped. But his eyes…when he looked at James, his gaze didn't seem to focus.

"Shit, man, are you high?"

Devin's body weaved. "Got to…h-help…Tess…"

"Just how the hell are you going to help Tess?" He jerked his head toward the wall of photos. "You been stalking her? You been after her?" When the hell had those photos been put up? James had been in that building the previous week doing a survey.

Set-up. Feels like —

"Not me…h-help Tess…" Devin's voice was slurred.

Yeah, the guy was definitely on something. And…

James unclenched his jaw. "What did you take?"

"N-nothing…"

Lie. "What did you want to tell me about that hospital corridor and Tess's attack?"

For an instant, some of the confusion seemed to clear from Devin's eyes. "Tess. She was hurt."

"Yes, she was. Who the hell hurt her? Was it you, did you —"

"Marilyn," he breathed.

"What about her? Where is —"

"Marilyn…hurt her."

James's blood iced.

***

Just as Cole reached out for Marilyn, she lunged forward. Her right hand flew up, and she plunged something into his neck.

It was…

Shit.

A syringe. He threw out his own arm, trying to grab her. But she laughed and danced back. Screw this. He fumbled for the gun in his holster.

Only…

His fingers weren't working quite right.

"Down, down you go," Marilyn sang out.

He looked back. The elevator doors had closed. It didn't seem like the elevator was moving, though. Had she stopped the elevator?

Everything started spinning. Black dots filled his vision, and—when the hell had he collapsed on the floor?

She crouched next to him. Patted his cheek. "Why don't you just enjoy the trip? When you wake up, it will all be over."

Trip? What trip—

The black dots danced more before his eyes, and a wave of heat enveloped him.

Fuck me.

CHAPTER SEVENTEEN

A sharp knock pounded at the door. Tess had been pacing near the kitchen, but at the knock, she snapped to attention.

The knock came again.

She crept toward the door. Crept at first, then moved fast. Faster. Her hands slapped against the wood as she leaned forward and put her eye to the peephole.

Marilyn?

"Tess?" Marilyn shouted. She swayed a bit. "Tess, please, let me in. I don't feel so well…"

Tess fumbled with the locks. She yanked open the door. Distantly, she was aware of a fast, hard beeping.

Christ. The alarm. I should have disengaged it before I opened the –

Marilyn fell into her arms. "Help…me."

Tess pulled her inside. The stupid alarm kept beeping, but she ignored it for the moment. It could just wait.

But Marilyn winced. Her hand went to her forehead. "What is that? Just...turn it off. Please...turn it off."

"No, that alarm will bring help." She could see a red outline on Marilyn's cheek. Someone had hit her? "You need help. The cops can come and we'll get an ambulance and —"

"Turn it off!" Marilyn cried. Tears trickled down her cheeks. "It hurts...my head. Please." She grabbed Tess's hand. Held tight. "We'll call an ambulance," she whispered. "Just...turn off the alarm."

Jaw locking, Tess slid away from her. She headed for the alarm panel. That morning, Cole had gone over the new alarm system with her. He'd told her all the codes. Told her how the alarm system was even equipped with cameras and how the feeds would go to her phone.

"Please..." Marilyn whispered from behind her.

From...very close behind her.

Marilyn was on her feet. Still swaying but inching closer to Tess.

Tess's fingers were poised over the keypad. "Where's Cole?"

"Who?"

"He went downstairs to find you. Did you see him?" She was staring at the alarm.

A whimper came from Marilyn. "N-no. I didn't. Please...*turn it off.*"

Tess fisted her fingers. "No."

"What?" That one word. It didn't sound so weak. Not so desperate. In fact, it sounded angry.

"I'm not turning off the alarm. I want the cops to come. I want help to come." She spun to face one of her best friends. "You should have seen Cole. He went downstairs to find you. *Where is Cole?*"

Marilyn screamed. She lunged at Tess, and Tess realized there was something in Marilyn's hand. Something she'd yanked out of the pocket of her scrubs. A syringe? Oh, hell, no.

Tess caught Marilyn's wrist with both of her hands, and she squeezed as hard as she could. "What are you doing?"

Marilyn screamed again. A loud, guttural scream. She kicked at Tess, a sharp jab right to Tess's knee. Tess felt her knee buckling. Shit. But as she fell, Tess hauled Marilyn down with her. They hit the floor. Rolled. Twisted. The syringe shot across the floor, and Tess fisted her right hand and plowed it into Marilyn's side.

"Get the syringe!" Marilyn yelled.

Wait…*who* was she yelling that to?

Tess craned her head to the right. She could see a man's expensive, leather shoes. He was standing just inside her doorway.

I didn't lock the door back when Marilyn came inside. She fell into my arms, and I didn't even shut the door. Oh, God.

Marilyn wasn't working alone.

Tess's gaze whipped upward. She frowned at the man. No, that didn't make sense. How would he be working with Marilyn? Why?

Why is Marilyn doing this?

He didn't reach for the syringe. Instead, he gave Tess a rueful smile. "Hi, Dr. Barrett."

She shook her head and scrambled to her feet. Her knee felt weak, but it was holding her, and, blessedly, her alarm was still beeping. Help would come for her. She just had to buy enough time for that help to arrive.

"I'm really sorry to involve you in all this," he said, voice regretful. "Because you seem like a nice enough person, and you did try to help my brother."

She was staring at Morgan Waller. He was wearing an expensive suit, his hair was perfectly styled, and his features reflected just the faintest hint of sadness.

"Of course, it would have been better to simply let the addict die," he continued in his regretful tone. "He was a waste, and I was tired of cleaning up his messes."

Her breath came faster. "Your brother…he's dead."

"Yes. I killed him."

Oh, God. He—

Marilyn grabbed her. "Gotcha." She sank the syringe into the side of Tess's throat. Tess screamed. Her hands flew up and her nails raked down Marilyn's face.

Marilyn screamed, too.

As Tess felt the drugs sweeping through her body, she thought...*Gotcha, too, bitch. I've got your DNA under my nails.*

Though, that wouldn't necessarily help with the whole matter of *staying* alive.

Black spots were dancing before her eyes. Her body felt slack and heavy, and it was her worst nightmare. Her past had come back to torture her.

She was thirteen and in a dark alley. The handsome stranger was grabbing for her —

He had blue eyes.

Bright, blue eyes.

Why hadn't she remembered that detail before?

The past vanished.

"We have to turn off that fucking alarm!" Marilyn cried out. "It's driving me crazy. It's —"

"I'll take care of it. Give me a second!" Morgan reached out to lock his fingers around Tess's shoulders.

Tess tried to scream. Only a whimper came from her.

"Sorry I had to involve you," Morgan told her. His face came in and out of her vision. "But your boyfriend needs to learn that you don't mess with my world and get to vanish without a trace. He'll get what's due to him."

Wait...this...this *was* about James?

"Turn off the alarm right now, or I will kill you here."

He'd dragged her before the alarm panel. He lifted her hand. Held her fingers as she slowly typed in the code. The alarm...stopped.

But an instant later, her phone rang.

"That's the alarm company." His breath blew over her ear. "You give them your verbal code and you tell them that you're okay. If you don't, I will put a bullet in your heart."

Marilyn had grabbed Tess's phone. She shoved it to Tess's ear.

Tess could barely focus. Maybe they shouldn't have pumped her full of drugs *before* getting her to talk.

She felt the gun dig into her.

Tess whispered the code. Said she was okay.

"Good girl," Morgan praised.

She wasn't a girl. She was tired of being fucking *good*.

And why was everything so very dark?

Morgan repositioned her so that he was carrying her in his arms. She lost time for a moment, and when she managed to open her eyes again, they were in the building's elevator.

Wait...was that...on the floor... "Cole?"

"I gave him more than I gave you. He was in the way." Marilyn stroked back a lock of Tess's hair. "I didn't want this for you. You were supposed to be good. Supposed to be better. I forgave you for what you'd done. I even thought that you'd *helped* me. But then you went out and fell for that killer. You even told me so. I mean, I tried to give you an out this morning. I came by, before things went too far—"

Too far? Was she serious? Everything was *too far*!

"I was giving you the chance to reject him. You didn't. You stood in your kitchen and told me you loved him. *Him*. A killer."

"I told her all about James," Morgan added. "She knows exactly what he is. And he's far too much like her brother."

"There's no going back now." Marilyn's fingers lingered on Tess's cheek. "This is all on you. Your choice."

Tess couldn't make sense of what they were saying. Her body was numb. Blackness leaked across her vision and—

Ding.

They were moving. Exiting the elevator. A few moments later, she could feel the sun on her face. Feel the breeze blowing against her. She could—

"My girlfriend is ill. We're taking her to the doctor," Morgan announced.

Who was he telling that to? Who was—

Tess cracked open one eye. Saw a woman…with a stroller?

"I'm a nurse," Marilyn supplied quickly. "We've got her. Don't worry."

"H-help…" Tess whispered.

Marilyn patted her arm. "Don't you worry, dear. We are going to help you."

They put her in the back of a car. Drove away.

And she couldn't speak. Couldn't fight. Could barely feel at all. No, her *body* could barely feel. Her heart and soul could feel plenty. Inside, deep inside, she was terrified. Desperate. She was being taken away. They planned to use her against James.

They were going to kill James. Then her.

No. I can't let it happen. I won't.

"Aw, she's crying," Marilyn said. She wiped away Tess's tears. "Don't worry. You're my friend. I'll make sure it doesn't hurt."

***

James raced into Tess's building. He'd tried calling her — over and over again — but she hadn't answered. He'd tried to reach Linc and Blair. *Nothing.* Tried to get Cole.

Cole's phone just rang and rang.

Where was everyone?

The building was deserted. No real surprise since he knew the tenants on the first floor were on an extended trip to Europe, but…

The silence seemed too oppressive. Too complete.

He'd called an ambulance for Devin. Had gotten Barnes to stay with the guy until help could arrive. Devin's words kept playing through his mind.

Marilyn. Why would Marilyn be behind this mess?

He'd had to go the long way over to Tess's place. His GPS had rerouted him because of some damn car accident. It had cost him precious time. He jabbed the button for the elevator. The doors slid open and—

"Fucking hell!" James lunged down. Cole was slumped in the corner. At first glance, he thought Cole was dead. Cole was not moving, and James didn't think he saw the guy breathing. He put his hand to Cole's throat as he searched for a pulse. Nothing. Oh, dammit, he was—

A light beat. A thready pulse.

Still alive.

James yanked out his phone. Called nine-one-one and barked orders as fast as he could. He needed…

"They t-took…her…" Cole whispered.

At least, that was what he thought Cole whispered.

"J-just left…h-hurry…"

What? James threw out his hand and hit the emergency button on the elevator. The doors stayed open as he listened to the calm nine-one-one operator tell him to assess the situation and—

"The situation is fucked to hell and back," James snapped. "I need help for my partner, right *now.* Get an ambulance out here because I don't know what's wrong with him!" He couldn't see any signs of injury. In fact, physically, Cole looked fine. But his speech was slurred and his eyes wouldn't stay open. His pulse was barely there and it sure seemed like —

Drugs.

James felt his heart squeeze. Cole had been drugged. Devin had been drugged.

And, years ago, Tess had been drugged and attacked.

"G-go...after her..." Cole's voice was weaker. "H-hurry..."

"Who took her? Was it Marilyn?"

Cole didn't speak, but...had that been a nod?

"And Marilyn...did she drug you?"

Another...possible nod?

"Fuck."

"*Sir,*" the nine-one-one operator said in her crisp voice. "I need to know more about the victim, will you tell me —"

"He's been drugged and he needs a hospital, right the hell now. Get an ambulance here and *help* him." He squeezed Cole's hand. "I need you to hold on, got it? Help is coming."

Cole's face had bleached of color. "Go...*Tess.*"

He'd said that *they* had just left with Tess. "Who was with Marilyn?"

Cole's lips moved. He didn't speak. He...he started to spasm. His eyes flew wide and there was terror in his gaze.

"Fucking hell!" James roared into the phone. *"He's dying!"*

***

The ER was absolute chaos. Latonya Wilson ignored the twisting pain in her back and the tension in her shoulders as she headed for the next patient—the man sprawled out on the exam table that waited for her.

She'd been told he was a gunshot victim. That he was probably high on drugs.

That he'd seized once in the ambulance on the way over.

That the patient was shouting and saying things that didn't make sense.

She donned her gloves, she squared her shoulders, and she—

The patient's head turned toward her. His face was haggard, his eyes wild, and terror cloaked his expression. "Help…me." He grabbed her hand. "Please."

Dr. Devin Goddard was on her table.

Begging for help.

Her breath caught. What in the hell?

"Please…"

"I help everyone who comes into my ER." She nodded. "You're going to be okay, Devin. Just breathe and relax."

"T-Tess…"

Her heart squeezed. "What about Tess?"

"I'm...sorry..."

***

James watched the ambulance drive away. James had followed the nine-one-one operator's desperate instructions. For a moment, he'd been sure that he was losing Cole. No, he *had* lost him. Because Cole's heart had stopped. James had given him CPR until the EMTs arrived, and when they'd roared onto the scene, they'd gone to work on the Wilde agent immediately.

They'd kept up the CPR. They'd injected Cole with something. Maybe Narcan?

They'd worked like hell, and they'd gotten him back.

Now Cole was being rushed to the hospital. Cole was — hopefully — going to make it. *But what about Tess?*

James rubbed his chest. He felt as if someone had ripped out his heart. He'd stayed with Cole. Lost his chance to find Tess, and he was about to lose his mind. She was out there, somewhere. Hurting. Maybe dead. When the EMTs had taken over, he'd done a desperate search of her apartment.

There had been no sign of Tess. He'd called the alarm company and been told that, yes, the alarm had sent out a distress signal. A signal that had been canceled. Tess had even spoken with an agent, confirming that she was safe. Though, after prompting from James, the agent had admitted that Tess had sounded…strained.

Strained? Jesus. She'd probably been terrified. He had no doubt that Tess had been forced to cancel the alarm call. Now she was gone, and he was breaking apart.

"Um, excuse me?"

James glanced back. A woman with dark hair, deep brown eyes, and a pensive frown stood close by. A baby was cradled against her, and the woman rocked back and forth as she soothed the child.

"Can you tell me what happened here?" she asked.

Damn. Where to start? "A man was injured. He's being taken to the hospital."

She bit her lower lip and kept moving her body, doing that thing that moms always did where they stayed in constant motion to calm their babies.

He started to turn away.

"Was this related to the woman with the nurse?"

James jerked toward her. "What woman?"

"The woman who was so sick. The nurse said they were taking care of her. She came out of this building." The young mother tilted her head toward Tess's building. "The man was carrying her."

Breathe. "Can you describe him for me? I need as much information as you can give me."

The baby began to cry.

She murmured softly to him, stroked his back, but kept her eyes on James. "Something was wrong, wasn't it? I could tell. I just — it all felt off. And I swear, she asked me for help."

Her words tore his heart to shreds. "Please tell you me what you remember about the man."

But the young mother winced. "I'm not so good with faces. He was good-looking. His clothes appeared expensive. His hair was dark. I think."

Hold on to your control. Let her talk. Give her time —

"I'm not good with faces," she said again as she rocked the baby, "but would the car's license plate help?"

He stopped breathing.

"Because I'm really good with numbers. And I memorized it as they drove away."

***

"I need to know what's happening with my partner." Linc slammed his fists into the check-in counter at the ER. Blair's blood had dried on his hands. *Blair.* He yanked his fists back as the administrative clerk frowned at him. "She was rushed to the back, and no one will tell me anything." He was about to go insane. He'd ridden in the ambulance with her. Kept her hand tightly in his. He'd talked to her the whole way.

Even when she'd stopped talking to him.

"Sir," the clerk began, his voice firm, "you need to take a seat in the waiting area. We will be back with you as soon as we know more." A pause. "And you said this was your partner? As in…your wife? Your girlfriend? We need to know your legal relationship to her so that—"

"Fuck my legal relationship to her."

The clerk's eyes widened. "Sir, you need to calm down."

"I can't calm down. That's my partner in there. She was bleeding and she was unconscious, and I need to know that she's all right." He was losing his damn mind. "Look, she's not my wife. She's not my girlfriend. She's my—" *Everything.* No, no, he couldn't say that. "I have to know how she is. Get me someone who knows—"

The ER doors burst open. Those damn doors had been bursting like crazy in the short time he'd been there. All hell seemed to have broken loose in the city. But he wasn't so worried about the city.

He was worried about Blair.

His Blair.

EMTs shoved in a gurney, and Linc caught a fast glance at the man on there and…

"Holy shit, *Cole?*" Linc bounded toward him. "What the hell happened?"

A security guard pushed him back. "Sir, you need to move. The staff has to work on him."

Cole's lashes flickered up. He blinked. Seemed to focus on Linc for a moment. Then his eyes rolled back in his head.

The security guard's hand pressed hard to Linc's chest.

"Is he...a partner, too?" The question came from the same administrative assistant.

Linc's head swiveled toward him. *Don't freak out on the hospital staff. Do not —*

"I need to speak with the family of Blair Kincaid." A female doctor had just appeared near the swinging ER doors.

"That's me!" He ran away from the security guard. "I'm her family."

"Ah...but you said you were her partner —" It was that damn administrative guy again.

"I'm both." He staggered to a stop in front of the doctor. Her dark hair was pulled into a long braid. She wore green scrubs, a stethoscope circled her neck, and her eyes were smudged with shadows. "How is Blair?"

"She was in a car accident?"

A hit and run. He nodded.

"She's fine. We contained the bleeding and assessed the additional damage."

He couldn't swallow. "What additional damage?"

"Her broken ribs. Her head wound. The lacerations on her arm and side." Spoken crisply. "Don't worry. She's in recovery now. She should be fine."

He choked down the lump in his throat. Blair was okay. "Thank you." His gaze darted to her name tag. "Dr. Wilson. Thank you very much."

Her smile was tired. "You're welcome. But, now I have to go. We're short staffed, and I have other patients who need me."

Patients like Cole.

What in the hell happened to Cole?

Even as the question registered, even as he watched the doctor turn and stride back through those swinging doors, he realized…

If Cole is here, where's Tess?

His hands slapped over his body. His phone was gone. Had it been left in the wreckage? He'd…yeah, okay, he'd lost his control when Blair had been injured. His whole focus had been on getting her to safety.

He'd thought that Cole was protecting Tess. Thought that James was clear back at the club.

But things weren't fine. Nothing was fine.

He rushed back to the administrative desk. "I need to use your phone."

The clerk lifted a brow.

"*Please.*"

The guy slid him the phone. "Everything is always easier when you ask nicely. Manners go a long way in this world."

With his middle finger, Linc punched in the number he had memorized for James. It rang once, twice, and…

"Who the hell is this?" James demanded.

"Yeah, happy to hear your voice, too," Linc threw back. "Where are you and what in the hell is happening?"

CHAPTER EIGHTEEN

Tess opened her eyes. She jerked upright, realizing that she was in…a bed?

Yes, some fancy bed. King-sized. The covers felt like soft down. The wooden, four-poster was huge, and the heavy furniture in the room reeked of money. "What?" She shook her head. Oh, bad move. The room spun. Nausea rolled in her stomach, and she thought that she might black out again. Her hands rose and they were—cuffed? She stared down at her cuffed wrists. She twisted her hands. Tried to yank them free of the cuffs. The metal bit into her skin.

"You woke up faster than I thought."

The room was spinning and so was Marilyn.

Marilyn smiled. Only it looked like an evil grin. "How do you feel?"

"Like crap." Her throat was bone dry. Her heart raced. Her cuffed hands shook.

Marilyn hummed and came closer. "I didn't give you nearly as much as I gave Cole. Didn't want him waking up and bothering us.

Actually…" She leaned toward Tess. "He probably won't wake up at all."

The blonde was so close to her. Tess lifted up her cuffed hands and *lunged* —

She fell off the side of the bed and crashed into the floor.

"That was sad," Marilyn told her. "Did you think it was going to work out differently? Like, in your head? Did you think you were going to hit me, knock me unconscious, and escape?" She crouched next to Tess. "Or maybe you thought you'd get this from me." She pulled a capped syringe from her pocket. She was still wearing her scrubs. How many syringes did the woman have ready to go? Seemed like a limitless supply. "Maybe you thought you'd shoot me up the way you shot up my brother all those years ago. And you'd kill me, too."

Had she just heard that right? Marilyn's brother?

Tess stared into Marilyn's bright blue eyes.
OhmyGod.

Marilyn smiled again. The evil grin. "At first, I was grateful to you."

What was happening? Was this all some hallucination?

Where was James? She'd like to see James now. Right now.

"He hurt me, too, you know. I think that's why he picked girls my age. I did research on it later, cause, you know…" She waved the syringe vaguely in the air. "Trying to figure out why he wound up like he did. Trying to make sure I didn't end up the same way." She leaned closer. "In case it was genetic or something."

No. *No.*

"He used to watch me. Then he'd touch me. Mom caught him once. Told him to never touch me that way again." Marilyn glanced at the syringe. "But she kept letting him live in the house with me. That was when he started going out to hunt. I followed him once. I watched *him.* And he would whisper to me about them. Those girls that he hurt."

Okay, Tess was going to vomit.

"But then you stopped him. I didn't know it was you, of course, not right away. I knew *someone* had stopped him. He wrecked his car on the way home. Heard the cops telling mom that he was high. A mix of drugs. That was what he did. He gave all the girls drugs." She bit her lip. "He gave me drugs. I remember that."

"Marilyn….*please…*"

"Took me years to figure out it was you. I was all Nancy Drew like. Checked hospital records, tracked down leads. Then found you." She smoothed back Tess's hair with her left hand. "When I met you in that library, I liked you. I decided that maybe you had helped me. You got rid of him. My life got better. And, we even became friends. The more I was with you, I realized that you were good. So good."

Tess's body was shaking. She didn't know what Marilyn had given her, so she didn't know what to expect her body to do. She couldn't think of Cole, not then. Couldn't think of what might have happened to him.

She had to survive. Had to get past this moment. Once she was free, then she'd figure out everything else.

Cole was trying to help me. Just to help me.

No, she slammed the door on that thought.

"Your new boyfriend wasn't so good." Marilyn stopped stroking Tess's hair. "Barnes tipped me off, but I didn't learn the real truth, not until Morgan came into the hospital."

Crap. So that memory had been real. Morgan was involved. But why?

"He's a killer."

Morgan was a killer? Tess pushed up onto her knees. Every movement made her head swim sickeningly.

"He's killed dozens of people, and you fell for him."

Wait, she was talking about James? Not Morgan?

"You let a killer into your bed. You knew what he was, Morgan told me that you knew, and you didn't care." She nodded. "There's something wrong with you. You were supposed to stay good. Supposed to stay better."

Better than what?

"But you didn't. You fell for him, and now, I have to make you pay."

This was insane. "We've…been friends…for *years.*"

Another nod. "And we would have kept right on being friends." A despondent sigh. "If you hadn't fucked a killer and liked it."

"Are you…serious? You…after what *you* did to Cole…to *me…*"

Marilyn's face hardened. Her lips parted—

"Yeah, I don't think she quite gets how illogical she is," a male voice announced.

Morgan Waller had just sauntered into the bedroom. He stood a few feet behind Marilyn.

Marilyn scrambled to her feet. "I'm not illogical! I'm doing what's right! You told me that James Smith was evil! You told me she knew everything he'd done. She didn't care, she was as tainted as my brother."

How had Morgan even known about Marilyn's brother?

Tess knew she needed to get off the floor. She needed a weapon. She needed a damn miracle.

"Your brother *was* a sick fucking freak, dear. Just like *my* brother." He peered around at Tess. "They were friends, you see. Her brother and mine. Isn't that chummy?"

That wasn't the word she'd use to describe things. More like—*horrific?*

"Want to know who gave Marilyn's dear brother the drugs he used on his victims? *My* brother did. He was always getting his hands far too dirty."

No, this wasn't happening.

"I recognized Marilyn when I went into the hospital. I'd seen her a bit growing up. We ran in the same social circles, you see."

What circles would those be? The rich who sold drugs? Who hurt young girls?

But Marilyn had been hurt, too. Hurt and damaged, and Tess hadn't seen the truth. Marilyn had put up a mask, and Tess had believed it.

Because I was wearing my own mask. Because I didn't let her get close. And she didn't let me get close. And I thought that was normal.

"Marilyn, I..." Her throat was so dry. She cleared it. Tried again. "I want to help you."

Marilyn glanced down at her with huge eyes.

Morgan wrapped his hand around Marilyn's shoulder. "No, don't listen to her. Tess is lying. She wants to hurt you. I *told* you that. Her new boyfriend kills. He assassinates people who do bad things. She was going to get him to turn on you. As soon as she learned the truth—and you knew, Marilyn, deep down, eventually, she would learn it—Tess was going to get him to kill you."

Marilyn's lower lip trembled.

"No." Tess pushed up. Her knees wanted to buckle—especially the right one—but she grabbed onto one of the bed posts. "I wasn't going to do that! You were my *friend*, Marilyn!"

Morgan smiled and leaned closer to Marilyn. His voice was like the pleased hiss of a snake as he told her, "Were. Did you hear that? She said you *were* her friend. Not any longer. She's done with you. The truth came out. She'll get Ghost to kill you."

Ghost. Goosebumps covered her. She stopped focusing on Marilyn. Turned her attention to the mastermind. "You knew who he was."

He lifted a brow.

"Did you see him at the hospital?" Her mind was running slowly, so it was hard to piece things together. "The night your brother attacked…you were there. James was there. He waited for me after…" He'd brought her fudge. Her favorite. "You saw him." He must have seen him. "You saw *us.*"

"Recognized him because I had an old photo of my prey, courtesy of a corrupt government handler I had bribed a long time ago. That photo was burned into my head." A muscle jerked along Morgan's jaw as he stepped back from Marilyn. "It's hard to forget the man who came to destroy your world. In and out, leaving nothing behind but death. The big, bad, infamous Ghost. Couldn't believe that I'd been searching the world for him, and he'd decided to come right to me in Savannah. Talk about some crazy luck."

"Who did he take from you?" Maybe if she kept him talking, she'd get stronger. The more time that passed, the stronger she'd be. Then she could attack.

"My father. Sure, the old bastard was a killer and he controlled one of the biggest drug empires on the coast..." His eyes glinted. *"But he was mine."*

Her heart raced far too fast. "Wasn't your brother *yours,* too? Wasn't Frederick yours? You killed him." He'd told her that...hadn't he? Back at her apartment? Dammit, things were still so jumbled and foggy.

He nodded. "What else was I to do? I'd given him chance after chance. He didn't learn. And he wasn't about to drag me down with him." A shrug. "In the end, Frederick proved useful, though. His death got the cops to turn their attention to your so-called James Smith. Bet that was a new one for him. Getting hauled into a jail cell."

"And you think...you think you're going to kill him? Use me as bait somehow and kill—James—"

"I'm not going to kill him. I thought about it. Had actually planned his murder many, many times in my mind. But then I discovered a better ending."

Her breath choked out in relief.

"I'm going to kill *you.*" He waved a hand around him. "This place? It's one of his many holdings. In case you didn't realize it, the guy tends to collect things. I'm going to set it up so that your body is found here, with direct evidence to tie you to him. The cops will be called. Hell, *he* will be called. He'll be found over your poor, broken body, and then he'll spend the rest of his life in jail." Morgan nodded. "Fitting for him, I think. Losing his life would be too quick. He needs to be locked away. To be shut in, to slowly fade away until he is nothing more than a ghost…"

"Wait." Marilyn rolled the syringe in her fingertips. "What do you mean about her being 'broken'? Because I don't want her to hurt. I can just give her some more meds, and she'll go to sleep. This syringe is powerful. One jab, and she won't ever wake up again. Everything will be okay."

Her gaze snapped to Marilyn. *"Nothing is okay here, Marilyn."*

Marilyn backed up a step. Her shoulder rammed into Morgan.

"He's going to kill us both, Marilyn," Tess fired at her. She *was* getting stronger. "How can you not get that? He used you. He's not going to let you walk away because you're a weak link. You might tell someone the truth one day, and he can't have that."

Marilyn looked up at him. "She's wrong."

He reached for her hand. Curled his fingers around hers. Slid the syringe from her. "No, darling, she's not."

He pushed off the syringe cap.

"*Marilyn, run!*" Tess shouted.

Marilyn's head jerked toward her.

He shoved the needle into Marilyn's arm.

***

He'd found the car, thanks to Barnes and to help from Wilde techs. They'd accessed traffic cams and traced the vehicle all over the city.

And back to one of my homes.

The car was just sitting in the driveway.

Fucking balls.

He even knew who'd driven it. The license and registration had gone back to Morgan Waller. Only, that wasn't the guy's real name. He'd changed his name four years ago, right after the death of his father and the seeming collapse of his father's business. As soon as James had learned Morgan's real last name, everything had clicked. He remembered Morgan's father.

Sometimes, there were a whole lot of monsters in one family tree. In the case of the Waller tree, hell, that bitch was corroded from the inside.

James cased the house, then slipped around the side. This was his house — and the bastard was a fool to choose one of James's own homes in his plans. James knew how to get inside. Knew every single space on that property.

Getting in undetected wouldn't be a problem.

I'm coming, Tess. Baby, I swear, I'm coming for you.

And he would destroy anyone who got in his way.

***

He dropped the syringe. Marilyn was on the floor. Her body trembled. Tess surged forward, but Morgan grabbed her.

"Please, let me help her!"

He locked one hand around her neck. "Why?" Morgan seemed genuinely curious. "She was going to kill you. Even if I hadn't come along, eventually, she would have done it. She'd been stalking you for years. You should have seen all the photos I found at her place." He shook his head. "I think her brother messed her up far more than anyone realized. You were her savior and her villain. She loved you and hated you, and that mix of emotions can never be good."

He wasn't strangling her. In fact, it seemed he'd tried to put his fingers on her neck in the exact spots where his own brother's had been. But he wasn't squeezing, not yet.

"Family can be a burden. You love them. You hate them. You even have to kill them." A shrug. His nostrils flared. "You wouldn't know, though, would you? Since you never had a real family."

So he'd dug into her life. The last thing she cared about right then. "Your father…if he was so bad…why do you care—"

"He wasn't bad *to me.* He loved me. Trained me. And I owe him this. Hell, do you have any clue how many people want your lover dead? It's like, a freaking line. I was the lucky one. I managed to get details from his old handler, even got that lucky picture of him. Fucking rare. Like I said, that's how I recognized him at the hospital. A little more digging, some confirmation, and, well, here we are."

She saw a movement behind him. The faintest flicker. No sound though. No rustles.

She kept her eyes on Morgan. Didn't let her expression alter.

"It's going to wreck him." Morgan beamed at her. So confident in his power. "He doesn't get attached to anyone. But he kept going back to you, over and over. I think he was obsessed."

"It's called love."

"Whatever. He'll be destroyed when he finds your body. The same way I was destroyed when I found my father. I lost the business after his death, did you know that?"

Uh, did it look like she knew that?

"Our enemies swarmed in. The government swarmed in. I had to reinvent myself. New name. New business. Frederick—hell, that asshole had his mother's maiden name. He was my half-brother, born on the side when my dad was still married to *my* mom. When I went looking for a new name, I thought, why not use his?" His nostrils flared. "When you lose everything, it makes you desperate. I've been desperate for a very, very long time. That desperation is ending." His hand began to tighten on her throat. "He has to know you suffered."

Did she look like a freaking prop for a man's pain?

"It's going to hurt a lot."

He thought she was just going to stand there and take it? "Yes," Tess breathed. "It will." She slammed her left knee into his groin. As hard as she could.

His hand jerked back.

She lifted up the handcuffs and slammed them into his face. They hit him with a hard crack, and she saw blood explode from his lips and nose. Tess lunged past him.

"*I've got you.*" James was there. She'd seen him slip into the room. Had known that she needed to keep Morgan focused on her, and she'd done her job. She'd also shattered Morgan's nose. A damn *fine* job.

James grabbed her. Shoved her behind him.

Morgan spun around. Only — when his hand came up, he had a gun aimed at James. "Freaking Ghost…"

"The one and only."

James had a gun, too. She saw it gripped in his right hand. And when he shifted forward a bit…wait, was that a second gun tucked into the back waistband of his jeans? Her cuffed hands slid beneath his coat and she grabbed the weapon. It felt surprisingly heavy in her grip. She'd never fired a gun before, but there was a first time for everything.

Morgan laughed. "Can't believe we're face to face. Kinda like meeting a celebrity, you know, one you hate."

James blocked her from seeing most of Morgan. He was using his body to shield her. Tess glanced down at the floor. Marilyn didn't appear to be moving. Her blonde hair spilled around her head.

"Why am I not dead yet?" Morgan wondered. "Why haven't you pulled the trigger? Have you lost your touch, Ghost?"

"Drop your weapon, asshole. Drop it now, or I will pull the trigger."

"I think you won't. I think you don't want to kill with her watching." More laughter. "You want her to think you're something special, but you're not. You're a criminal. You're evil. Rotten through and through."

"He was going to k-kill me," Tess said. Her palm was sweaty around the gun. "Pin it on you."

A growl broke from James.

"Yes, well…so much for that plan." Morgan didn't seem particularly worried.

Why not? He should be terrified. *She* was terrified.

"Guess I have to go with option two," Morgan continued and then he—ducked for cover?

He hit the floor. Yes, it definitely looked as if he'd just jumped for cover.

James didn't move. Tess was rooted to the spot.

Slowly, Morgan lifted his head. "Where are my men?"

Now James laughed. A cold and mocking sound. "The men you had hiding around *my* place? Are those the ones you're asking about?"

A grudging nod.

"I took care of most of them. My backup took care of the rest." Another spine-chilling laugh. "You didn't really think I came out here alone, did you? See, my days of working solo are behind me. Now I always have a team."

Morgan lunged to his feet. His finger began to tighten on the gun's trigger.

Bam!

Bam!

Two shots. Two hits that had Morgan jerking back like a puppet on a string.

Only one of those shots had come from the gun James held.

The other shot had come from Tess's gun.

James rushed toward the bed. Morgan's body had crashed onto it. Morgan's weapon had fallen to the floor, and James kicked it out of the way.

Blood soaked Morgan's shirt. The two bullets had gone into his chest, and when Tess stumbled to him, she saw that one had—

His heart. It went in his heart.

She didn't know if it had been her shot or the one James fired. And it didn't matter. This man had been prepared to kill her. He'd been ready to kill James. She'd had to fire. She'd *had* to do it.

She could feel the tears on her cheeks, and she didn't care. She could feel the blood on her hands, and she realized—

I'm trying to save him. She'd dropped her weapon and put her hands on Morgan. *I know it won't work. But my hands are on his chest. I'm trying to stop the blood.* She was moving by rote and she couldn't stop herself. Someone was dying. She was supposed to step in. She was supposed to help.

Morgan's eyes were on hers.

The life faded from his stare.

"We have to call the police," she whispered. His blood was warm. She was cold. "We have to get the police here."

James curled his hands around her shoulders. "Baby, tell me that you're okay."

She'd just shot a man. Killed— "Marilyn!" She jumped off the bed. Rushed to her but—

"No." James caught her in his arms. "No, baby, there isn't anything you can do."

Tess shuddered against him.

"I just checked. She's gone."

Marilyn was gone. Morgan was dead.

"Baby, are you *okay?*"

Her head tilted back. She stared into his eyes. Those blazing eyes of his. The eyes that had found her across a crowded club. The eyes that had looked into hers and seemed to see her very soul. Was she okay?

Somewhere, a siren screamed in the distance. She didn't know who'd called the cops. Hell, it had probably been a neighbor. Someone who'd heard gunshots. She'd told James to call the cops. An instinctive response from her but she hadn't seen him pull out a phone.

"Baby, please, talk to me. Tell me that you're all right. God, I need to hear—"

"Cops are coming!" Linc had just burst into the room. "We've got a dozen injured men outside and—fuck me!" His gaze scanned the floor. "Two dead here?"

Her body trembled. Her hands were going numb on her. Why were they doing that? Just what had Marilyn given to her? Tess had thought that she was getting stronger with each moment that passed, but…

Had that been adrenaline?

Her heart was racing so fast. Pounding and pounding and pounding. Her throat was desert dry. Her lungs felt as if they were bursting.

"What are we going to tell the cops?" Linc demanded quickly. "Are we ready for them?

Hell, Ghost, as a former detective, I can tell you that we need to be prepared for — "

"I killed the bastard on the bed. It was me. I shot him twice. Used two guns to do it." James bent and picked up the gun that Tess had dropped. He held it tightly.

Putting his prints on it.

"He kidnapped my lady, and I came after her. I killed him. I took out his guards. That's the story." He glared at Linc. "Got it?"

But that wasn't the story.

James caught her chin in his hand. "You don't need this on you, baby. You don't need a damn thing on you. Let me take care of you. Let me get you out of here."

She wanted out of there. She wanted away from the bodies and the pain.

"I am so fucking sorry," he murmured. His forehead pressed to hers. "He was from my past, and he tried to hurt you because of me. I won't ever let something like this happen again. You'll be safe." He kissed her. A deep, hard kiss. "I swear it, I will make sure you're safe."

His words were distorted. And the black dots were popping up near her vision again. Not good. Pinpricks danced over her face. A sure sign she was about to pass out. "James…"

Her stupid legs had buckled.

He caught her. Lifted her up. "Tess? What did they do to you?"

"Drugs…" A whole lot of them. She'd thought they were getting out of her system but…

Adrenaline is crashing. I'm crashing. Need to get to ER.

"It's going to be all right." He turned. Rushed out of the room with her. "It's going to be all right. I'll get you whatever you need." His voice was ragged. His hold desperate. "Tess, I love you so damn much. Please, please don't leave me."

She wasn't going to leave him. In fact, she wanted to spend the rest of her life with him. He was hers. She was his. That was what mattered. "I love you," she managed to tell him. That was important. So very important. And so was one other thing. One other thing that she *had* to say. "And *I* freaking shot him. I'd do it…again, in a…heartbeat."

No one was going to hurt James. If any SOBs tried, they'd find her standing in their way.

"Now, hold tight," she whispered, "because I'm pretty sure I'm about to pass out."

***

He held her tight.

James lifted Tess into his arms and he held her as tightly as he could.

"She…okay?" Linc asked, voice halting.

She had to be okay. There wasn't any other option for him. "I killed him. When the cops ask, *I* fired the shots." He pulled her closer. She was breathing. Her heart was beating, but God, what drugs had they given to her?

He kept remembering how Cole had started convulsing on him. "Baby, stay strong. Please, just stay strong."

"Uh, about the shots, I thought she just said —
"

Sirens were louder. Screaming.

His head jerked toward Linc. "*I* killed him. I'm not letting her risk anything else for me. I'll take responsibility for everything."

Linc winced. "Yeah, bro, don't really think she's gonna let you do that. But good luck trying."

CHAPTER NINETEEN

"I killed him." Tess sat up in bed, her eyes flaring wide, and she made her confession again as she said, "I shot him." Her voice came out strong and clear. No weakness at all.

Latonya blinked at her.

The machines around Tess hummed and beeped.

And the police detective who stood in the corner—Detective Wesley Cade—raised both of his brows. "Just who is it that you're confessing to killing, Dr. Barrett?"

"No one."

Tess's head turned to the right, and there he was. James sat in the chair next to her bed. He was leaning forward, his hands between his spread legs, and his eyes were on her. Dark shadows dipped under his eyes, the stubble on his jaw was thicker, and the faint lines near his mouth seemed deeper.

God, he was gorgeous.

"She didn't kill anyone," James continued grimly. "She just woke up after going through hell. Your ass shouldn't even be in here now. She didn't confess to a thing." James reached for her hand. Squeezed it. "Baby, I told you—"

The detective stepped forward and cleared his throat. "Two bullets hit Morgan Waller. Two bullets from two different guns. Both guns were claimed by James Smith."

"That's because they were both mine. I shot with one, then the other." His voice was flat. "How many times do I have to tell you the same thing?" His hold on Tess's hand was so careful.

She smiled at him. "Liar."

His brows pulled low.

She felt good. Tess had no idea how long she'd been in the hospital, but an IV fed into her arm. Whatever she'd been given, it had certainly helped her.

"I shot him, Detective Cade. Morgan was going to kill me and James, and I shot him in self-defense." Her shoulders squared. "And I also killed Marilyn's brother. Though, God, that was a lifetime ago."

Now the detective didn't just step forward. He bounded forward. "You did *what?*"

"I killed her brother, but, at the time, I didn't know he was her brother. He was just some bastard who picked me up off the street when I was thirteen, drugged me, and tried to rape me. I fought, slammed a needle into *him,* and when I woke up in a hospital…" Her gaze slid around the bright, stark white room. "I tried to pretend it all had never happened."

"*OhmyGod.*" Latonya grabbed Tess's other hand. Squeezed hard.

Tess straightened her shoulders even though she felt her paper hospital gown starting to dip. "Before she died, Marilyn confessed that her brother had attacked other girls." She'd woken with her mind sharp, her heart aching, and her past determined to be exposed. *No secrets.* "I want to find out who all he hurt. I want the families to know what he did."

"This is insane." Latonya appeared dazed. "This is—"

"This is what Dr. Devin Goddard told me, too," the detective announced.

Devin? Tess frowned. Okay, her mind was sharp, but she'd sort of forgotten about him.

"He said that Marilyn confessed her brother's crimes to him. He wanted to tell you everything, but he didn't get the chance to do it. He was jumped by Morgan Waller. From what I can piece together, Marilyn had given Waller a syringe of drugs to use on Devin. They set him up to be found by James Smith over there." An incline of his head toward James. Then Wesley whistled. "For some reason, it seems those two thought that you'd find Devin, surrounded by pics of Dr. Barrett, and immediately kill him. Hmmm. Wonder what they know about you that I don't?"

James just shrugged. "I did shoot him."

"Yes, well, Devin was armed. Courtesy of Waller. Guessing he thought if you saw Devin with a gun—combined with all those pics of Dr. Barrett—you'd attack."

She wasn't sure what pictures he meant.

"But you didn't kill him."

Her hold tightened on James's hand. "He's not a monster, detective."

She saw James's mouth curl a bit.

The detective's gaze swept over James. "One thing is for sure, Marilyn Montgomery and Morgan Waller both hated you."

"I stir that emotion in a lot of people," James allowed.

"My team is digging into Morgan's background. And just so you know, that witness who reported seeing you at Frederick Waller's apartment? He recanted. Confessed that Morgan paid him to lie."

No expression crossed James's face. "That's because Morgan killed his own brother."

"Yeah, yeah, we, um, found the murder weapon at Morgan's place." He released a hard breath. "Such a freaking tangled mess. And to top it all off, I'm hearing whispered intel that Morgan Waller might have actually been some sort of hitman."

Tess stiffened.

"An assassin, if you can believe that shit." Wesley rubbed the back of his neck. "That sounds crazy, I know, but I'm getting some rumbles from government sources that indicate this fellow was a professional. Went by the name of Ghost."

Tess stopped breathing.

"I'm thinking a lot of people will be glad to hear he's gone." Wesley inclined his head to James. He gestured between James and Tess. "He tried to take out the wrong folks this time, huh?"

Tess was trying to school her expression, but the machines around her were beeping faster and faster with every second that passed.

"It still bugs me, though. Why'd he get so fixed on you two? Don't quite understand that part. Everything else, hell, it almost seems like it is being tied up in a nice, neat bow for me."

"Doesn't seem so neat to me." Tess's hospital gown scraped lightly over her arm. "Not when I was drugged and almost killed. Nothing neat about that."

Immediately, remorse filled the detective's eyes. "No, of course not, I was just trying to figure out why —"

"He and Marilyn were working as a team," Tess said. "Maybe he did it for her."

Wesley seemed to absorb that. His stare drifted from Tess to James, then back to Tess. "Could be. I've heard some people will do just about anything for love."

He knows. He knows there's more. He knows —

"Rest up, Dr. Barrett. I'm sure I'll be back with follow-up questions — lots of them — but, until then, you just take care, all right?"

She jerked her head in agreement. She'd definitely rest up. Sure thing. Yes, a thousand times yes. And then—

He left.

The machines kept beeping a little too fast.

"OhmyGod."

Tess turned her head to stare at Latonya.

"What is going on?" She shook her head. Several times. "Marilyn is dead."

Tess's heart squeezed.

"She tried to kill you. She tried to kill Devin. She was...she was apparently stealing drugs from the hospital, over and over. Had been, for months. Maybe years. And she—" Her breath choked out. "I never really knew her, did I?"

Latonya was still holding one of Tess's hands. James held the other.

Tess squeezed Latonya's fingers. "I want to tell you about my past. I want to tell you *everything* about me."

Latonya nodded. "I want to hear it." Tears were in her eyes. She licked her lower lip. "Devin was talking pretty wildly when he first came in. One of the things he told me was that Marilyn had been the one in the corridor. The one who attacked you. He saw her doing it. Confronted her, and she confessed that she'd been stealing drugs. Apparently, they had...a thing, and she begged him not to turn her in. She spilled everything about her past to him and tried to convince him to stay quiet."

"But he started feeling guilty," James added quietly, "and that's when he called you, Tess, wanting to talk."

So many secrets. Drowning them all.

A nurse knocked on the door and then slipped her head inside. "Dr. Wilson? We need you."

Latonya nodded. Her stare lingered on Tess. "I want to hear everything," she said again. "But for right now, I'm just glad you're alive."

And Tess was pretty damn glad to *be* alive.

Latonya hurried away. The door closed softly behind her.

James's gaze was so bright as it slid over her face.

"I knew you'd find me," Tess blurted. "It was just a matter of time."

"I was scared as hell that when I got there, I'd find your body."

Pain was in his words. Not just pain. More like agony.

He stood. Brought their joined hands to his lips and pressed a kiss to her knuckles. He was always doing that. And every time he did it, warmth spread through her.

Voice ragged, he told her, "My past almost killed you."

"Actually, I think it was *my* past, too."

Another kiss on her knuckles. "I'm not sure what I would have done if I hadn't found you alive." He released a ragged breath. "I want you so much, but the truth is...You shouldn't be with me. I'm no good for you."

"You killed to keep me safe. You tracked me down when I was missing. And I'm pretty sure you just tried to take the fall for me pulling the trigger."

He swallowed. "Baby, I'd kill for you any day of the week, and I'd go to jail a hundred times before I let you take the fall for anything."

That was...scary. Sweet. James. "It was self-defense. Neither one of us is going anywhere."

His gaze darted away from her.

Um, hello, *bad sign.* "James?"

"I can't be sure that someone from my past won't find me again."

The machines were going crazy. A nurse was probably going to run in the room any moment to check on her. "I thought the detective just said that it looked like Morgan was the assassin."

"Yeah, Wilde is putting out that story. Creating some false evidence to back it up. There will be enough gasoline on that fire to make most people who knew about Ghost believe that he was Morgan Waller." A pause. "*Most* people. I can't be certain others won't eventually try to find me. And I can't keep putting you at risk just because I love you so much that I want you with me every single moment."

"No." She shook her head, hard. "No, I did *not* just wake up from whatever nightmare that was to have you tell me that you can't put me at risk."

"Tess—"

"I take my own risks. I make my own choices. And you know what? I love *you* so much that I want to be with you every single moment, and I don't care if I have to make sacrifices to do that. We can both make sacrifices. You want to join Wilde? You want to work with them? Fine. We can make that happen. We can make anything happen, if we're together. Because I realized something about us..." Before she'd passed out, but, hey, she'd been kicking butt until that point. "We're pretty scary together."

His head tilted. "You're okay...with scary?"

"I think I'm in love with it."

Hope lit his eyes.

"I love you, James. I don't care about your past. I want your future. That's what matters to me. I want us to have a future together, so don't even think about pulling some dramatic bullshit where you try to leave me in order to protect me."

His lips began to curl. "Do you think I'm the dramatic bullshit type?"

"When you believe you're protecting me?" Tess didn't even miss a beat. "Absolutely. One hundred percent."

His smile stretched. "You're really all right."

"I'm all right," she whispered back. Sure, she was practically twitching to get her hands on her own chart so she could see what had happened to her and just what Marilyn had given her, but...

I'm all right.

She was alive. James was alive. They had a future waiting. Their future. They could do anything they wanted to do with it.

Anything.

"I was afraid," he admitted starkly. "I've never been so scared about anything in my life. If you'd died, I swear, I don't know what I would have done."

"I didn't die."

He nodded. "Loving someone that much, it can make you weak."

Something she'd learned when she'd fired the gun... "It can also make you strong."

"Yes." He leaned forward. His lips skimmed over hers.

Her eyes closed and, for a moment, she simply savored his kiss, but when he pulled back, her lashes lifted, and Tess asked him, "Will you be strong with me?"

"Always."

"Will you be weak? Strong, weak, happy, in love—everything? Will you just *be* with me?"

"Sweetheart, you are my one. My only. I will love you for the rest of my life."

The beeping steadied. "Good," Tess told him. "I'll love you that long, too. Maybe even longer."

He kissed her once more.

She knew they had a real chance for their future. As long as they were together, they could face anything that came their way. She wasn't afraid, she wasn't holding back. It was time to grab her future with both hands.

And never let go.

***

"Okay, let *go*," Blair growled as she glared at Linc.

But he kept his hand wrapped around her wrist, his fingers on her pulse. "I'm just making sure you're okay."

She rolled her eyes. "That's what the monitors do. You don't have to physically check my pulse every five minutes."

His lips pulled down. Total pout. "I'm helping."

He had been helping. Actually, he'd been with her pretty much constantly. Watching over her. Frowning and grousing when he didn't think the staff was helping her enough. Though, they had definitely been helping enough. He was excessively fretting over her and it was…too much. "What's up with you?"

He caressed her inner wrist.

A little shiver skated over Blair's body.

Immediately, his gaze jumped to her face. "Are you cold?"

No. "Yes."

A decisive nod. "I'll get an extra blanket for you."

And he did. He was back moments later and the guy seriously tucked the blanket around her. When he leaned close to her, his head dipped her way, and for a moment, her eyes dropped to his mouth.

No. No, no. Her eyes whipped back up. "Thank you."

Linc stared at her. "I can't let anything happen to you."

The machines gave a fast beep. Stupid monitors.

"After all, you're the best partner I've ever had." A rueful smile. "And breaking in another partner would just be a pain in the ass if you died."

Her eyes narrowed. "Right. Wouldn't want to inconvenience you."

He eased back into his chair. The one that he'd pulled up right beside her bed. "Losing you would be a huge inconvenience."

Blair shook her head. She closed her eyes.

"You didn't thank me for saving you."

Her eyes flew open.

"But there will be time for that later." Linc smiled. Flashed his dimples. He always thought he could charm her with those. "After all, we'll be on a new case together before you even know it."

"I can't wait," she muttered. Her eyes drifted closed again.

"Neither can I," he said softly. So softly she almost didn't hear him.

She tried to sleep. Tried to calm her thoughts. Linc had briefed her on the case. She knew that the bad guys were dead. Thanks to traffic cam footage that had been recovered, they'd discovered that one of Morgan Waller's thugs had been the one to hit them. He'd been arrested, and he'd been more than happy to roll on his dead boss.

She knew that Cole was in recovery—he was going to be okay. Tess was okay. James was okay. The team had made it, though the case had sure been one hell of a lot harder than they'd anticipated.

Heck, I didn't even know it was a case when I first came to Savannah—

His fingers curled around her wrist once more.

She didn't open her eyes. "Linc…"

"I'm just checking you…"

She didn't tell him to let go. In fact, with his hand on her wrist, she felt a little bit better. Sleep tugged at her. Sleep or…maybe it was the pain meds. Maybe they were pulling her under. Either way… "Thanks," she whispered.

"For what?"

For what? He'd asked for the gratitude mere moments before. "Saving me." Her breathing steadied. Her body went lax.

Did he press a kiss to her temple? Felt like it. Felt like…

"Anytime, B. Anytime." A pause. "I would never have left you. And I never will."

EPILOGUE

"He's staring," Latonya told her with a firm nod. "Mr. Tall and Dangerous has his eyes locked on you."

Tess turned her head and saw the gorgeous guy at the bar lift his beer toward her in a silent salute. Just seeing him made her heart race. Always happened. She smiled, waved, and turned back to her friend.

"Yeah, okay, he's looking at you like he could eat you alive." Latonya took a sip of her drink. "Come to think of it, that's pretty much the only way he looks at you."

He was heading toward her. A fast glance showed the crowd parting quickly before him. Eagerness pulsed inside of Tess. She was so different from the woman she'd been the first time she'd entered this club. The past didn't chain her down any longer. She wasn't hiding her secrets. Detective Wesley Cade had joined a task force to help track down all of the victims killed by Marilyn's brother. They were going to get their justice. Their families would get closure.

Latonya touched her hand. "You're sure about this?"

Tess had told Latonya everything. They'd cried together. They'd mourned together. They'd stood over Marilyn's grave and hugged each other.

The past was ugly and twisted, but the friendship Tess had with Latonya was one of the most beautiful things in her life.

"Because if you're not sure about him, this whole club is full of guys." Latonya waved her hand vaguely to the left. "You can always try them out."

The two men who happened to be standing toward the left immediately perked up and locked their attention on Latonya. They began to advance.

"I'm sure about him," Tess replied. "He's what I want."

The two men were almost at the table. Latonya shooed them away, well, she started to, but then she told them, "Give me two minutes." Her stare returned to Tess. "I want you to be happy."

"And I want *you* happy."

Latonya smiled at her. "We make ourselves happy in this world, don't we? We go after what we want, and we take our happiness."

Yes, they did.

"So go take some happiness, and I think I'll go take some, too."

Tess hugged her friend, tight. "Thank you for standing by me."

"Yes, just so you know, if I ever get a crazy killer on my trail, I'll be turning to your guy and his Wilde friends for help. They'd better keep my ass safe, too."

James had reached their table. He cleared his throat. "You have a standing order of protection, Dr. Wilson."

"Damn right I do." She stood. Her gaze darted to the two men who'd been eager to approach her. "By any chance, do you know anything about them? Can't be too careful, it would seem."

"The guy on the left is a stock broker. No criminal record. One ex-wife. The man next to him owns three tattoo shops. No previous marriages, no criminal record, and, in fact, he was a cop for three years."

"Huh. Choices, choices. Thanks." She slanted a glance at him. "Do you know this much about everyone in your club?"

James shrugged.

She gave him a half-smile. "You'd better love my friend with your whole heart. If you don't, I can make you sorry. I'm a doctor. That means I can kill you in lots of ways that no one will ever detect."

Face serious, he told her, "I swear, I love Tess with my whole heart."

"Okay then…" She smiled at the two waiting men. "Night." She sauntered away.

James reached for Tess's hand. His fingers curled with hers. She rose and followed him through the crowd. She wasn't in the mood to dance or drink or to be surrounded by a hundred strangers that she didn't know. She was only in the mood for him.

They headed up the stairs to the VIP space. Went straight to the same room they'd used that first night. Tess shut the door behind her. Locked it. She squared her shoulders. "Did you make a decision about Wilde?" About the job offer they'd made him.

"I did. Told them I wanted to work freelance. When the cases are big enough, when they need me, I'll be there." His arms lifted and his palms pressed to the door behind her. "But where I want to be, where I need to be, it's here with you. I'm going to keep running the club and handling the other businesses that I've — "

"Collected?" Tess inserted smoothly as her hands slid between their bodies. She unsnapped his jeans. Pulled down his zipper.

"Ah…*yes*."

"I would have gone to Atlanta with you." Her hands were already on his cock. Squeezing him. Stroking him.

"I know…but…oh, God, baby…for now, you want Savannah. I want…*yes, yes*…" His eyes blazed. "I want to make you happy."

"We make ourselves happy," she whispered. Her mouth pressed to the strong column of this throat. A lick. A suck. A kiss. "But just so you know, I'm very happy right now."

"Me, too. Me—*oh, hell, yes.*"

She lowered to her knees. His cock was right there, and she had to take a lick. And a suck. And then if you were going to play, you had to play all the way.

Tess took him into her mouth. Her head bobbed and he groaned, and his hands clamped over her shoulders as he gritted out her name.

Tess loved that she could drive him wild. Loved that he needed and wanted her so badly because she needed and wanted him the exact same way. He drove her crazy. He gave her so much pleasure.

She wanted to always do the same for him.

Her lips feathered over the head of his erection. She slid him inside—

In a flash, he lifted her up. Carried her across the room. Tess laughed as she kicked off her shoes. He stripped her in record time, and then he was pushing her legs apart. James ripped open a foil packet, rolled on the condom, and drove deep inside of her.

She moaned as he filled her. Her head tipped back. He felt so good. Perfect.

"Like you were made for me."

Her eyes opened. She'd been thinking the exact same thing.

"Like you were meant to be mine." He kissed her. "And I was meant to be yours."

She tightened around him. He growled, withdrew, thrust.

Her nails raked over him. He still had on his t-shirt! She wanted it out of the way. She wanted to feel every bit of his body against her. She wanted —

The climax slammed into her. Tess opened her mouth to scream his name, but his lips took hers. He swallowed the cry even as he came inside of her.

The pleasure washed over her. Going on and on, and she felt like she was floating. Like she was touching the best paradise in the world.

Her heartbeat slowly returned to normal. Her eyes opened.

James smiled down at her. "I want new ground rules, Tess."

Her breath was still panting out. He was still in her.

"Sex without strings doesn't work for me."

It didn't work for her, either. They'd been in this same room when she'd first told him that she didn't have sex with strangers.

And he'd told her that he thought they would be incredible together.

They *were* incredible together. "What do you have in mind?"

He gazed down at her. She'd never seen him look more tender. She smiled up at him.

"Tess, will you marry me?"

She felt her eyes widen.

"I will give you anything you want, I swear it, just will you consider—"

"You are the only thing I want. And yes, yes, I will marry you." She yanked him down toward her. Kissed him wildly. Felt so much joy pour through her veins.

This was right.

He was right.

They were right.

He wasn't a ghost. He was a flesh and blood man. He was her man. And they were going to keep being absolutely incredible together...

For the rest of their lives.

The End

A NOTE FROM THE AUTHOR

Thank you for reading GHOST OF A CHANCE! And if you're curious about Blair and Linc…their slow-burn romance will be told in CROSSING THE LINE. These partners are about to break all the rules as their attraction breaks past their control. Times are going to get hot, hot, hot for them as the danger mounts. Prepare for a funny, sexy, *Wilde* time in CROSSING THE LINE.

If you'd like to stay updated on my releases and sales, please join my newsletter list.

http://www.cynthiaeden.com/newsletter/

Again, thank you for reading GHOST OF A CHANCE.

Best,
Cynthia Eden
www.cynthiaeden.com

ABOUT THE AUTHOR

Award-winning author Cynthia Eden writes dark tales of paranormal romance and romantic suspense. She is a New York Times, USA Today, Digital Book World, and IndieReader best-seller. Cynthia is also a three-time finalist for the RITA® award. Since she began writing full-time in 2005, Cynthia has written over eighty novels and novellas.

For More Information

- *www.cynthiaeden.com*
- *http://www.facebook.com/cynthiaedenfanpage*
- *http://www.twitter.com/cynthiaeden*

HER OTHER WORKS

Wilde Ways

- Protecting Piper (Wilde Ways, Book 1)
- Guarding Gwen (Wilde Ways, Book 2)
- Before Ben (Wilde Ways, Book 3)
- The Heart You Break (Wilde Ways, Book 4)
- Fighting For Her (Wilde Ways, Book 5)

Dark Sins

- Don't Trust A Killer (Dark Sins, Book 1)
- Don't Love A Liar (Dark Sins, Book 2)

Lazarus Rising

- Never Let Go (Book One, Lazarus Rising)
- Keep Me Close (Book Two, Lazarus Rising)
- Stay With Me (Book Three, Lazarus Rising)
- Run To Me (Book Four, Lazarus Rising)
- Lie Close To Me (Book Five, Lazarus Rising)

- Hold On Tight (Book Six, Lazarus Rising)
- Lazarus Rising Volume One (Books 1 to 3)
- Lazarus Rising Volume Two (Books 4 to 6)

Dark Obsession Series

- Watch Me (Dark Obsession, Book 1)
- Want Me (Dark Obsession, Book 2)
- Need Me (Dark Obsession, Book 3)
- Beware Of Me (Dark Obsession, Book 4)
- Only For Me (Dark Obsession, Books 1 to 4)

Mine Series

- Mine To Take (Mine, Book 1)
- Mine To Keep (Mine, Book 2)
- Mine To Hold (Mine, Book 3)
- Mine To Crave (Mine, Book 4)
- Mine To Have (Mine, Book 5)
- Mine To Protect (Mine, Book 6)
- Mine Series Box Set Volume 1 (Mine, Books 1-3)
- Mine Series Box Set Volume 2 (Mine, Books 4-6)

Bad Things

- The Devil In Disguise (Bad Things, Book 1)
- On The Prowl (Bad Things, Book 2)

- Undead Or Alive (Bad Things, Book 3)
- Broken Angel (Bad Things, Book 4)
- Heart Of Stone (Bad Things, Book 5)
- Tempted By Fate (Bad Things, Book 6)
- Bad Things Volume One (Books 1 to 3)
- Bad Things Volume Two (Books 4 to 6)
- Bad Things Deluxe Box Set (Books 1 to 6)
- Wicked And Wild (Bad Things, Book 7)
- Saint Or Sinner (Bad Things, Book 8)

Bite Series

- Forbidden Bite (Bite Book 1)
- Mating Bite (Bite Book 2)

Blood and Moonlight Series

- Bite The Dust (Blood and Moonlight, Book 1)
- Better Off Undead (Blood and Moonlight, Book 2)
- Bitter Blood (Blood and Moonlight, Book 3)
- Blood and Moonlight (The Complete Series)

Purgatory Series

- The Wolf Within (Purgatory, Book 1)
- Marked By The Vampire (Purgatory, Book 2)
- Charming The Beast (Purgatory, Book 3)

- Deal with the Devil (Purgatory, Book 4)
- The Beasts Inside (Purgatory, Books 1 to 4)

Bound Series

- Bound By Blood (Bound Book 1)
- Bound In Darkness (Bound Book 2)
- Bound In Sin (Bound Book 3)
- Bound By The Night (Bound Book 4)
- Forever Bound (Bound, Books 1 to 4)
- Bound in Death (Bound Book 5)

Other Romantic Suspense

- One Hot Holiday
- Secret Admirer
- First Taste of Darkness
- Sinful Secrets
- Until Death
- Christmas With A Spy